BLACKENED

a novel

TIM McWHORTER

Manta Press, Ltd.

Blackened
ISBN: 978-1-7357289-2-6 (paperback)
ISBN: 978-1-7357289-3-3 (ebook)

Published by Manta Press, Ltd.
Pickerington, OH 43147

Cover Design by Tim McWhorter
Author Photo by Julie A. McWhorter

Printed in the United States of America

PROLOGUE

"Come on, baby." He spit out the words while planting brewery-scented kisses up and down her quivering neck. "Here I am helping you out. Don't you wanna return the favor?"

The man smelled of grease and beer. The combination, as much as his actions, churned her stomach. She squirmed under his filthy touch. The tow truck driver's ravenous hands remained unshakable. Lifting her dress from behind had been his first breech of professional courtesy. Pinning her against the door of his tow truck, as her disabled Accord hung off the back, had ratcheted things to an all-new level. She was beyond irritated at this point. She was downright terrified.

"Just a kiss, baby. Let's start with that." The creep wasn't taking no for an answer. "Give ol' J.D. a kiss."

Her free hand searched the depths of her oversized purse for something she could use to fend the driver off, all the while cursing herself for not listening to her father, for not maintaining her car better. She tried not to panic, but the situation was escalating. Alarm was warranted.

She looked up and down the deserted road. The lack of a single car in the last half hour only reinforced what she already knew: she was on her own. No one would be coming down this road anytime soon. Probably why the guy felt so bold to begin with. It was just him and her, surrounded by trees as far as she could see. Her car had broken down in the middle of Ohio's own version of Yellowstone. She wanted to scream, but knew the effort would be wasted.

Her probing fingers brushed against the hard shell of her cell just as something over the driver's shoulder caught her eye. Behind him, the thick, overgrown brush parted. A man emerged from the trees. A large man, as formidable as any she'd seen. Relief flooded through her like rainwater rushing through a street after a downpour.

Her momentary lapse of anxiety proved short-lived.

Bent at the waist, one arm across his stomach, the man lumbering toward them appeared injured. The nearer he drew, the more visible his injuries. Her heart sank. Thick, mud-colored blood trailed over the man's shoulders. It streamed down both sides of his chest like a fireman's suspenders. The back of his bald head was leaking.

She stared at the man over the tow truck driver's shoulder. When their eyes met, hers grew wide. His feral. What she saw brought no comfort. 'Murderous intent,' a phrase from the crime shows she watched with her roommate when neither of them had a Friday night date.

Oblivious to the approaching danger, the tow truck driver continued his groping ways. He tore at her pink dress strap with his teeth. He tried to rip it free as his bulk pinned her against the door of the truck. She felt his yearning against her leg.

A thought struck her, freezing the blood in her veins. Could the two men be working together? Was one man's job to hold her up while the other laid in wait until the time was right? The thoughts of what the two of them together might have in store were too horrifying to bear.

The man from the woods raised his free hand as he stumbled onto the shoulder of the road. When she saw what the man held in his hand, it answered her question. They weren't working together. In fact, the tow truck driver was about to be as surprised by the other man's presence as she'd been. The revelation did nothing to ease the fear growing within.

The tow truck driver rose onto his toes. He arched his back, releasing her. His head tilted back. His throat bulged. A scream exploded from somewhere deep inside; a place so deep only the damned know its depths.

The next few moments played out in slow motion.

The truck driver's head snapped forward. His eyes doubled in size as his body pinned her to the truck. Mere inches from her face, the tip of a long, bloody knife burst through his chest. It pointed at her accusingly, calling her out on every mistake she had ever made. The upturned blade had sliced through the driver without resistance, sliding through his body like the hole had already been there, just waiting for the knife to come along and fill it.

She retreated, shrinking away from the oncoming threat as best she could. The truck's steel door limited her progress. The blade stopped just short of her throat. It hovered like the deadliest of hummingbirds, suspended in the air. She fought the urge to swallow, fearing even doing so would cause the blade's tip to prick her trembling flesh.

The blood-slicked blade taunted her for what seemed like hours before retreating. The driver's blossoming red chest swallowed it with a slurping sound as quickly as it had appeared. When the man from the woods drew back his arm, she watched in magnified horror as gravity reached up and grabbed the truck driver's body. It drew him toward the ground. With a final, wet sucking sound, the lifeless corpse that had been so threatening only seconds before, slid off the curved, sword-like knife and crumpled into a ruined mass at her feet.

A barrier no longer separated her from the killer.

Her breakfast churned in her stomach, threatening to join the growing puddle of crimson spreading over the gravel.

The knife rested beside the injured man's leg. Gore ran down its length in waves. It was as if the steel itself had been mortally wounded in the assault.

The man turned his attention. Wild eyes looked deep into hers. In them, she saw his plan. Her breath caught in her chest.

Frantic and consumed by fear, she turned away from the truck. She tried to run. With her first step, the heel of her right shoe wobbled, then snapped. There was no second step.

She hit the ground.

She screamed.

Moments later, an exhausted and barely conscious Corwin Barnes held a wadded piece of pink dress to the back of his head as he steered the tow truck onto the road, spraying a cloud of dust and gravel into the air, covering two more in his vast collection of nameless bodies.

ONE YEAR
LATER

CHAPTER 1

My hands would never be clean again.

I'd been working at Tipsword's Auto Repair for three months, and the grease and oil had wasted no time working their way into every crease on my fingers, every line on my palms. Thin, black, crisscrossing slashes like the veins on a leaf. It didn't matter how hard I scrubbed, or how long. Nineteen years old and already scarred for life.

An outside to match my inside.

I had just rotated the tires on a beat-up Ford Explorer and was washing my hands at the sink when Dallas Tipsword, the business's owner and namesake, stalked past, Wade hot on his heels. Wade was in his late twenties, an Army reservist, and Dallas' nephew. The guy was good. He knew his way around an engine the way a neurologist knows his way around a brain. Unfortunately, he also knew his way around a 12-pack of beer. He wasn't much of a mechanic—or employee, for that matter—when he couldn't find his way out of bed after an all-night bender. And it seemed to happen more and more frequently.

This was the point Dallas was making as he stormed through the shop on his way to the office.

"Can't have you working for me if I can't depend on your ass to be here!"

Dallas, himself, was a character. The guy looked like every sixty-two-year-old Vietnam vet ever portrayed on television. He had a salt and pepper ponytail and a chest-length beard to match. He even wore the obligatory tie-dyed t-shirts and flip-flops on the weekends. The first time my dad met him, he told me that if Dallas could sing, The Grateful Dead could revive their career. I didn't quite get the reference, but I took his word for it.

When it came to his auto repair shop, however, Dallas was all business. He had only two rules: be here on time, and be ready to work hard. That was all he asked of me as an employee, and in my inexperienced opinion, it seemed reasonable enough.

"Looks like it's just you and me now, kid," Dallas said, returning from his office.

"Oh, yeah?" I said, reaching for a paper towel. It was all I could muster at the moment. To be honest, the confrontation between my boss and his nephew had made me a little uncomfortable. It didn't take much nowadays. I'd developed an allergy to confrontation and drama in the last year.

"Today was the last straw." Dallas ran his fingers through his graying beard. "I needed that kid here at eight a.m. to finish the job he started yesterday. Not 11:30. Told Mrs. Cutter her Buick would be ready by ten, and I hate like hell not having a job done when I say it'll be."

"Sorry I wasn't much help on that one," I said, working the damp paper towel into the crevice around my thumbnail. The Buick had come in with a busted spring. Unfortunately, I hadn't yet been trained on busted springs. Dallas had to get in there and get his hands dirty. Ordinarily, he wouldn't have minded, but the first thing I learned about the auto repair business was that nobody likes to finish a job someone else has started. To be honest, Mrs. Cutter hadn't looked all that upset about having to sit and flip through a magazine for forty-five minutes, but Dallas sure was.

"No worries," he said. "But we have a few cars lined up right now. Nothing too serious. All things you can handle. Probably pick up some extra hours this week, if you want 'em. Till I can bring someone else in. I'll help as much as I can, but I got a million other things to do. Haven't quite figured out how to make the business run itself."

With the conversation at its end, Dallas walked over and pressed the green button on the wall to raise the nearest overhead. As the rickety door started its slow ascent, I cringed at the laboring grind of the motor. The rustling chain reminded me of the lift that had lowered my best friend's casket into the ground.

"By the way," he said, once he'd raised the door and the motor had fallen silent, "looks like there's a package in on the counter for you."

I scowled. "Really?"

Odd. I'd never received a package at the garage before. Nothing beyond the auto parts I'd order and have dropped off by the Napa driver. But, I hadn't ordered anything all week. Unless Claire or one of my parents had dropped by and left it without saying hello. Which seemed unlikely.

Dallas shrugged. Spinning a keyring around his finger, and whistling one of the oldies tunes in his repertoire, he headed out toward a red Civic that awaited him in the parking lot.

I finished drying my hands and tossed the crumpled paper towels into the trashcan before venturing into the office. I pulled my cell from my jeans pocket and checked the time.

Claire was supposed to pick me up for lunch around noon. My stomach was telling me it was getting close, and it was rarely wrong. My phone read 11:51 am. I glanced out the window, but didn't see Claire's car anywhere.

On the front counter, right where Dallas said it was, a small, white box sat among a collection of auto parts catalogues, grime-covered tools, and filthy white Styrofoam cups peppered with black fingerprints. When I was a kid, every Valentine's Day, my mother would give me a box of homemade fudge from Mrs. Marshall's candy store back in New Paris. She always included a handwritten note, reminding me to hide the fudge from my chocolate-addicted father. The box sitting on the counter looked very similar to all those fudge boxes. A piece of white notepaper taped to the top had 'LUKE' written across it in big black letters. There was no question who the box was meant for, yet there were no instructions, either. The note offered no hints at what was inside, nor whom the box was from.

I picked up the box.

It didn't weigh much. Made me wonder if there was even anything in it. When I held the box to my ear and shook it, something inside rattled. Whatever it was, it sounded small and loose and nothing at all like fudge. I'll admit to being a little disappointed. Like I said, I was hungry, and who doesn't like fudge? I worked the clear strip of tape holding the box closed until it pulled free.

When I lifted the lid, tufts of wrinkled, baby blue tissue paper fluffed up. I chuckled. *Let me out!* I imagined the tissue paper being held against its will. At the very least, it had been used before. Crumpled and wrinkled and a little dirty, stuffed into the corners more to take up space than for decorative presentation.

One piece poked up further than the rest, and I took hold. When the large clump of tissue paper came free, I gasped and dropped the box. It didn't slip out of my hand. It wasn't even on accident. I dropped the box on account of what was inside.

CHAPTER 2

The dead teenagers were everywhere. That's what the news referred to them as. 'The dead teenagers of New Paris, Ohio.' Like it was some kind of honorary f'ing title. Everywhere I went, reminders of last year's tragic events followed. The ghosts of the first two missing students would have been difficult enough to ignore. I hadn't known them all that well. But there were the chimeras of Becca and my best friend, Garrett. Both murdered. Both still hanging around town. Across the high school's parking lot. Watching me stuff my face with fries at the McDonald's. Lounging sad-faced at my kitchen table, like neighborhood children wishing I'd come out and play.

Rather than facing my demons head on, I simply left. Though, it wasn't entirely my decision. My parents thought it would put a cap on my recovery if we sought unfamiliar surroundings, somewhere away from New Paris and all of its ghosts. When it was all said and done, we ended up a whole half hour away. Dayton, of all places. Dayton. Ohio. Not exactly across the country, but I guess my parents felt it was far enough. I mean, we couldn't just up and move to the Black Hills of Utah or disappear into the cornfields of Nebraska. There were my parent's jobs to consider, after all.

At least I hadn't left too many people behind. Less than a

month after the town had laid four of its youngest and brightest to rest, Garrett's parents packed up his sister and left New Paris, heading somewhere out west. Our friend, Cricket, moved back to Mumbai once his father had completed the work he was here to do. So, there wasn't much left for me in the blip of a town, anyway.

The only friend who'd remained was Claire, whom I'd grown even closer to over the past year. We were dating now, brought together by the heartbreak and loss of mutual friends. And even though she had helped me through so much, Claire was away most of the time. While I was still doing my stint in the nuthouse, she was busy portraying a freshman at a liberal arts college near Columbus.

Sorry, mental health facility. That's what I'm supposed to call that place. Not a nuthouse. I spent seven weeks in the Sovereign Knolls Mental Health Facility, and I think the boredom made me crazier than I was when I checked in. Talking. That's all we did. I spent countless hours talking about my fears, my anger, and my difficulty distinguishing between the two. Talking in groups. Talking to my team of therapists. Not just one, mind you. A team. Four of them, to be exact. All with PhDs and yachts floating in the Florida Keys, thanks to my parents and me. It wouldn't have surprised me at all to learn there was a yacht named after me. Something like 'Teenager Overboard' or 'Luke's Insanity.'

Seven weeks I spent answering the same questions over and over. Was I still experiencing nightmares? (I wasn't) Did I still fear the boogeyman? (I didn't.) For the most part, at least. What precious little time they allowed me to be alone, I spent studying for the final exams I hadn't been able to take at the end of my senior year. Something had come up, and I'd had to postpone test-taking for a while. It's kinda hard to take an exam when you're laid up in the hospital with both a shattered ankle and psyche.

Post traumatic stress disorder. That was what they called it. What I 'had,' like it was some sort of disease or something. The patronizing result of unimaginable trauma. My particular trauma stemmed from the fact, not only had I been the one to find the remains of New Paris' missing girls in the basement of an abandoned church, but I'd also had a front-row seat to another girl losing her head right before my eyes. I lost my best friend. And if that was enough, I narrowly escaped the blade of the man responsible for it all. He'd done everything in his powers to add me to his grisly list of victims, but I got away. Only me. It didn't make me feel lucky. Or even fortunate.

It left me with more than one person's share of stress.

Besides the nightmares, the blackouts were the scariest part. My blackouts weren't the kind where I'd get light headed or faint. Mine were the kind that stole time away. Some people refer to it as 'losing time,' but I always felt like mine had been stolen. I had brought none of it on. Either way, they resulted in not knowing what the hell I'd been doing. One minute I would be standing in the kitchen loading the dishwasher, and next thing I knew, I'd be sitting in my truck out in front of the house, not knowing how I got there. The doctor's assurances that these episodes were common did nothing to ease the anxiety they brought. Being told other people dealt with blackouts as well didn't make me feel any better, either. Just because other people have cancer doesn't make yours any less shitty. The only thing that helped with the blackouts was when they stopped.

Like the limp I'll walk with for the rest of my life, I think he will always be with me, too. The boogeyman, that is. His once frequent jogs through my mind have diminished to an all-time low at this point. I can get through most days, sometimes even weeks, without a single thought of Corwin Barnes. But what my parents feared most, and the main reason they swept me away from our home in New Paris, was that Corwin Barnes was still thinking about me.

In escaping from Barnes, I'd taken out his equally demented stepdaughter. I won't lie. Having taken a life myself only added to the trauma. That the world was probably a better place without her didn't matter. There was also the fact I thought I'd killed Barnes, too. It turned out I hadn't. The cops never found him. The body was gone when they got there. Which meant he was still out there somewhere. And pissed. He was probably really, really pissed.

That point was driven home when I received the little white box at Tipsword's Automotive. Opening it answered two nagging questions: yes, Barnes was still thinking about me; and no, turns out Dayton wasn't far enough after all.

I stood at the counter—hands trembling, heart racing—staring down at the empty box and the three white bones lying on the grimy tile floor beside it. The bones, small and somehow locked together, formed a finger. A class ring, silver with an emerald green stone, lay a couple of inches away. Small balls of crumpled, blue tissue paper surrounded both items.

Who the finger had belonged to remained unknown.

The class ring was Garrett's.

I knew it without having to pick it up and take a closer

look. My heart thumped against my chest, not from fear, but from the implications. It didn't take a genius to realize that if it was Garrett's ring—and no amount of wishing would make it not so—it was most likely Garrett's finger.

My disgust turned to fear.

I could see Dallas through the large, plate-glass window separating the office from the shop. He stood beside the red Civic with a pneumatic drill in hand, looking back at me. The look on his face told me the look on mine puzzled him. I offered an Oscar-worthy grin and threw in a bullshit head nod. I wasn't sure he bought the validity of either, but they were convincing enough for him to return his attention to removing the wheels of the elevated sedan.

With my heart pounding to beat all hell and my stomach tying itself in knots, I bent down to retrieve the box. After a moment's hesitation, and a quick wipe of my clammy hands on my pants, I used a piece of tissue paper to scoop the skeletal finger and ring back into the box. Metal hit bone with a dull clank. A wave of cold electricity shot down my spine, standing my neck hair on end.

I had just straightened when a car horn blast nearly put me through the ceiling. I spun around with more alarm than was warranted and looked out the front window. Between the painted white and red lettering spelling out 'Tipsword's Automotive,' I saw Claire's silver Toyota Prius parked out front. A graduation gift from her parents.

With a deep breath, a sizeable cringe, and a sense of how wrong it all was, I stashed the box behind an oil filter display where it would stay hidden until I returned to deal with it after lunch. I didn't want Claire to see it. I didn't want her to know what was inside. Not because I didn't think she was strong enough to stomach it. I witnessed her dissect a gopher embryo in Advanced Biology at the start of our senior year. She'd been the only girl in the class who didn't excuse herself to the restroom at some point.

Claire would have stomached it just fine.

I didn't want her to see what was in the box because Garrett had been her friend, too.

CHAPTER 3

I spent most of the next hour paying little attention to my burrito, and even less attention to Claire. Even though the conversation was one-sided, it didn't stop her from holding her end of the bargain. She told me about the job she might get for the coming summer, and the girl in her dorm who was juggling two guys at once. All the things important in her life, but only registered as white noise in mine. I was normally a better listener, but today, I just stared at my half-eaten lunch. I wasn't as hungry as I'd been before opening the little white box. The only time I looked up from my food were to take inventory of the faces coming into the restaurant.

If Claire suspected something was bothering me, she didn't show it. After all, seeing me off in my own little world was nothing new to her. Over the past year, I'd made a habit of retreating inside myself from time to time.

"So, where are you today?"

"Huh?" I knew a question had been asked, yet wasn't sure what that question was. I'd just been called on in class, caught staring out the window.

"Nothing," she said, grinning between bites of taco salad. "So, enough about what's going on in my life. How's everything at the garage? I haven't checked in much, with finals and all."

"Alright." I poked at my burrito's insides with the world's least durable plastic fork. "Wade's gone. Dallas canned him today."

"Just leaves you, then?"

"For now. Told me I can get all the hours I want the next couple of weeks."

"That's good," she said, swishing around the iced tea in her Styrofoam cup. "Maybe you can get those rims. Start fixing up the truck like you've been wanting."

The mention of the truck turned the small amount of food in my stomach into something that would hold a large ship in place. The old Chevy 1500 had been Garrett's. His parents gave it to me before they left town. It's what Garrett would have wanted, they said. I'd been driving it ever since, trying to save enough money to fix it up the way Garrett had always talked about. Part of me shared his vision. Mostly I just wanted to make him proud.

I laid the fork down, crumpled my napkin, and dropped it onto the red plastic tray in front of me. I pushed my chair away from the table. "I'll be right back."

For the first time since picking me up, a look of concern came over Claire's face.

"You okay?"

"I think I'm gonna get sick."

And I did. I made it to the men's room and into the first stall before doubling over and emptying the contents of my stomach. It only took the one time to do the job. The second and third round of heaves were for good measure. Luckily, the awaiting toilet was cleaner than I would have expected.

As I knelt beside the porcelain john, one knee on the ground, stomach lurching as if considering a fourth round, I wondered why I was even here. Seeing the bones from my dead friend's finger was disturbing. But I'd seen so much worse in the basement of that church; unimaginable things no person should ever see, much less a punk teenage kid. All I could figure was it was hitting too close to home.

As he knew it would.

Because that was the other thing. Bones and ring aside, there was also the Corwin Barnes aspect of it. Creeping fear was keeping my stomach from settling. Fear he had found me. Fear he was coming my way. He was out there, somewhere, and if he had discovered where I worked, he most likely knew where I lived, where I went, and who I spent time with. He could even be watching Claire and me while we sat eating lunch.

My blood grew frost.

I scrambled to my feet.

The thought of Claire sitting out there alone…

I flushed the toilet, washed my hands, then took a look at myself in the mirror. The face that stared back at me said two things. One, I looked like shit. Considering the latest turn of events, I might just need to get used to it. And two, unlike the first time I faced Barnes, I wouldn't be able to handle this on my own. I had to tell someone. Just who, I wasn't quite sure yet.

My mind started sorting through the possibilities as I exited the restroom and made a beeline toward Claire.

CHAPTER 4

The entire ride back to the garage, I remained as quiet as I'd been at the taco joint. Add my abrupt disappearing act in the middle of lunch, and I was sure Claire suspected something was wrong at this point; something more than my usual awkwardness. She was a smart girl. Way smarter than me. Whether she believed it was a simple stomach problem or something more, she didn't press. I appreciated that. I wasn't ready to let her in on what was going on just yet. I also knew I couldn't keep her in the dark for long.

Part of me wanted to protect her from the emotional aspect of the small box's arrival. She'd been friends with Garrett, too, and this would rip off her emotional scabs, just as it had mine. There was also a part of me, albeit a small part, afraid she would think I was having a PTSD relapse. In the back of my mind, there was always the fear I would say or do something that would cause people to give me that look. The look saying, 'Is this it? Has he finally lost it?' I guess that problem would be solved once I actually showed her the box and all its contents. Though I wasn't looking forward to that, either.

Still, the knowledge that I had to tell someone nagged me like a determined pit bull with a taste for pant leg. My parents? I should tell them for sure. Sooner rather than later. They would get the police involved, most likely a good thing. There was only one issue. My parents had just started letting me out of their sight without staying up all night worrying. Just because my fragile psyche had been dealt a blow today, didn't mean I was in a hurry to do the same to theirs. I wasn't telling them just yet, either.

As Claire steered the Prius into Tipsword's parking lot, I decided there was only one person to whom I could go. Only one person who didn't have a direct stake in the matter.

Dallas sat perched on his stool behind the front counter as I climbed out of the car. The large front window brought the entire office into view. It didn't take long to start wondering just how vulnerable I was while at work. The entire front of the building was more glass than anything. You could see everything going on inside. That realization poured the queasiness back into my stomach. I'd been feeling better since we left the restaurant, but now I wondered if stomach problems were something I might have to get used to.

Despite the creeping sensation of neighborhood eyes watching me, I stood outside the office until Claire pulled away. As she did, I waved. She blew me a kiss in return. And just like that, she was gone. I scanned the street and nearby buildings—without really knowing what I was looking for—before ducking into the office.

The bell above the door announced my arrival.

Dallas glanced up from his muscle car magazine. It was his passion. In the far corner of the shop sat a '66 Chevy C10 Stepside he had spent the better part of five years restoring. The engine, transmission, and everything else under the hood were primed and ready to go. It was the weathered midnight blue body with its patches of grey primer that still needed work. But, according to Dallas, it wouldn't take much longer now that he was divorced, and the 'Dragon Lady' wasn't standing in his way, bitching about the time and money he spent on it. Whatever the excuse, he'd been divorced a couple years now, and the truck still sat there.

"How was lunch?" he asked, before tipping his head back and robbing a small bag of chips of its last remaining crumbs.

"Good," I lied.

He looked at me for a moment, crunching the last of his lunch before speaking his mind.

"Bullshit."

"What?" I crossed over to where the water cooler sat under a stack of clear plastic cups. I had the worst taste in my mouth, and I feared if I didn't get water soon, I would be stuck with it forever.

"Bullshit," he repeated, as matter-of-factly as the first time. He hadn't said it like he was calling me out. Just calling it like he saw it.

I wasn't offended. It was actually the opening I needed.

Twenty minutes later, I'd laid it all out for him, both figuratively and literally. The white box and its contents lay spread out on the counter . We were lucky no customers had come in during that time. Not sure how we would have explained it all. I told Dallas everything. I told him about the missing girls, the abandoned church, Garrett, Becca, and Corwin Barnes. Especially Corwin Barnes. Afterward, I stood there leaning against the counter and waited for a reaction, letting it all sink in. Every couple minutes, I looked out the front window and wondered if Barnes might be watching. I also wondered just how long the paranoia would last.

Dallas picked up the length of bones and eyed it closer; plucking it off the counter like it was a pen or piece of gum. I guess his time in Vietnam had left him immune to things like severed body parts. He turned it over in his hand, bending his head toward it like a jeweler. He even brought it up to his nose at one point and took a whif. Just as I was wondering what he was thinking, he saved me the effort of asking.

"They're glued." He held the bones up and bent them slightly at the joint. "Probably super glue or something. They wouldn't stay together on their own, and you don't see the glue once it dries like you would a wire. That's how I'd do it, too. Nice work actually. Guy knows his stuff."

It wasn't quite the reaction I had expected. But then that's why my first thought was to come to Dallas. His was the no-nonsense, level-headedness I needed.

"Are you positive this is your friend's finger?" he asked.

I took a moment to answer. It was such a strange question to ask someone.

"Pretty sure," I said, hoping it wasn't, but willing to bet it was. "I know for a fact it's his ring. Even has his initials on the side."

I looked out the window again. This time, an old, black SUV sat in the parking lot of the barred-up liquor store across the street. I couldn't remember if it had been there earlier or not. The reason it caught my eye now was because it had backed into the parking spot, not pulled in. Like the driver was on a stakeout or something. I swore the someone in that seat was looking back at me from the shadow of the vehicle's tinted interior. The man wore glasses, and though I didn't recall Barnes wearing them, I figured he could be now. Unfortunately, it was the only feature I could make out. And that was only because the glasses glinted in the sunlight when the guy moved his head.

Turns out, it was a false alarm. A moment later, an older woman in a black and white dress and carrying a brown paper bag exited the liquor store and climbed into the passenger side of the SUV. A moment later, the vehicle pulled out of the parking lot and onto the street, heading westbound. It afforded me a better look at the driver and confirmed what I suppose I already knew.

It wasn't Corwin Barnes.

"Okay, well," Dallas started, bringing me back to the present, "assuming it *is* from this Barnes guy, and he *is* back in the picture, the obvious first question is, what are you going to do?"

"I don't know," I admitted, glancing back at the now empty parking lot across the street. "Guess that's why I came to you first. And don't bother asking me why you specifically, because I doubt I have a good answer for that, either."

He looked at me.

I acted like I didn't notice, turning my attention once again to the world outside the window.

"What about your parents?" He ran his fingers through his beard. "They need to know. Then the cops. Maybe not even in that order."

"I know," I said, and it was a good question. Dallas seemed to have an entire arsenal of good questions, and I didn't have answers for any of them.

"Maybe tell your parents and let them deal with the police?" Dallas suggested.

I nodded at the logical order of things. Still, I was glad I'd told Dallas, and made him aware. I mean, the guy was ex-military, for crying out loud. That couldn't hurt.

The NAPA parts delivery truck pulled up out front, and I

quickly set about putting the bones and the ring back in the box.

"I'll tell them tonight," I assured Dallas, pressing the box closed.

"Maybe you should go tell them now," he said. "I can handle things around here for the rest of the day."

"No," I said, sliding the box into my pocket. Maybe getting some work done would clear my head. "I can finish my shift. If he wanted to kill me so bad, I'd be dead. He's trying to scare me."

"And is it working?"

I ignored the question, and after giving my boss a sidelong look, slipped through the door leading into the shop.

The rest of the day passed uneventfully. The worst part of it was having to walk out to the truck after my shift was over. It was a tense couple of seconds, which included Dallas' eyes on me from the back door. The neighborhood wasn't exactly Beverly Hills, and the alley behind the garage could hardly be confused with Rodeo Drive. Between the dumpsters and the skeletons of cars we sometimes pulled parts from, there were more places someone could hide out back than a creepy old church. It was a poor man's carnival funhouse, and the effect it had on my heart rate was the same. But I made it to my awaiting truck safely enough and started the short drive home just as the sun set behind the Gem City's darkening buildings.

CHAPTER 5

When I first got the truck from Garrett's parents, my father kind of wrinkled his nose about it sitting out in front of the house. It was an eyesore, he said, and it was hard to disagree. It was big and blue and rust was taking over around the wheel wells and tailgate. With its 35" tires and four-inch lift, the Chevy was too tall to hide in the garage. Since it had been Garrett's, my father made no more than the initial fuss about the truck before dropping the subject. My mother may have turned his ear, like she was so good at doing. Now all our neighbors were lucky enough to gaze upon Garrett's pride and joy every night.

I was sitting in the truck in front of the house that evening when I first saw the box. The day's second box, perched on the stoop beside my mother's sprawling fern. A plain, Amazon brown box. It was the size a toaster might come in. Unable to stop it, my mind started listing all the body parts that might fit inside.

Since my parents parked their cars in the garage and entered the house through the kitchen, I was the only one who used the front door. Therefore, I was the one most likely to find the package. I got the uncomfortable feeling Barnes knew this. The thought of him watching me come and go stood my hair on end.

I took a quick glance around and checked all three of the truck's mirrors. Nothing seemed out of the ordinary. No unfamiliar vehicles were parked on the street. No strange shadows lurked beneath lampposts that had recently lit up. Still, I didn't take for granted the possibility Barnes wasn't nearby.

I closed the driver side door and glanced once more up and down the street before rounding the truck and walking up the sidewalk. The goal was to limit my time in the open and not draw attention. I took the two steps leading up to the front porch and scooped up the cardboard box all in one motion.

The first thing I noticed was, like the box left for me at the shop, this one was also naked. No labels or writing of any kind. The second thing I noticed was the box was light. Like there was nothing inside but air. Though, as I held a box up to my ear and shook it for the second time that day, I could make out a slight rattling sound. It couldn't be much, but something certainly awaited me inside.

With the heightened rhythm of my heart urging swiftness, I fumbled with my keys before unlocking the door, stepping inside, and then slamming it shut behind me. Once I'd made sure the door was locked and secure, I peeked through the window beside it. Nothing.

Only then did I dare flip on the hallway light.

The kitchen, like the rest of the house, was on the small side. A simple room in a simple house in a rather quiet and simple neighborhood in north Dayton. The word 'nondescript' described it all to a T. Enough to seat people at the table and still be able to move around the kitchen, we had set the rectangular dining table against the wall under the window overlooking the narrow side yard. On the table is where I dropped the box. I was in no hurry to open it. I wanted to search the house for parents before doing anything.

However, the search was quickly deemed unnecessary. In the middle of the table was a small notebook my mother usually kept off to the side where odds and ends like the mail or car keys gathered. Now the notebook was front and center, opened to the middle with a pen laying on top. My mother had left a note. Closer inspection revealed the note was meant for me.

Apparently, my father had a business dinner, one that actually allowed my mother to accompany him this time. I read the double underlining of the words 'woo-hoo' in parentheses as either excitement or sarcasm. I wasn't sure which. Anyway, they wouldn't be home until late. The note also mentioned a twenty-dollar bill in the savings jar if I wanted to order a pizza.

The words 'fuck that' came immediately to mind. No way in hell was I opening the front door for anyone. I knew what Corwin Barnes looked like. He'd taken up residency in my head for the better part of a year. But, changing one's looks wasn't all that hard. Nor would I put it past him to use a pizza delivery kid as a means to drop in.

No, the door was locked, and it would stay that way.

I went around and closed all the blinds covering the downstairs windows. I considered turning lights on in every room, but stopped short. I bristled at the thought of spending the evening alone, but that would have been an entirely new level of paranoia. I wasn't a child, after all. I wasn't scared of the dark.

I made sure the back door was locked, as well as the side door leading to the garage. Before locking the garage door, however, I made a bold move. I stuck my head in and flipped on the light. The garage was empty. Both cars were gone. My mother must have met my father at the restaurant. From the doorway, I gave a cursory glance around. No one crouched behind the trash cans. No one hid beside the cabinet where my dad stored his bags of lawn fertilizer and bottles of windshield washer fluid. The coast was clear. There was no serial killer intent on harvesting my bones lurking about. I wasn't sure I expected him to be. Still, checking it off the list made me feel better. I flipped the light back off, then closed and locked the door.

Since I'd lost the bit of lunch I'd eaten, I found myself surprisingly hungry, despite the seed of fear germinating in my stomach.

I poked my head in the refrigerator and sorted through packages of lunchmeat and plastic containers full of leftovers. All the while, the question of whether I should call the police nagged at me like a lost child tugging the sleeve on a stranger's jacket. When it came down to it, I felt I should talk to my parents first, and would do so as soon as they got home. No more stalling. Finding where I worked was one thing. If Barnes knew where I lived, then my entire family could be in danger. And that was unacceptable.

The image of Corwin Barnes holding his bolo knife to my mother's throat popped into my head. I cringed. That backward sloping blade had separated Becca's head from her body with little resistance. Imagining it pressed against my mother's skin piqued a charge of anger somewhere inside me. I shook my head as if it were an Etch-a-Sketch. Doing so didn't clear the image from my mind, but it knocked it out of focus long enough for me to grab a container and shut the refrigerator door.

In my rush to secure the house, I'd nearly forgotten the cardboard box. Or, had I? Perhaps, subconsciously, I'd busied myself the last ten minutes for that very reason. Now, however, as I set a blue Tupperware container of three-day-old beef stroganoff on the table, the box proved difficult to ignore. The phrase 'if it had been a snake, it would have bitten me' slithered into my thoughts. Thankfully, I was fairly certain a snake wasn't inside. The box was too light.

With my heart rate rising, I slid the bowl aside and went to the utensil drawer to retrieve a knife. Six or seven gleaming blades stared at me from the bottom of the drawer, each wanting their turn with the box. After a few seconds deliberation, I chose a small paring knife with a black handle sufficient enough to slice through tape. I grabbed my father's long carving knife as well, just for the heck of it. I'd seen him sharpen it more than I'd seen him use it, so I knew it would get the job done. Whatever that job might be.

I started on one end and slid the paring knife into a seam along the top. The clear packaging tape put up little fight against the sharp knife. Within seconds, I'd cut through the tape that sealed both sides of the box top and the seam running across the middle. And just like that, I was in. The thumping of my heart resonated all the way into my ears.

I set the knife down and stared at the box for at least a minute, trying to work up the nerve to look inside. Garrett's body had been found in the tool shed beside the abandoned church. Barnes had tied him up and slit his throat, otherwise, his body was intact. Was it possible Barnes had taken off one of my friend's fingers without being noticed? Sure. Anything was possible. But, it was unlikely much else could have been missing without it being reported. Even an article of clothing. In today's world, details like that don't make it past the rumor mill. I would have heard about it. I wasn't so naïve, however, to think all the information gathered and inventoried that night had been shared with me. Especially given the state I was in. Maybe the finger bones belonged to Garrett, maybe they didn't. Maybe whatever was in this box belonged to Garrett, maybe it didn't. There was only one way to find out.

I swallowed hard and opened the box.

The empty box. Empty except for a folded sheet of paper. No bones, no personal effects. Certainly nothing as dangerous as a snake. Pulling out the piece of paper, I braced myself. I told myself I could handle whatever the note or letter had to say.

I was wrong. Because it was more than a note. Way more. Photos of my mom, my dad, Claire, and ultimately, myself, were taped to one side of the sheet of paper.

My heart caught in my chest. I ceased to breathe. On the bottom of the page, in one-inch, handwritten, black letters was a message…

'IMAGINE ALL THE PARTS OF YOU I COULD FIT IN THIS BOX'

Unfortunately, having seen Barnes' handiwork up close, imagining it was all too easy.

CHAPTER 6

With the empty box sitting in the garage, and the threatening note laying on my dresser, I stood at my bedroom window overlooking the back yard and the elementary school beyond. The school grounds, like the night itself, were still. The swings hung idle, the basketball, tetherball, and hopscotch courts empty. There wasn't even a dog being walked. The night went about its business as if nothing out of the ordinary had happened that day.

The same couldn't be said for me.

My entire world had changed.

With my bedroom lights off, Bring Me the Horizon's *It Never Ends* shredded my wireless speaker. The carving knife I'd carried through the house and set on my nightstand rattled from the pounding bass. I closed my eyes and breathed deep. This kind of music was supposed to be off-limits. The doctors feared the artillery fire rhythms and rage-soaked screams would stimulate my brain too much; which, they said was bad for my mental stability. But, that was a year ago, and the sounds of waterfalls and rain they'd prescribed wouldn't cut it. Not tonight. I needed music to match my current emotions. Fear was most prominent, but anger had also reported for duty. It smoldered in the back of the room like a bully who'd been stood up to. Besides, it was nearing midnight, and I needed something to keep me from falling asleep until I could talk to my parents.

And that sure as hell wasn't a job for the soothing sounds of water.

In the hours since I'd opened the second box, I'd left three messages on each of my parents' cell phones. None of the calls had been returned. That I hadn't heard from either of them caused only slight alarm. It wasn't beyond the norm not to hear from them. Neither used their phones like they should. They weren't teenagers, after all.

Still…

He's out there somewhere.

The thought had returned throughout the day. Looking out my window, it somehow took on an entirely new meaning. It wasn't just the trigger to a campfire ghost story. Corwin Barnes *was* out there. Somewhere in the city, somewhere in the shadows. Behind the neighbor's evergreens. In a car parked down the street. The large plastic tunnel on the school's playground with the bubble window that faced our house. I wondered if he could see me standing there, framed by my window, blending into the darkened room behind me.

A shiver rolled through my shoulders.

I closed the blind and stepped away from the window. By the glow of the blue light on my speaker, I made my way over to my bed and laid down. Staring up at a ceiling concealed in black, I wondered what the police would do once I informed them. Maybe more importantly, I wondered how long it would take them to do it. Barnes knew where I lived, where I worked, and the names and faces of the people closest to me. He could make a move on any of them, at any time. That he hadn't come after me yet, somehow bothered me the most. What was he waiting for?

In discussions with my therapists about Barnes and why someone would do the things he did, I learned all about Antisocial Personality Disorder. Barnes was a sociopath, which allowed him to kill and dismember his victims without remorse, empathy, or regard for society's laws. Repurposing the bones and selling them for a profit also meant he dealt with at least some psychosis, which put him more in the psychotic category. It seems ol' Corwin fit both bills. I couldn't care less what they called it. Either way, taking innocent human beings and turning them into a commodity was just plain fucked up.

Coming after me was something entirely different, though. There was no financial gain to be had. Nothing for Barnes to garner other than the personal satisfaction of ridding the world of my presence. It was revenge in its purest form; cold, personal and calculating.

It had been almost twelve hours since I'd opened the first box, the one delivered to Tipsword's. That made for a long day lost in thought and worry. Needing a distraction, I shut off the music, grabbed the remote off the nightstand, and clicked on the television my father had mounted on my wall last year hoping to lessen the blow of having to move away. I told him it did, but wasn't sure. Maybe a movie or some bad reality TV would take my mind off things until my parents got home. It shouldn't be too long. They rarely went out, and when they did, they were usually home in time for the eleven o'clock news.

With tonight being the rare exception, I wasn't yet worried, but wondered if I should be.

It took only a few moments to discover there was nothing on. Friday nights were the worst for cable programming.

Anyone with a life was out doing things, having fun, being a functioning member of the bustling world. If I didn't have to work the next morning, I would have been out doing things, too. Then, I thought about the boxes and whom they were from, and I remembered the real reason I was staying in tonight.

After settling on Conan, I dropped the remote onto the bed beside me. Dressed in a grey pinstripe suit with a red and white tie, the talk show host was debating Mark Wahlberg on who would look better in nothing but a pair of boxers. The audience was cheering, encouraging the actor to stand up and remove his shirt. I don't know if he ever did, because that was about the time the stress of the day caught up with me, and I fell asleep.

CHAPTER 7

Cavernous.

That's how I would describe the emptiness beyond the doorway. Pitch black. Hollow. Where the steps led, I did not know. They disappeared into a swirling dark fog that started about seven or eight steps down. The murk churned angrily, like a storm brewing at the bottom.

I had the pestering feeling I'd been here before.

My hand groped the wall beside me. Instincts told me a light switch would be there somewhere. My fingers found the rectangular plastic plate first, then the switch.

I jerked my hand back.

Something wasn't right. The switch wasn't the hard plastic it should be. The object on the wall was soft and fleshy. It felt almost like a fingertip, only smaller. My skin crawled at the possibilities. I took a deep breath and reached back up. I felt nothing out of the ordinary this time. I felt nothing at all. The entire light switch was gone. My hand caressed nothing but cold plaster.

I ran my hand all over the wall. There had to be a switch somewhere, though it eluded me. It was only when I'd stepped down onto the first step and reached far out along the wall that my fingertips brushed against the corner of the switch's plastic plate. It was located ridiculously far down the wall, much further into the stairwell than it ever should have been. It was almost as if the basement itself was trying to lure me down the steps, pulling the carrot farther and farther away. At least the switch was the normal hard plastic this time. No flesh.

Déjà vu hit me full-on as I flipped the switch. The dark fog disappeared, chased by the pale-yellow light of a lone, naked bulb hanging at the foot of the stairs. Its weak illumination revealed a grimy, cracked, and uneven concrete floor. A familiar stench rose from the cracks like steam. Long forgotten rot. I was no longer in my bedroom. I was in an awful place. A terrible place.

I was back in the church where I'd first crossed paths with Corwin Barnes.

Saying a wave of apprehension washed over me right then would be like saying having a limb lopped off would hurt a little. Not only was it an obvious statement, but so much so it was embarrassing to even point out. My hands trembled, my neck and forehead broke in a slick sheen. My heart felt like a drummer keeping time in a death metal band. Still, I ignored the nagging urge to turn away from the stairs, to run out of the place before it could get its claws in me a second time. I had to ignore it. If I was here again, I was here for a reason. I just didn't know what that reason was.

Garrett?

A soft murmur came from somewhere deep in the bowels of the basement. If it was possible for a murmur to sound familiar, this one did. The tone's inflection was one I recognized, and it urged me on.

With a confidence born more of righteousness than bravery, I took the first step. Then the second. Before I knew it, I was halfway to the bottom. Or halfway to the top, depending which side of me you asked. By nature, I was equal parts optimist and pessimist, swaying back and forth between the two like a windblown tree. With each step, the grimy floor grew closer, the pained murmurs louder until eventually, I'd gone too far to turn back.

As soon as I planted my feet on the concrete floor, the murmurs stopped. It was as if I had triggered something or breached some invisible barrier. I waited a moment and listened. No sounds replaced the low, guttural moaning. There was only silence.

And shadows.

The entire basement was awash in foreboding gloom, black as tar, beckoning from just outside the glare of the naked bulb. It was just like the first time, and I couldn't shake the growing dread over what I might find in the church's bowels this time around.

I would find nothing, I told myself, without some kind of light to penetrate the dark corners. And if there was anything to find down here, it only stood to reason the darkness is where it would reside. Hiding. Waiting. Reaching into my pocket for my cell phone, I came away with nothing but small wads of lint. Searching the rest of my pockets, I came up just as empty. Unless I stumbled upon another source of light down here, which seemed unlikely, this was as good as it was going to get.

The sound of shuffling caught my attention from somewhere to my left. The sound came from the same area I'd found Becca hanging by a hook. The realization sent a tingling sensation tiptoeing across the base of my neck. Then the soft shamble ceased. As I stood listening to heavy silence, I questioned whether I'd heard anything at all.

When the sound returned, I felt a strange sense of relief. I took comfort in the fact I hadn't been hearing things. The realization I was no longer alone, however, stomped the out that comfort like a burning twig before it could become a forest fire.

"Hello?" Miraculously, I got the word out with only a hint of a tremor in my voice. In fact, I sounded somewhat confident. In reality, it was a confidence I didn't feel, and I hoped like hell it wasn't about to be tested. "Is someone down here?"

"Luke."

The voice was soft, familiar. I knew the lips that spoke my name all too well. Hearing it come from the shadowy depths made my heart stop beating.

"Luke... help me... please."

A spark flickered deep in the shadows. A candle sat on the floor, and as its flame grew, it illuminated the space above it. A person hung in that space. Someone I was intimately familiar with. It wasn't Becca this time. It wasn't Garrett. It was Clair. She hung from a rope, not by her wrists like Becca, but by her neck.

The thick sinewy rope looped around my girlfriend's throat, so tight I wasn't sure how she could even speak. Purplish rolls of neck skin bulged through the gaps of the rope that, at initial glance, looked like long, corded fingers. It was the only way she could have been hanging there. Her arms were both gone, severed at the shoulder. Her legs, also gone. There was nothing but a torso. Nothing but remains.

Although open, her all-white eyes held no life. They stared off into a space that didn't include me. There was no rise and fall in her chest, no movement at all. She didn't appear to be alive, although I was sure it had been her voice calling out to me.

Something in my heart fractured and gave way. I wanted to run to her. I wanted to wrap my arms around her and lower her down.

Fear kept my feet planted.

Before I could choose a means of action, a form emerged from behind Claire. A man stepped into the candlelight and smiled. Not just any man. Corwin Barnes. The man I once thought I'd rid the world of, leaving him for dead beside a lake a year ago. After all this time wondering if he would come, he'd answered that question. Answered it in the affirmative. Not only had he found me, but he now stood a mere ten feet away.

Pure evil carved Barnes' face into a smile. A sour taste formed in my mouth. His crooked teeth, grey and foul, projected this way and that, as if they couldn't all get on the same page. Scars decorated his bald head in no uniform fashion, telling no story. They were just there. The rough scar cutting across his temple appeared more recent, the result of blunt force trauma. Something deep inside me recognized the scars as a job well done—only not done well enough.

Despite there being no breeze, the candlelight flickered.

Barnes' smile faded.

"I believe you know this one," he said, his snarled lips barely moving. He turned to Claire, and after bringing back the jagged smile, nudged her torso. What remained of my girlfriend started swinging back and forth like a side of beef. With each arc, the rope squeaked from rubbing against the overhead wooden rafter. Back and forth. To and fro. Each tiny shriek of the rope caused a shutter to cut through me.

Looking into my eyes, Barnes gave Claire a second

shove, this time harder. It was on her outward swing, when she was furthest away from Barnes, that I glimpsed what he held in his right hand; what he had been hiding in Claire's shadow all along.

The bolo knife.

That familiar blade glinted in the flickering candlelight. When I saw it, Barnes must have recognized the fact in my expression. His expression changed. His smile faded. His wild eyes gave birth to a rage he hadn't possessed earlier.

A scream erupted from Claire's dead, constricted throat. High and shrill, it curled the hairs on the back of my neck. It sent shivers dancing down my spine. I clamped my hands over my aching ears, but it did little to muffle the scream. Claire's once lifeless eyes were now very much alert.

"Luke! Run!" Her high-pitched shriek echoed throughout the darkened room and into the far reaches.

Barnes took a step toward me.

With few options, I did as Claire had instructed. I turned and I ran. I took the stairs two at a time, hoping to accomplish two things: put distance between Barnes and me; and put myself closer to the open doorway at the top of the steps.

Only it wasn't open. Not anymore. Even though I'd left it open. *Damnit!* It was as if the church itself was lending Barnes a hand, making sure I didn't get away a second time.

I crashed into the towering wooden door with as much momentum as I could build, hoping to either bust it open or break it down altogether. I had no preference and would have been good with either outcome. But the door didn't budge. It felt like it had hunkered down and braced itself for impact. The throbbing pain shooting through my shoulder offered testimony to the fact.

The footsteps behind me were slowing now they'd reached the stairs. Wood creaked under each deliberate step. I cowered against the door, jiggling the handle, too frightened to turn and look. My heart raced faster with every clomp of a heavy boot on wood, throttling my chest from inside. I pictured Barnes taking his time to creep up the stairs, knife in hand, savoring the knowledge I had nowhere to go. This was it. This is where I would die. Corwin Barnes was finally getting his man.

I awaited death with eyes seized shut.

I imagined how much it would hurt when the tip of the bolo knife slid its way into my back and freed my blood.

Just as Barnes' hot breath hit my neck, the door opened. Flew open, in fact, and I tumbled into a room full of bright light and voices. I didn't recognize any of them, but people were talking. Bantering. There was a woman's voice, and what sounded like two men, but neither of them was Barnes.

I looked around with eyes still trying to focus. Corwin Barnes was gone. So was the dark stairway. The dingy basement had transformed back into my bedroom, and I sat in bed, wrapped in damp sheets.

Safe. Alive.

The television blasted from high on the wall above my dresser. On its screen, the Channel 7 traffic reporter stood in front of a quad of screens, pointing to the activity on each. Tiny red and white lights formed intermittent rows as Dayton's early morning rush was getting underway.

And as my heart rate slowed to normal, I knew what had to be done. I also knew who would have to do it.

CHAPTER 8

"Honey, I don't think it's there anymore."

My mother paced the living room like an expectant father. The detective and I stood to the side looking on. The roots of her auburn hair were showing her age, and with trembling hands, she kept tucking strands of it behind her ears. Her frenzied expression had that, 'oh, no, it's happening' look. In her defense, it was early morning, and she hadn't had her coffee yet. Even if she had, getting hit first thing in the morning with what I had hit her with would have unnerved any parent. I'd started her day by dropping the 'B-word.'

Barnes.

In the kitchen, my father was on the phone, trying to track down one of the original investigators of the case from a year ago. His voice rose from time to time, and we could hear his frustration all the way on the other side of the house. The robust smell of fresh brewed coffee was also making its way in, so I suspected my father was one step ahead of my mother in that regard. If he hadn't been on the phone, he would have been pacing right along beside her. His face had gone about as white as a person's could when I first broke house protocol and spoke of he who should not be named.

"I'm pretty sure they bulldozed it once all the remains were recovered and the investigation was done." My mother paused a beat before voicing the word 'remains.' A year later, and the whole ordeal was still difficult for her to talk about. I sometimes wondered if I was the only member of the family that should have been talking with therapists after it all went down. Truth be told, it would have done my parents some good, too.

I had a sense my mother was wrong about the old church being bulldozed. Call it denial, call it a mother's attempt to protect her son, but I think she would have given me that line regardless of what she knew to be the truth. Maybe it was the dream, maybe it was my Spidey sense masquerading as a gut feeling, but the derelict house of anything-but-God needed to be checked out. Someone needed to make sure Corwin Barnes wasn't back in the dismemberment business and wasn't using his old workshop in the bowels of that abandoned church to do it. I knew it was just a dream, and not some psychic premonition, but still. Corwin Barnes was back. It was worth someone going out to have a look-see.

"We'll look into it," said Detective Morgenstern, a tower of a man with a sculpted jaw and spiral notepad. Unfortunately, his pen hadn't been working nearly as hard as that jaw since he arrived. He had barely written anything I'd said in the last ten minutes, so I was less than confident he would follow through on his assurances. He and his dark grey sport coat seemed to only be going through the motions. If his smile was supposed to be comforting, it was failing miserably. It came across more like, 'I'm just trying to get out of here and get to McDonald's and that hot little blonde who smiles when asking me how much sugar I'd like in my free cup of coffee.'

"Do you even know where I'm talking about?" I asked, not keeping the frustration out of my voice, nor trying very hard to. Fear was fueling my attitude. The dream was still very vivid in my mind.

"Abandoned church," the detective said. "Preble County. Burns murders. Got it."

"Barnes!"

"Barnes. Right." He made a small notation on his pad. Whether it was a correction, I couldn't tell.

I still wasn't convinced, but I'd already decided not to waste any more time trying to persuade this guy. Either he would look into it or he wouldn't. There were other cops. There were other options.

"Detective, what are your thoughts on the packages?" My mother shot a sidelong glance at the two boxes resting on the coffee table. Both still held their contents, both sealed tight in their own separate plastic bags. Tests were being ordered on all of it, Morgenstern had assured us. Fingerprinting and the like.

"If those aren't a direct threat," she continued, "I don't know what is. Especially the second one. At the very least, it means that psycho is somewhere close. At most, it means he's coming after my son. If not all of us."

When the detective said, "Now hold on," I decided once and for all I didn't like the guy. "We don't even know who dropped off the boxes. Could just be a prank."

"But, it's his ring—" I started, before the detective cut me off by holding up his notebook like a stop sign.

"Now, this Corwin Barnes," he continued, "if he's responsible for what you said he was, then he's in the system. There will be a standing warrant out for him. I'll look into it."

"And in the meantime?"

"In the meantime, ma'am, you folks might check

yourselves into a hotel if it would make you more comfortable. There's not enough here to justify a security detail. Just make sure we have a contact number so we can get in touch if something turns up."

"Including Corwin Barnes?" I asked.

"Especially Barnes."

The emphasis on the word 'especially,' the slight nod and narrowing of his eyes. It was all for show, designed to instill confidence he would show up and kick Barnes' ass if need be. At least after his stop off at McDonalds. It may have just been frustration, but I now had even less confidence that the good detective would check out the church. And a moment later, when he closed his notepad and stuck it in the pocket of his sport coat noting nothing about the church, there was no confidence left to be had on my part. I only hoped my father was having better luck in the kitchen.

"Hey, so," I said as the detective reached down and picked up the bags of what was now evidence, "about the church…"

"We'll see what we can do," the detective said, smiling and nodding as he turned to head out.

"So, that would be a no," I said, shaking my head. I don't think the detective heard me. If he did, he didn't show it. One person heard me, however, and she let me know about it.

"Luke," said my mother, in a hushed, yet still authoritarian voice. "I'm sure the police will do their job and check out all the possibilities. Give 'em a chance."

I couldn't tell if my mother was temporarily delusional or trying to ease my fears. Fears she probably shared, but found wiser to keep to herself for the time being. Or who knows? Maybe she was right. Maybe we could trust the cops to serve and protect us, and I was just being paranoid and anxious. This entire ordeal had me on edge, probably knocking me back a few steps in my recovery. A relapse is what they called it. My team of therapists would love the opportunity to get back inside my head and poke around. Make another payment on those yachts.

It was when my mother was walking the detective through the foyer, showing him to the door, that my already rough start to the day turned even worse. It wasn't so much that my mother said the words, 'oh, hello,' it was how she said them. Hesitantly. Pensive. Without explanation, I knew what those two words meant. I also had a pretty good idea to whom she'd said them.

I'd been texting Claire all morning and getting no response.

A moment later, when my mother returned to the family room, Claire followed close behind. Her face was as pale as a wet paper towel, her shoulders slumped forward. Her arms cradled her upper torso like there was a nip in the air.

Shit.

I think I'd kept the thought in my head. Maybe not. Maybe I said it under my breath. I can't be sure. I was focused on the redness of Claire's eyes. I went over and wrapped my arms around her like it would make everything better, even though I knew it wouldn't. The reality of it was, she was in just as much danger as anyone close to me, and knowing that made me feel like shit. Down deep, I knew she had a right to know. This just wasn't how I wanted her to find out.

With a reassuring caress of Claire's shoulder and a sympathetic smile for me, my mother left the room.

"Your dad," Claire said. "He let me in. But he was on the phone, so I just stood there in the foyer."

Shit. Shit. Shit.

"So, you—"

"Heard everything," she finished. "Well, at least the last few minutes of conversation. It was enough."

"I'm sorry," I said, and pulled her in even tighter. The uncertainty in her haunted eyes was killing me. She was like a baby deer that'd just seen its mother get sideswiped by a sedan. Lost. Scared.

"I knew something was wrong yesterday," she said, face nuzzled against my chest. "At lunch. Something more than your usual detachment. Thought I'd see if you wanted to grab coffee before you went to work this morning. I guess... I guess now I know what was bothering you."

We stood there for a quiet moment, a frightened and worried young man trying to console a frightened and worried young woman. But there was something else, too. Despite the fear, or rather because of it, a flicker of genuine anger sparked inside me, trying to catch flame. When I felt the shudder run through Claire's body, the flame caught.

And I was no longer just afraid.

I was pissed.

CHAPTER 9

Claire's parents still lived in New Paris, but since they were on an Alaskan cruise, mine felt it best she stay with us for the time being. Especially since Barnes had included her photo in his threatening note. Claire had an older sister who worked as a lobbyist in DC, but after much debate, we decided it was best not to drag anyone else into this matter if we didn't need to. 'No reason to put any more innocents in harm's way,' was how my father put it.

Later that day, while I went to work and tried to concentrate on something other than Barnes and getting dead, my mother and Claire packed a few things and checked into a hotel with decent security on the other side of the city. Far enough it would hopefully throw Barnes off our scent, but still close enough to continue life as we knew it. Although, the life I'd known had transformed. For the second time. It was a holiday weekend, and except for my having to work a few hours that Saturday morning, we could all lie low for the next couple days.

In typical Ohio fashion, Memorial Day weekend was off to a soggy start. Rain clouds had parked themselves over the city, making for a gloomy day. Too gloomy for putting on a happy face, so I didn't bother trying. I only hoped the hours would pass quickly since we had a backlog of cars in need of repair.

The people of Dayton were rough on their vehicles, which was great for business.

Dallas worked alongside me, replacing the brakes on a newer model Nissan. I didn't mind. He wasn't a typical boss, at least from my limited experience. He was about as easy going as they came. We listened to music. We talked about things. We discussed the prospect of me working through the weekend, picking up some of those extra hours he'd mentioned the day before. Dallas tried to backpedal, though, after I told him about my dream. He felt my time might be better spent taking care of my own business.

I assured him that wasn't the case.

"I just need to check it out," I said, wiping my black hands on an already soiled towel. The rag had once been red, but you never would have guessed it. "See if it's even still there."

"And if it is?" Dallas asked, eyebrows raised. He eyed me while leaning on a lever, lowering the black SUV back to the ground.

I just shrugged. It was a good question, one I hadn't yet thought of. What if the church *was* still there? Hell, what if Barnes was there? What would I do? I'd dealt with Barnes on his turf once and made it out alive. Could I do it again? I wasn't sure. I only knew the cops wouldn't check out the church, and more than anything right now, I felt a survey of it was warranted. If Barnes was back to work, it was possible he was using the same place that had concealed his activities so well the first time. Not to mention a place he obviously felt comfortable, as secluded as it was.

Was he that stupid? Somehow, I didn't think so, but it meant everything to find out for sure.

"Well," Dallas said, opening the door to the Nissan and

climbing inside so he could back it out, "I sure as shit ain't lettin' you go out there by yourself. When you thinkin' of goin'?"

A flash of light shocked the dimly lit garage. Crashing thunder followed. Within seconds, the raindrops that had been dancing on the metal roof for the last hour turned things up a notch. It sounded like an angry mob was trying to break in from above. The noise drowned out the corner radio that was always tuned to the classic sounds of either the 60s, 70s or 80s.

"Soon," I said, speaking loud enough for Dallas to hear. "Sooner the better. But this time, it's got to be daylight out. I'm not insane enough to go out there at night again." Then, right on cue, an icy chill ran down my spine, settling into my lower back.

"Well, then, looks like today would be less than ideal," Dallas said, just before another well-timed clap of thunder. "What do you say we go out there tomorrow morning, see what we can find?"

While I wasn't keen on waiting another twenty-four hours, I wasn't excited about going out there in this weather, either. It was storming the last time I stepped foot in that church, and things didn't go all that well. Call it being paranoid, I don't care. I also didn't like the idea of going by myself. I'd already determined asking either of my parents was out of the question. Neither would have gone for it, and would have only tried to talk me out of it. And if I was going back out to the church, I couldn't think of anyone better to have by my side than an ex-soldier with weapons experience. So, if Dallas was willing to go as long as we waited a day, then waiting a day is what I'd do.

"Meet here around nine?" I asked, raising the overhead

door so Dallas could pull the Nissan out.

"Sounds like a plan," he said, glancing up at the clock above the office door. "In the meantime, your ass is still mine for another ninety minutes. Would be nice to get some work out of ya for a change."

Dallas's jab brought a grin to my face. I had to say, it felt good to have my ass wanted for something other than killing it.

I spent the rest of my rainy Saturday huddled in a hotel room trying to learn Euchre and assuring my mother I was okay. My father and I shared a room, while Claire stayed with my mother in the one adjoining it. It was my mother who insisted we split up that way, despite the fact both Claire and I were creeping up on twenty and had even spent the night together on occasion. It wouldn't be appropriate, my mother said. We left the connecting door open all day and didn't close it until we went to bed. Even then we left it open a crack. Just in case. Security still trumped decency.

CHAPTER 10

"There's gotta be a McDonald's around here somewhere," Dallas muttered. His eyes scanned the passing landscape like a junkie in search of a fix. "Fuckin' White Castle or something."

We rode in silence for the next half hour, watching acres of trees race past the windows, keeping our eyes peeled for a McDonald's or a 'fuckin' White Castle.' Occasionally, we'd pass by a group of houses and an abandoned gas station that was now either a tanning salon or pizza shop. A Dollar General here and there. But, that was as close to a fast-food restaurant as we'd come across. Little green signs on the side of the road told us the names of the towns. The only remarkable thing about any of them was that someone had taken the time to name each one of them. And here I'd thought New Paris was small.

"Anyone else getting nervous?"

I had all but forgotten Claire in the back seat. She'd been so quiet the whole time. But then, we all had. A sense of hushed contemplation hung inside Dallas's beat up Jeep Wrangler. I guess we were all feeling a little uneasy about the church and what we might find there. That Claire had come along for the ride only added to my uneasiness. But, once I'd tripped up and mentioned my plan to her, she'd insisted. No matter what I said. I wasn't sure if she wanted to be there for me, or if a part of her wanted to see the place once and for all, satisfy her own morbid curiosity.

"Nope," Dallas said, answering Claire's question through a mouth full of jalapeno-flavored potato chips. His hunger had gotten the better of him, and he'd given up on finding fast food along the back roads of western Ohio. Coming across a gas station in Camden, he'd pulled in and loaded up on chips, Twizzlers and enough coffee for the three of us, even though Claire and I had both said we were good. It amazed me what passed for breakfast with this guy.

To answer Claire's question, I offered only an encouraging smile and a brave face. I wasn't sure she bought it, but the last thing I needed was to let my girlfriend know I wasn't just a little nervous about going back to the church, I was damn near petrified. The feeling grew the closer we got. I wasn't so afraid of the church, or what we might find there. If I had to bet all the money I had, I'd bet it on not finding anything. What had me most worried was the prospect of starting all over with the doctors when it was all said and done. When I'd said goodbye to them months ago, I'd hoped it would be for good.

CHAPTER 11

Nothing about the trees themselves looked familiar. None stood apart from the others, creating a landmark I might recognize. No oddly shaped trunks someone would want to capture for a calendar. Together, however, the trees in one area created an almost tangible feeling of foreboding. Something was just a little off about this stretch of woods.

Call it a survivor's intuition.

"Slow down," I said, my eyes absorbing nothing but green through the windshield. It was the first time I'd been around so many trees in a year. The Jeep slowed at the same pace my heart rate accelerated. Something told me we were getting close. Perhaps it was the butterflies that sprang to life in my stomach.

"You sure this is the road?" Dallas asked, taking in the same surroundings, but not seeing what I did. Let alone sensing what I sensed. "How can you tell?"

A moment later, we crept past a gravel driveway with a large pothole like a casual acquaintance you think you recognize, but aren't sure. I felt myself nod, the driveway, like a magnet, drawing my eyes to it as we passed. I found myself turned so far around in my seat I met Claire's anxious stare from the back seat. I held her gaze for a moment before turning back around.

"We need to go back," I said. "That was it."

"Okay," Dallas said, his usual boisterousness gone. "I'll turn around in the next driveway."

"Yeah, that'll be awhile."

A hundred yards later, Dallas settled on a place where the shoulder didn't drop away from the asphalt road quite so sharply. The broken, grey pavement just sort of morphed into the strip of gravel along the edge. Dallas slowed the Jeep again and turned the wheel hard to the right. Leaving the edge of the road produced a slight jolt before Dallas swung the wheel back around to the left. Gravel pinged against the Jeep's undercarriage. If it bothered Dallas, he didn't show it. Once all four tires were back on the road, he pressed the gas and we headed in the opposite direction.

As we travelled back toward the driveway, the twin black lampposts guarding the entrance came into view. They leaned in opposite directions. Thick green strands of ivy snaked up their lengths. The glass of the lanterns were cracked and cloudy. They looked just as I had remembered, with one glaring exception. Now hanging from each post were strips of faded yellow police tape, like paper streamers from a parade float. The tape fluttered in the breeze, an eerie addition to an already unsettling scene.

"I'd say you're right," Dallas said. "This is the place." He brought the Jeep to a stop in the middle of the empty road. Claire leaned forward in her seat until she was looking over my shoulder.

"Wow," she muttered, her hand finding out just how tense my shoulder could get. "I've always tried to imagine it, but it's even creepier than I thought."

"The crime scene tape kinda drives it home, doesn't it?"

Dallas said.

I didn't respond to either of them. All I knew was the doctors had been wrong about my progress, because I must have been clinically insane for coming back here. Like Charles f'ing Manson insane. But not as bad as that dude in Milwaukee who had a taste for people.

The large pothole greeted me as it did last time. And just like last time, it resembled a small pond because of all the rain the day before. I didn't know how deep it was, and it still stretched across the entire mouth of the driveway. If we were going to continue on, there would be no going around it except on foot.

I unbuckled my seat belt.

"Shouldn't be a problem for this old girl," Dallas said, having apparently read my thoughts.

And it wasn't. After a slight pause, Dallas steered the Jeep into the drive. He didn't lack confidence in the Jeep's abilities, so I could only think the pause was for my benefit. Like he was giving me a chance to change my mind. I didn't say a word, and instead braced myself for what loomed ahead. With nothing more than a couple of soft bounces, we navigated the pothole with ease. Admittedly, the part of me still questioning this little trip was disappointed. Rough terrain would have been a good excuse to turn back.

Tree limbs intermingled above us like a child's fingers clasped in prayer. They created a tunnel effect, and we made our way through it like we owned the place. As we meandered up the driveway, I found that the daylight offered an opportunity to sightsee I hadn't had last time. There were things I hadn't noticed before, things I had. And then there were things I wished had been a dream, but weren't.

The small mound that hid the forsaken cemetery from view crept up on our right. It was that cemetery where Garrett and I discovered three freshly dug graves. Two had been filled back in, while one had been waiting to be. From what the police told us, they had retrieved the remains of two of the missing girls from the freshly dug graves during the investigation. What I didn't know was whether the graves had been filled back in. Were there now three gaping holes in the ground where the deceased should be resting? I didn't care enough to ask Dallas to stop the Jeep. I didn't even mention what was on the other side of the unremarkable hill. I simply allowed it to fade into the distance as we drove passed.

The shivers that went through me, I also kept to myself.

CHAPTER 12

I like to think my mother had just been wrong, that she hadn't outright lied to me. That maybe she'd even heard wrong herself. But, if she knew the truth and chose to tell me otherwise, I guess I couldn't blame her. She was only protecting her child. A child that, after this latest decision, obviously needed protecting. From himself, if nothing else.

As soon as the dilapidated building came into view, Dallas hit the brakes. I hadn't had to say anything about taking things slow. We were on the same page. Though taking it slow didn't stop my heart from leaping up into my throat as the dingy white church emerged through the trees.

Suddenly, it was as if the Jeep's air-conditioner had stopped working. The air inside turned stifling. The back of my neck grew damp, as images I'd tried so hard to forget flooded my mind. I tried to stop them. They played like an old silent film, one right after the other. Only these images weren't black and white. The colors were just as vivid as when I'd first seen them. Over and over they came to mind as my breathing started coming in short, rapid bursts.

I jumped at the touch of Claire's calming hand on my shoulder.

"I'm alright," I lied, but doubted she believed me.

Dallas shifted the Jeep into reverse and backed to where it

would be hidden by a trio of pines before cutting the ignition. For a quiet moment, the three of us sat there, staring through gnarled branches at an old abandoned church that held too many horrific memories for me to have returned. But I knew why I had come. And despite the voice in my head saying, 'Dude, this is a bad idea,' I also knew I hadn't come all this way just to turn back at the parking lot.

In therapy, one thing they taught me was how to control my breathing when I feel myself stressing out. So that's what I did. Taking air in through my nose, I counted to four, then released it through my mouth to a seven count. I repeated these steps several times over the course of a minute until I could feel myself relax.

"Ho-ly shit." Dallas pursed his lips and whistled. "If the inside looks anything like the outside—"

"Believe me," I cut in, "it's much worse."

Although I'd been there before, this was my first time seeing the church in daylight. The once-white clapboard building was now a dull, dirty dishwater. Streaks of dark grey wood showed through cracked and peeled paint. Where there had been a few black shutters, the church's siding was now bare. Several shutters lay in the grass, propped against the building, like they'd done their best, but simply couldn't hang on any longer. Sheets of weathered plywood covered the windows like Band-Aids.

I couldn't help it. I tried focusing on the church itself, but my eyes were drawn to the rubble that used to be the storage shed behind it. The place where Garrett had taken his last breath was now only a defeated pile of wood and sheet metal. I wasn't sure how I felt about someone destroying it. It was possible I was only disappointed someone else had gotten the pleasure of doing so before I could.

"Looks like all points of entry have been sealed," Dallas said, pulling my attention back to the church. "We should be able to approach undetected from any side. Especially on foot. We'll need to be on the lookout for any kind of tripwire or homemade alarm system, though."

Somewhere down deep, I felt myself smile. Dallas' combat instincts were kicking in, and I couldn't be happier.

"Well," I said, my breathing having returned to normal, "we didn't come all this way just to look at the damn place." I looked first to Claire, who smiled, yet unsure, and then to Dallas.

"Did you bring it?"

Dallas nodded his head. "Glove box."

I reached up and pulled the silver handle on the black dashboard. The door sprung open like it was gasping for air. There, among stacks of endless paper—from fast food napkins to unpaid parking tickets—laid a handgun, its finish black and dull.

"Colt M1911," Dallas said. "Forty-five cal, semiautomatic. Same gun that got me through 'Nam. She's old, but still operates as smoothly as she did back then. I've got others, newer 9mms and such, but I've never gone into battle without Prudence here. Never will."

Ignoring the obvious question, I reached into the dark space and pulled out the first handgun I had ever held. Its weight surprised me as I looked it over. It was much heavier than I expected. Easily a couple pounds. When I recognized I was doing a poor impression of someone who knew what they were doing, I handed the gun over to Dallas. The smile on his face caught me off guard. I wasn't sure if it was pride, or that he hoped he'd get a chance to use it today. Or, should I say 'her?'

Without further discussion, Dallas opened his door and stepped out.

I looked back at Claire once more.

"No turning back now," she said. Her ever-present smile was working overtime, trying to convince me everything was going to be okay.

Opening the door and stepping out onto the soft ground, I hoped like hell it was right.

CHAPTER 13

The air had an earthy smell to it, the kind a fresh rain leaves behind. I stood beneath a tangle of tree limbs, breathing it in like I was in line at Cinnabon. An occasional raindrop fell from one branch to another. A small animal scurried off toward a clump of bushes. I took a moment and let the soothing atmosphere of the woods reign me in.

Things would change soon enough.

"Alright," I said, once Claire had climbed from the back seat and I could shut the door, "here's the deal."

We gathered together in front of the Jeep like kids huddling to call a play in a game of schoolyard football. It was the same kind of planning session, I guess, but I wasn't about to tell either of them to go deep.

"We stay together as much as possible," I continued. "Nobody goes off exploring on their own. At the very least, we stay within eyesight. Okay?"

I got nods of understanding in return. They knew what I was asking of them. I was also pretty sure they knew why.

"No tire tracks," Dallas said, scoping out the muddy and overgrown parking lot from where we stood. "A good sign. In fact, doesn't look like another vehicle's been through here for quite some time."

Claire and I both nodded. It was indeed a good sign.

"Well," I said. "If nobody's got any questions..."

We broke the huddle and started making our way along the grassy edge of the parking lot. The scared kid with way too many reasons not to be here, but one enormous reason to be; his smart and beautiful, red-headed girlfriend who ignored the dangers and insisted on being there for moral support; and the Vietnam vet with a graying ponytail, a closet full of tie dye, and an eager handgun named Prudence tucked into the back of his jeans.

We were quite the team.

Dallas made a beeline for the stoop, where crime scene tape crisscrossed the doors like a yellow spider web. Through the mass of plastic strips, I could see a silver chain wound through the door handles. I called out to Dallas, but stopped myself. It wouldn't hurt for him to take a look, make sure it wasn't there for decoration.

And it wasn't. After a moment, Dallas came down off the stoop shaking his head and falling in beside us.

Staying as close to the building as possible, we made our way across the front of the church, tromping through tall grass and overgrown flowerbeds littered with more weeds than anything. We shot occasional glances up at the boarded windows and continued around the side of the building just as the sun peaked over the treetops. The day was supposed to be a hot one. The sun would beat down on us soon enough. It was yet another reason to find our way inside the church, and I needed all the motivation I could find to get me to step foot in that building again.

As soon as we turned the corner, my eyes were once again drawn to the pile of rubble that had once been a tool shed. It pulled me toward it like gravity. Claire and Dallas followed.

The grass was still wet from the rain the day before. My tennis shoes soaked up the moisture like thirsty sponges.

"What is it?"

I left Claire's question unanswered, as if I hadn't heard it. I didn't know how to answer her without bringing her unnecessary pain. Garrett had been her friend, too, and I didn't want to tell her this was where he'd died. Where he'd suffered. *Where I'd left him.* None of us said anything. It seemed my companions were content to remain quiet, to leave me alone with my thoughts. I appreciated both their silence and their understanding. They may not have known why this pile of wood was important, but somehow, they knew it was.

There were a million thoughts cluttering my mind, all vying for attention. I didn't know which deserved my focus more. I thought about Garrett and what I'd learned of his time spent in the shed. I thought of how I'd run past the shed while trying to escape that night. The police assured me it wouldn't have mattered, that he was probably already dead at that point, that there wasn't anything I could have done. I wanted to believe it. I really did.

Still...

Something in the pile of damp wood and rusted sheet metal caught my eye. I knelt and lifted one board to get a better look. It was black on one end. Charred black. Several of the boards sported the same marking. Someone had tried to light the pile on fire. I had to smile. It was a hell of an idea. Despite their lack of success, I was grateful for the vandals' attempts, whoever they were. I couldn't have wished for any better way to wipe that shed from existence.

A thought came to me as I rose to my feet.

"Happen to have any matches on ya?" I asked Dallas.

"Even better," he said, pulling something from his pocket. It was an old, silver Zippo. The kind with a lid you had to open before you could strike it. "Haven't used it in a long time, but I still carry it around. It was my father's. Gave it to me the day I shipped out for the Army. More of a souvenir now, but it still lights."

To prove his point, Dallas flipped the lid back with his thumb, then pressed down on the little wheel. It took two tries, but the flint finally sparked. Blue flame shot up about an inch. I watched it dance for a few seconds, my mind racing with thought, until Dallas flipped the lid closed again. He handed me the lighter. It was warm, and I said thanks before sliding it into my front pocket. In the three months I'd been working for Dallas, I'd never seen him smoke a cigarette or cigar. So, the fact he carried a lighter only added to my speculation he smoked a little marijuana. I'd also decided it wasn't any of my business. I just found it interesting.

"Thanks," I said. "I'll give it back when we leave."

"Not a problem," he said.

When I felt like standing there staring at the pile of rubble was growing ridiculously unproductive, I turned away. And then I saw it. A piece of plywood covered the basement window. The very window I had climbed out of a year ago. There had only been one.

I walked over to it.

I nudged the piece of plywood with my toe. As expected, it didn't budge. Bending down, I discovered eight very stout screws holding it in place. Even after I'd stood up, I couldn't help but stare at the covered window. My thoughts returned to that night. My chest felt like it was being compressed by the metal window frame all over again.

I'd been standing there awhile when Claire broke the silence.

"It's okay, Luke. There are other windows. We'll find another one."

"That's not it," Dallas said, before I could speak. "There's something significant about this one. Ain't there, Chief?"

I thought about my answer and whether I wanted to voice it. I was anxious. I also figured it didn't hurt to let them in on a few things. They were here, after all, offering aid and support. They'd earned the right to know.

So, with a deep breath and tears pooling in my eyes, I shared with them the significance of the basement window.

CHAPTER 14

Sheets of plywood covered the church's tall stained-glass windows. Some were held in place by only a few haphazard screws, while others, covering more accessible windows, were hung with enough screws to hold a two-story house together. Somebody really didn't want anyone inside the church. Odds were, it was the local police wanting to keep out thrill seekers and drunk teenagers looking for some place to fornicate. Whether it was working or not, we would soon find out.

The back door was also secure, though you wouldn't know it by looking at it. It appeared normal enough. It looked like we could walk right up, open the door, and walk on in, which Dallas tried to do. But, I remembered how Barnes had barricaded it from the inside with wood planks. Even though there was a slight possibility the police had seen reason to take them all down, considering the lengths they had gone to in keeping people out, I couldn't think of a good enough reason.

Finally, as we made our way around another corner and checked the far side of the church, it was Claire who discovered a way into the secured church.

"This one's not screwed down," she said, looking up at one sheet of plywood in particular. Proving her point, she gave it a shove, and the bottom of the plywood swung from side to side. All the screws except one in the very top center had been removed, giving the illusion of being secure for anyone who didn't take the time to investigate further.

The implications set off alarms in my mind. I was glad for a way in, but wary of the fact someone was already using it in secret. And not just once. More than likely, the illusion was seeing repeated use. Why else hide the fact they'd been there?

Moments later, as we stood peering through a busted-out window into the church's darkened sanctuary, it was Dallas who broke the silence.

"Got a flashlight in the Jeep," he whispered. "Not sure why I didn't just grab it. Guess I figured we'd be able to see since it was light out. Be right back."

Before I could say anything, Dallas disappeared around the corner.

A wave of déjà vu came over me. Only it wasn't just a feeling. I had been there before when Garrett took off to explore on his own. It wasn't the first worrisome thing that happened that night, but it was so far the biggest. Standing on the stoop of an abandoned church in the middle of an unfamiliar forest, a storm of Biblical proportions bearing down, it forced me to brave the darkness alone. I had no idea where Garrett had gone, and no idea where I was. This time, I knew where Dallas had gone, and that he would be right back. A luxury I didn't have that night. It was one of the few times I could remember getting angry at Garrett.

An emotion I couldn't imagine feeling now.

Dallas didn't take long. The poor guy must have run all the way to the Jeep and back, knowing I was already on edge. Or, maybe it was the excitement that propelled him.

"Alright," he said, breathing harder than when he'd left, "who's up first?"

The smile on his face. The wild and hungry eyes. They told me all I needed to know. The guy was actually excited about the adventure looming ahead. And eager to get started. I couldn't fault him, I guess, having to sit on all that military training for all these years.

I, on the other hand, had no military training, nor was I excited about what might or might not be waiting for us on the inside.

I gestured toward the window. "After you."

CHAPTER 15

Shards of glass crunched underfoot as we climbed through the open window and into the pitch-black sanctuary. Ironically, pitch black was just the way I remembered it. Still, the church's floor plan came back to me almost immediately. I knew where the mudroom was in proximity to where we stood. The pulpit stage. The stairwell to the loft. The little side room that had been used as a playroom slash classroom. After our eyes had adjusted, Dallas found a broken armrest from one of the pews and used it to prop open the sheet of plywood.

The ray of sunlight coming through the open window helped, but we would still need Dallas' flashlight and the light from our cell phones to find our way around.

But light wasn't the only thing the open window offered. A strong, mustiness hung in the air. The sanctuary smelled like sweaty gym shorts left in a locker over summer break. Odds were, the roof leaked, causing the inside of the church to stay damp long after the rain outside was gone. The funk wasn't overpowering, just unpleasant. Like the rest of the building's overall atmosphere.

With Claire and Dallas at my side, I played the indecision game. The basement was calling my name, but I wasn't sure that's where I wanted to start. The very thought of the basement got my pulse up. We should probably end there. But what did I know? The only thing I was completely sure of was that, even though I'd never used one before, I wished I had a gun tucked in the back of my jeans, too.

Sensing Dallas's growing impatience, I made a decision.

"Let's go that way." I kept my voice low, nodding toward the stairs leading up to the loft. I forwent the pulpit area altogether, with the coffin that may or may not still be there. Like an old girlfriend who'd caused you way too much grief, I had no desire to see that wooden prison again. After all, I was on a fact-finding mission to see if Barnes had been back, not a nostalgic trip down memory lane.

"You got it, Chief." Dallas whispered, too, though with his deep voice, it didn't sound like a whisper at all. I looked to Claire, who was half concealed in shadow. Her silhouette nodded in agreement.

The set of stairs leading to the second floor shared a wall with the concealed window, so we didn't have far to go. With a flashlight and two cell phone screens leading the way, we made our way along the wall to the stairway. And we were anything but quiet about it. No matter how hard we tried, there was no navigating the shattered glass littering the floor. The crunching echoed throughout the otherwise silent sanctuary.

At the foot of the stairway, Dallas shined his military grade flashlight up into the second-floor abyss, putting to shame the weak ass light coming from my phone. There was a landing at the top of the stairs, and just beyond, a doorway. The dingy, white door stood open by a few inches. To say the long, dark opening didn't conjure up every haunted house movie I'd ever seen, would be the understatement of all understatements. Especially with the shadows viewing it by flashlight creates. After a few seconds with no movement or sounds from above, Dallas looked at me and gave a nod. I nodded back, and before I could change my mind, followed the path the flashlight laid out.

When the wooden stairs let out their first sharp creak, I froze. I looked back at Dallas. All he offered was a shrug. When I took the second step and produced a similar sound, I realized it was likely to happen every step of the way. The wood was old, neglected, and had undergone some warping over the years. Short of dismissing the second floor altogether, there was nothing I could do about the noise. So, without further hesitation, I climbed the stairs, doing my best to ignore the sounds that were like a wake up call to anyone hiding in the darkness.

I'm not sure when it happened, but at some point, I started feeling like we wouldn't be running into Barnes. There were no tire tracks in the muddy parking lot, no flattened soggy grass. There didn't seem to be any activity in the sanctuary, and so far, everything appeared quiet and dark. Just like an old, abandoned church should be. Key word, 'abandoned.' Except for a possible forest animal or two, we were most likely alone. That didn't mean he hadn't been there at all. There was a reason someone had removed the screws from the sheet of plywood and the window busted out. Neither of these were the work of a raccoon or opossum; I don't care how wily they might be.

The stairs deposited us onto the small landing, bringing us face to face with the open doorway. Adrenaline coursed through my veins. Its volume increased with every exploratory step I took in the only part of the church I wasn't familiar with. I did not know what awaited us beyond that door.

I felt a slight tapping on my arm.

"You're up front," Dallas said, thrusting his flashlight

toward me. As I took it from him, I wished our positions were reversed. Dallas told me he was behind me in all this, I just didn't know he meant it literally.

I slid my cell back into my jeans pocket, then trained the flashlight on the door in front of me. I used my foot to nudge it open. As the door swung inward, the hinges emitted a low, drawn out creak. Up close and personal, it was one of the scariest sounds I'd ever heard. Like a witch about to summon a demon. My neck hairs rose out of fear.

I stepped into the room and to the side, allowing my team a view as well. The ceiling was low. The space was cramped. I swept the flashlight over walls, catching a million floating dust particles in its beam. It also found a tiny, lone window at the far end of the room. Like the rest of the space, the window was on the small side. Not much larger than a box of cereal. The glass looked to have been painted over with black paint. It reminded me of the basement window. The two shared the same artist. Not to mention, the same artistic style, best described as "bleak."

A crash sent spikes up my spine.

I swung the flashlight around.

Claire had entered the room. At her feet, silver beer cans scattered in and out of the shadows, like rodents fleeing the light. The chaotic clanking of metal continued for several seconds before the room once again fell silent. Even if our being there had been a secret up to this point, it was a secret no longer. We had officially announced our presence.

"Sorry," Claire said through a scowl. "Must've been a stack of them."

Dallas giggled. "Honey, you just took kicking the can to an all new level."

The three of us stood still, taking a moment to let our hearts drop back into our chests. When the time came, it was Dallas who made the next move.

"Let me see that a sec," he said, reaching for the flashlight.

I graciously handed it over.

Starting with the cans at our feet, Dallas scanned the flashlight along the floor. What it revealed was a scene straight from a 'teens gone wild' horror film. Two mattresses took up most of the floor space. Less actual beds than old, filthy mattresses cast onto the floor. A soiled yellow bedsheet lay balled up at the foot of one mattress. The other mattress was bare, but just as stained. Empty travel-sized liquor bottles, condom wrappers, and cigarette butts littered the floor, explaining why one window had been made accessible. Three crushed red solo cups, a gold lipstick tube, and a neon green pair of earbuds added a festive splash of color to the otherwise drab and depressing display.

"Yuck," Claire said, and even though I couldn't see her, I imagined her cute little nose wrinkled up the way it does when her dog has gas.

"Eh, I've done it in worse," Dallas said.

And whether or not he'd intended to, he'd added levity to a situation desperately needing it. Claire and I shared a chuckle. Dallas offered a shrug. Which was just as funny.

Once we'd determined whatever had taken place in the room was plenty disgusting, yet most likely not the work of Corwin Barnes, we turned from the room and started shuffling our way back toward the stairs.

CHAPTER 16

The sound was like something smacking against the side of the church. Dallas snapped off the flashlight and the three of us held our breath. The last thing I saw before the world went dark was Dallas drawing his gun. I wasn't sure if that made me feel better about the situation or worse. It meant we had protection, sure. But it also meant there was something nearby we might need protection from.

A threat.

We stood for what must have been at least a minute, silent and still, as if our lives depended on it. For all we knew, they did. We stared into the dark landing, wondering when the sound might repeat itself. I pulled my phone from my pocket and clutched it in my hand. As much as I wanted to shed some light on the surrounding unknown, I kept my light off as long as Dallas did his.

With the church continuing to hold its tongue, I decided we couldn't stand there all day. One of us had to make a move. And with that thought, I approached the top of the stairs.

The sanctuary below was pitch black, like midnight on a moonless night. Despite the sun shining outside, its light no longer entered through the window. I breathed a partial sigh of relief. Apparently, there was no threat, after all. The sheet of wood we'd propped open had somehow swung back into place.

"Wind," Dallas whispered, his voice coming from just over my shoulder. It interrupted the quiet and scared the shit out of me.

More than likely, Dallas was right. It could have very well been the wind. Part of me, however, didn't trust the simplicity of it. My memory of this place and how things worked here wouldn't let me. The 'what ifs' started coming fast and furious. What if someone had seen the Jeep parked in the driveway? What if it was the people responsible for the mess up in the loft? What if it was Barnes?

What if we actually were in danger?

Since Dallas had both the flashlight and the gun, I elected him the leader with a hand to his back. He started down the stairs first, while I followed, clasping Claire's hand. We crept as quietly as the old wooden steps allowed, making our way down as a single, tight-knit group. We left the lights off, cautiously feeling our way. And not just because the plywood had fallen back into place. The handrail along the stairs was dry-rotted. If I put too much pressure on it, it swayed back and forth. I didn't know how much pressure it would take to topple it, but I was pretty sure I pushed it to its limit a couple times. The loud crack of splintering wood told me so.

When we reached the bottom of the stairs, Dallas put his hand out, telling me to stay where I was. I heard him shuffle away and instantly felt naked and vulnerable. I didn't like being separated. Outside was one thing. Inside, this house of horrors was a different story.

It took only seconds, but felt like a lifetime before I heard the crunching of glass, followed by a flood of brilliant sunlight into the room.

Dallas stuck his head through the window and surveyed the ground.

I did the same with the sanctuary. I couldn't see much. The large room was steeped in shadow and uncertainty. As far as I could tell, we were still alone. I wished I had the flashlight back. The light from my cell illuminated the space around Claire and me, but couldn't reach much beyond that.

"Where's he going?" Claire asked.

I turned back just in time to see Dallas disappear through the window. The sheet of plywood swung back into place, plunging the large room into darkness. I immediately determine I liked it better the other way.

"Shit." I felt my way over to where my boss had been standing five seconds earlier. With a deep breath, and fighting speculation he'd left us behind, I slid the sheet of wood aside.

Dallas hadn't gone far. Standing just below the window, he held the piece of broken pew.

"Yep." He shrugged. "Must've just fallen out."

"Great," I said, and chastised myself for doubting Dallas's integrity. It wasn't his fault. It was my insecurity. Mostly, it was the fact I had already been through so much in this church. I was going to question everything moving forward. Still, I vowed to never doubt Dallas again.

"Well, if it fell out once, it could fall out again," I said, while scanning the still tree line across the yard.

"I know." Dallas dropped the piece of broken pew onto the grass. He reached up and grabbed the sheet of plywood on both sides. After telling me to step back, he gave it a hard jerk. The sheet of plywood came away in his hands. The popping of the screw from the clapboard made a sound like a bone snapping.

"That should fix it," I said, and chuckled.

Claire, who had followed me over to the window, offered a grin. "I'd say so."

We extended our hands and helped Dallas back through the window. As much as I would have preferred it be the other way around, we couldn't leave just yet. Our business at the church wasn't finished. That fact was made clear when I turned back toward the sanctuary, and realized just how long we'd left our backs exposed. I shivered, despite the heat of the morning. It was that feeling of walking through a haunted house, stopping to glance behind you, and seeing something you hadn't seen the first time; something you missed.

"Enough screwing around," I said, with Dallas safely inside the sanctuary. "Let's check out that basement."

CHAPTER 17

On our way to the basement, we stopped at the wacked out classroom for the insane. Gone were the headless dolls and miniature chairs, leaving the room empty of everything except the chalkboard. It still hung cracked and haphazard on the wall. The phrase that had been written across it, not to mention my mind for several months following, was gone. There were no biblical quotes repeated over and over, no more talk of reaping or harvesting. What graced the chalkboard now couldn't be more unrighteous. In fact, it would have made a nun flee the room in shock.

Every curse word known to man was scrawled graffiti style in white chalk. Crudely drawn sketches of naked men and women covered the rest of the black board. The drawings were cartoonish, the breasts unnaturally large, the penises and scrotums equally so. These weren't the drawings of a talented hand. Most likely, it was the work of local teenagers. The same ones who'd built a shrine to a lack of parental supervision in the upstairs loft. Stupid kids. If they only knew what vile crimes against humanity had taken place inside these walls.

Or, maybe they knew. Maybe that was even the draw. Thrill seekers who hadn't lived the nightmare others had.

After only a brief stay, we left the classroom and its display of modern art just as we found it.

"That way," I said, pointing to the front of the church. Normally, the person who knows the way would lead the way. But at some point, we'd changed the rules. In our version of the game, the person who possessed the flashlight and gun led the way. We charged the nervous survivor and his supportive girlfriend with bringing up the rear. It made sense. Just because we assumed we were alone, didn't mean we couldn't be proven wrong at any moment.

As close as Claire and I stayed to Dallas, I stayed even closer to Claire. Her mood concerned me. She wasn't saying much, just kind of following along. Which wasn't like her. I hoped she wasn't sorry she'd come. I hoped she was simply taking it all in and processing through. When I looked over, she gave me a faint smile. At least I think she did, shadow engulfed most of her face.

I was too busy looking at Claire to mind where I was going. Hymnals were scattered everywhere. When I stepped on one, the book slid out from under my foot. I started to go down and grabbed onto Claire's arm to steady myself. I stayed on my feet, but there were consequences.

Claire's brief, but high-pitched shriek shattered the sanctuary's quiet.

Like line dancers, we crouched, one right after the other. We did the same with our lights. The echo from Claire's reaction bounced between the walls. Across the room, something small and furry scurried deeper into the darkness.

"What the hell," Dallas whispered.

"Sorry," I said. "I slipped."

"Me, too," Claire chimed. "Sorry, I mean."

We stayed low for almost a minute, my heart beating an elevated rhythm the whole time. Between the beer cans, the plywood swinging back into place and now this, my nerves were shot. I was ready to mosey on down the road, as my father would say. I didn't want to be here anymore. But we still needed to check the basement. If Barnes was back in operation, there was no better place for it. I couldn't leave without checking.

"Come on." I rose up, took a deep breath, then broke protocol. By the dim light of my cell phone, and without a weapon of any kind, I led the way to the front of the church. It was only another fifteen steps. This time I took them carefully, mindful of the scattered debris field.

I rounded the corner and entered the tiny alcove just off the entryway. The brass coat hooks still hung on the wall—still tarnished, still naked. After trading Dallas my cell phone, I shined the flashlight upon the doorway at the top of the basement steps. The door itself was gone. Standing at the precipice of the closest thing I'd experienced to Hell, my chest threatened to rip itself apart. It wouldn't have surprised me to learn my friends could hear my heart pounding.

This was the place.

The place.

Stepping foot in the church that stormy night hadn't been life altering. It was what I'd experienced at the bottom of those stairs that changed me forever. Not just my life, but me. The things I'd seen. The things I'd been forced to do to survive. They'd latched onto my psyche like leaches, and I'd carry those scars forever. It was all a bad dream I would never truly wake from.

And like a dumbass, I was going back down.

CHAPTER 18

The open doorway was a gaping black hole, darker than the rest of the alcove. Only a hole dug a mile into the Earth could be as black. To make matters worse, the light switch on the wall didn't work this time, no matter how many times I flipped it, nor how many times I cursed under my breath. I remembered how creepy and depraved the basement was with the light on. A luxury I wouldn't have this time around. Our flashlight and cell phones had done a decent enough job so far, but the basement was a whole other world. As much light as I could utilize while exploring it, the better.

The smell reached up from the dark before I even stepped down onto the first step. I pulled my t-shirt's collar up over my nose. The stench hinted at familiarity, yet was like nothing I'd ever experienced. A year ago, I discovered Corwin Barnes' cache of dismembered human body parts stewing in a pool of their own gore. The smell now was just as bad as it was then. Something about that fact launched a brick into the pit of my stomach. Surely someone had cleaned up and disposed of the remains during the investigation. Surely there wouldn't be any of it still down there.

Unless, of course, there were new body parts.

I stopped myself short, ignoring my subconscious. My desire to check out the basement diminished by half.

"My God."

The funk had apparently reached Claire. She gagged briefly, and for a moment, I thought she might get sick.

"God had nothing to do with that," Dallas said, as if he knew the Almighty personally and was sticking up for a friend. If the rising stench bothered him, he didn't show it. "That's one hundred percent death, right there. Cruel and shameful and stripped of all dignity. The God I believe in wouldn't be that messy about things."

I could hear Claire breathing again. Only now, it was muffled and through her mouth. Like mine.

Holding the flashlight out front, I lit up the stairs all the way to the bottom. The wooden steps were painted a light grey. This made the dark splatter patterns stand out in the bright LED light. My stomach soured. I knew what the spattering of blood was from. Moreso, I knew *who* it was from, and it took everything I learned in therapy to keep calm.

I closed my eyes and concentrated on my breathing. Four seconds in, seven seconds out. *Relax,* I told myself. *You can do this.* Four seconds in, seven seconds out. Gradually, my breathing slowed, but my heart rate didn't get the memo.

The first step was the toughest. The second proved a little easier, but the third put me right where I was standing when I'd lost Becca. When Barnes took the only good thing I did that night and ripped it from my hands. I took a deep breath and hastened to the fourth, fifth, and sixth steps.

Halfway.

I stopped and shined my flashlight up to make sure Claire and Dallas were following.

Dallas was right behind me. In fact, he could have been my shadow, he was keeping so close. Claire remained in the doorway at the top of the stairs.

"Sorry," she said, her arms folded across her stomach. "I don't think I can."

"It's okay, babe. Stay there. We won't be long." I looked to Dallas, who nodded discretely. We were on the same page. Whatever was down there emitting that God-awful smell, Claire didn't need to see it. She would be better off right where she was. At least that's what I kept telling myself while struggling to fight off images of my last moments with Becca.

The first thing I noticed when I stepped off the last wooden tread and onto concrete was the smell. It wasn't any worse down there. It wasn't any better, it just wasn't worse. Maybe I'd gotten used to it, if that was even possible. Whatever the reason, I found I could breathe through my nose without triggering my gag reflex. That, at least, was a move in the right direction.

The long, sturdy workbench still sat where I'd last seen it, shoved against the grey concrete wall directly across from the steps. It was the first thing my flashlight had been drawn to. As if it had no choice in the matter. The bench was as formidable as I remembered, and truly a marvel of craftsmanship. But then, it had to be to carry out the task it had been entrusted, and maybe even built, to perform.

Thankfully, there was no evidence of that task still being carried out. For the most part, the worn and scarred top of the wooden workbench was clear. There were no human remains, no flesh-eating beetles. A dark stain, nearly black, spread out over a third of the workbench's surface and trailed off the front edge. Training the flashlight onto the floor revealed a similar stain on the concrete. Only this one wasn't as much a stain as a slick of thick, dried blood. Its consistency resembled old bearing grease.

Before I could stop him, Dallas used the toe of his boot to draw a line through the viscid mass. The substance came off the floor like the worst flavor of ice cream ever, curling up onto the front of Dallas's boot. It took all I had to keep my breakfast in my stomach where it belonged.

"That was uncalled for," I said, shaking my head.

But Dallas just grinned and turned away, having apparently lost interest in the workbench and its dried blood. As he flipped on the cell phone and left me, I noticed his gun was back in the waistband of his jeans. I guess I wasn't the only one feeling that, perhaps the church no longer posed a danger. The old, abandoned building seemed to be just that: old and abandoned. A far cry from the way I'd found it the first time.

A thin, mousy sneeze startled me.

My neck muscles immediately seized.

"Sorry." Claire's soft voice drifted down from the top of the stairs. "Again. Just really dusty in here."

As the tension left my shoulders and I started to breathe again, Dallas joined me at the bottom of the stairs.

"Nothing over there," he said, no longer bothering to whisper. "Just an empty room, save for a few dead spiders."

"How do you know they were dead?"

"They didn't try to run when I stepped on them."

The two of us headed toward the other side of the basement, where I fully expected to find more of the same. And I was right. The larger of the basement's two sides proved just as empty as the one Dallas had already explored. Everything was gone, packed up and presumably disposed of with the rest of Barnes' operation. Even the large, menacing hook that had hung from the ceiling had been removed. Taken as evidence, it was probably sitting in a box deep in the bowels of a police station somewhere.

"Nothing left but bad memories," I said.

Dallas put his hand on my shoulder. "And maybe someday those'll be gone, too." He gave my shoulder a firm pat. "Come on. Let's get out of here before that smell permeates our clothes. Would hate to have to burn one of my favorite shirts."

I glanced down at his rainbow swirl tie dye. "I don't know. Burning that ugly ass shirt might be the best thing for it."

We found Claire sitting on the top step, knees drawn up against her chest, chin down. She looked more bored than frightened, and that's how I knew our work at the church was officially done.

"Ready to go?"

"Absolutely," she said, getting to her feet and brushing off the back of her jeans. "Could use some fresh air."

CHAPTER 19

Standing out front, we let the sun warm our skin and took one last look at a church that was all out of secrets. After everything the building had been through, I figured it was probably okay with it. I found it both a relief and a disappointment we hadn't found anything. At least nothing that had anything to do with Barnes. Once and for all, I had no more use for the old church.

And perhaps, no one ever should.

"Hey, Dallas." I turned the lighter over in my hand. "I noticed a gas can strapped in the back of your Jeep."

A knowing smile spread across his face.

"Right there with ya," he said, a youthful exuberance inflecting his voice.

The ride back to the city was a quiet one. We'd watched from the safety of the parking lot as the church and all its macabre history went up in flames. The inferno licked at the sky, rising higher than I would have ever guessed. I was thankful for the rain we'd had the day before; nothing around the church was likely to catch on fire. Most of all, I was thankful the church was gone.

We stuck around long enough to watch the completely engulfed structure collapse in on itself, filling the basement with its fiery ruin. The once-cherished house of worship was no more. It had gone up quick, like it was just as eager to be out of its misery as I was to send it there. When it became inevitable the swirling grey smoke rising into the sky had most likely been noticed, and the fire department probably called, we made our way to the Jeep.

No one said a word from the time we hightailed it out of there to when Dallas pulled into the alley behind Tipsword's and parked beside my truck. The three of us sat in silence for a full minute until Dallas broke it with the obvious question.

"Now what?"

I handed back his lighter. "Not sure." I'd been asking myself that very question the entire ride back and still didn't have an answer. The satisfaction I felt from burning down the church had faded before we'd gotten halfway home. Nothing had really changed. Barnes' threat still loomed. "I can't hide out forever," I said. "Unless the cops find Barnes, or determine someone else is just screwing with me, I guess I'm pretty much on my own."

"Hell, no." Dallas extended his hand. "Not anymore, you ain't."

As I shook his hand, a weight lifted from my shoulders.

"I'll be checking in on you at the hotel," he said. "Cruising through the parking lot, making sure there aren't any crazed killers skulking around."

"Dallas, you don't have to do that. Really—"

"The hell else I got to do?" he said, and gave me one of his grandiose smiles.

I smiled back and shook my head. It wasn't necessary for him to patrol the hotel parking lot, but deep down, I loved his enthusiasm. And the fact this gruff, military guy had apparently developed a soft spot for me? Who could hate that?

"Alright," I said, opening the passenger side door. "Guess I'll see you Tuesday."

Claire and I climbed out of the Jeep. After tossing Dallas a wave, I took Claire's hand and we walked over to where my truck sat waiting.

Instantly, I knew something was wrong. Before I had even approached the truck, the warm, fuzzy feeling in my stomach vanished. A cold, hard lump filled the void.

At some point, I let go of Claire's hand.

A folded sheet of paper sat tucked beneath the driver's side wiper blade. It wasn't mine, and it hadn't been there when we left. With my nerves starting to fire, I grabbed the paper. I opened it with trembling hands. That familiar lettering—big and bold and black—sent a chill down my spine. The tiny hairs along my neck stood up.

Where the fuck?

I looked all around, frantically checking my surroundings. The building. The dumpsters. The line of scrawny pines separating the alley from the row of chain-linked backyards. Somewhere in my periphery, Claire's anxious voice kept asking what was wrong. It came at me over and over, but I ignored her. My eyes were busy searching the area, my heart trying to break through my chest.

And as I dropped the letter to the damp gravel at my feet, it fell face up. Even from the ground, the words taunted me…

'SORRY YOU DIDN'T FIND WHAT YOU WERE LOOKING FOR'

CHAPTER 20

It was a Monday. Memorial Day, in fact. The day set aside to remember those who died serving in the United States military. A day people like Dallas, who fought and lost friends, hold sacred. And for everyone else, a day held sacred for entirely different reasons; barbecue, potato salad, and downing enough cans of Budweiser to drown the elephant in the room.

Dallas wouldn't let me work that day, and short of sitting around the hotel room, the last place I wanted to spend my day off was at a pool party at the house of my father's pompous boss. So, I was honoring the fallen by nursing overpriced coffee at a local Starbucks.

With the smell of burning wood still in my nose, I clicked away at the keyboard of my father's laptop. Trying to find anything on Corwin Barnes was proving more difficult than I'd expected. There were no exits on the information superhighway for Barnes-ville. I Googled his name both forward and backward, even though it didn't matter what order I entered the words. None of the search results brought forth the man I'd met a year ago. There were two Facebook pages for guys named Corwin Barnes. One was far too young, and according to the second guy's profile photo, restricted to a wheelchair. I wasn't surprised. I wouldn't think serial killers would be big on social media. If anything, it was just the opposite. A scouring of local newspaper archives and police records turned up old news about his arrest and conviction on animal cruelty charges, but nothing more recent than five years old. Nothing that would help me now.

I'd just started searching police records for the murders at the abandoned church when the coffee kicked in. And not in the boost of energy way you want it to.

I was well aware of the effect coffee had on my bladder. I'd chosen a small table in the back near the restrooms for that very reason. I'd feel relatively safe leaving the laptop unattended for a few minutes. At least that's what I told myself. I was still unnerved by our trip to the church the day before. Especially finding out we'd been followed. That's the only explanation I could think of for the wording of the note. Sleep was scarce, to say the least. Two questions kept me up: was Barnes following me everywhere I went? And if so, what was he waiting for?

There were only a couple people in the coffee shop. Both sat near the front of the store. I figured my things would be safe for no longer than it would take me to pee. The older business exec had his eyes glued to his own laptop, and the younger woman's eyes were fixed on a paperback copy of Gillian Flynn's *Dark Places.* Neither faced me. Nobody would even notice I was gone.

Less than three minutes.

That's how long I was away from my stuff. And that included taking longer than usual to wash my hands. It bothered me how stained they'd become. I scrubbed and scrubbed and they still never looked clean. Not completely. Luckily, I had a girlfriend who couldn't care less what my hands looked like.

But three minutes was apparently too long.

The table wasn't how I'd left it. Something that hadn't been there previously now sat square in the middle.

The short paper cup wasn't the familiar white with green logo Starbucks coffee comes in. The only similarity was the white, plastic lid. Yet there it sat, across the table from my father's laptop. Red with a playful white swirl design, the mysterious cup was impossible to miss.

I wouldn't call it alarm, but a milder form of it tugged at my chest. My heart rate crept upward. A scratchy-voiced man sang about a brown-eyed girl from the speakers mounted in the ceiling.

I stopped a couple steps shy of the table and scanned the place. *Who the hell put it there?* Only two tables sat nearby, both empty with their chairs pushed in. There was nowhere for anyone to hide. The only other people in the coffee shop were the man and woman near the front, and they were still as engrossed as when I went to the restroom.

Three frickin' minutes ago!

It wasn't until I approached the table that I noticed the white square beneath the cup. At first I thought it was a napkin. Upon further examination, I discovered it was a folded sheet of paper, very much like the note left on my windshield.

Apprehension soured my stomach, like week-old sushi. I reached down and picked up the cup, but not before giving one more glance around the room. I wanted to see if anyone was at least paying attention. They weren't. The man and woman couldn't care less what I was up to.

The cup was still warm. And full. I set it aside for the time being, more interested in the sheet of paper. My heart beat a couple beats faster than normal. Receiving notes and packages was becoming a routine for me lately, and not one I enjoyed.

The message on this note was shorter, but still written with the same handwritten letters…

A COMPLIMENTARY CUP OF JO.

There were only two baristas working the counter when I approached: a teenage girl with an independently artistic flair, and a guy with his dirty blond hair drawn into a man bun. The girl had made my cup of coffee perfectly, just the way I liked it. Her hardened scowl told me she was less than confident about the cup she was making now. It might have had something to do with the way hipster guy was looking over her shoulder. Like he was practically hoping she screwed up. He had a look of arrogance about him that said he took his coffee, and his training of newbies, entirely too seriously. If my mind wasn't otherwise preoccupied, I would have felt sorry for her.

"Hey," I said, setting the paper cup on the counter. But, that was as far as I got. I was rendered speechless by the set-jaw look the guy gave me. It was as if I was blasphemously interrupting a religious experience, and whatever I was about to say had better be important.

"Yeah?" asked Man Bun.

I pointed to the red and white cup. "Either of you set that on my table?"

Man Bun just looked at me.

It was apparently a dumb question. So, I didn't spend much time waiting for an answer. Any response from the guy would have undoubtedly come with a double shot of sarcasm. Normally, I would have been okay with it and even given some right back, but I didn't need his shit right now.

Even as I rushed toward the door, neither the guy on his laptop nor the lady with the book bothered to look up. Still, I asked if either had seen someone enter the coffee shop in the last few minutes.

"Young girl," the lady said, her eyes never leaving the page. "Blonde. Kinda dirty."

Busting through the door, I scanned the sidewalk, first to my left, then to the right. And that's where I found her. A blonde. Kinda dirty. She looked homeless, in fact, yet there she was, leaning against the building, counting out a thin handful of cash.

"Hey!" I said, turning in her direction.

She looked up and met my glare. If she was alarmed, she didn't show it. Like someone with nothing to lose, she simply slid the money into the pocket of her grimy oversized jacket and waited.

"What?" she asked as I approached. The young woman couldn't have been more nonchalant, as if being approached by angry strangers was a daily occurrence. Her eyes showed no fear. Her body registered no tension. In fact, the only expression she exhibited was indifference. Maybe a slight touch of defiance. She just stood there, waiting to hear whatever was about to come out of my mouth.

"Was it you?" I asked. "Did you put the cup on my table? The note?"

"Sure did," she said without hesitation. "Easiest twenty bucks I ever made. Didn't even have to stick my finger down my throat after."

Her bluntness surprised me, but her answer wasn't entirely unexpected. Walking up to her, I'd already determined if she was the one who put the cup there, it wasn't her idea. In fact, she looked all too eager to do someone a 'favor' in exchange for a couple fives.

"Who paid you to do it?" I asked. "Older, bald guy? Hideously ugly?"

She shook her head, scrunched her lips.

"Young guy. Kinda cute, actually, in a greasy Johnny Depp, Jack Sparrow kinda way. I woulda done him for—"

A high-pitched scream cut her profession of lust short; a bone-rattling wail from inside the Starbucks.

Turning on my heels, I sprinted up the sidewalk, leaving the blonde to lean against the building. What I saw as I entered the coffee shop stopped me only a few steps in. Behind the counter, the baristas stood facing each other. The teenage girl's hands covered her mouth, making it obvious where the scream had come from. What wasn't so obvious was why. It wasn't until I noticed the countertop that I understood.

A red liquid, most likely blood, covered the polished wood. It dripped off the front edge, creating a puddle on the tile floor. I say most likely blood, because, well, what else would it be at this point in Barnes' game?

"The cup," the girl behind the counter kept saying, the horror of its contents fresh in her eyes.

The red and white cup lay toppled on the countertop in the middle of the crimson slick, the lid sitting beside it. It hit me then why the cup had felt warm. It took all I had to keep from adding the coffee from my stomach to the growing puddle on the floor.

"Holy shit," Mr. Fifty-something said, his laptop and whatever he was working on all but forgotten.

Suddenly, the sound of convulsive vomiting came from

behind me. I turned to see the dirty blonde, bent, hands on knees. She was in the process of emptying her stomach of whatever she'd last eaten. The realization of what was in the cup she'd brought in had probably just hit her.

Quite literally, the cup looked to have been filled with the fresh blood of some girl named Jo.

CHAPTER 21

I gathered my things without a word and made to leave like I was late for an appointment. Except for the male barista, who was busy ruining a white towel by wiping red splatter off his arm, all eyes were on me. As I made my way to the door, I tossed my own nearly empty cup in the trashcan. When the barista finally noticed I was leaving, he yelled at me to stop.

I didn't.

Not until I'd gone around the side of the building to the parking lot and my waiting truck. Everyone inside the Starbucks must have either been in shock, not wanted to get involved, or flat out scared, because nobody followed. And I was glad. If they had come looking for an explanation, I would have been at a loss. How could I have possibly explained what had just happened? Or my part in it?

It took a few seconds of fumbling to find the right key and unlock the door. Tossing the laptop onto the bench seat, I slid in beside it and closed the door behind me. Two seconds later, I reached up and hit the lock. After several moments spent trying to slow my breathing, I pulled down the overhead sun visor and looked into the mirror held in place with two rubber bands.

The first question that came to mind was whether my eyes were always that wide. I didn't think so, but damn did I look alert. And I didn't think it was the coffee.

The second question was, who the hell paid that girl to bring me a cup of blood? *Greasy Johnny Depp type?* That wasn't Barnes at all. Not even close. Johnny Depp was short and wiry, whereas Corwin Barnes was tall and muscular. And bald. While playing Jack Sparrow, Depp's hair had been long, brown and wavy. It didn't make any sense, especially when it seemed like the girl had gotten a pretty good look at the guy.

So, what the hell was going on?

I flipped the sun visor back up and took a look around. There were only a handful of other cars in the parking lot. None of them had a driver or any other such occupants. Nor did I see anyone slinking around, looking lost or out of place. Whoever had given the girl the cup, they hadn't stuck around to see what would happen. They weren't like the arsonist, who can't help but hang back and watch his handiwork go up in flames.

I sat in the truck a few more minutes, slouched in the seat, trying to compile a mental list of who may have been responsible. I didn't get far. By its definition alone, I would have needed actual names or possible leads in order for it to be an actual list. I had neither.

It wasn't until a police cruiser pulled into the lot and parked in a spot up front that I sat up straight behind the wheel. I patiently waited until the officer had gotten out of the car, pulled on his dark blue hat and disappeared around the corner to the front of the building before turning the key in the ignition. When the V-8 engine roared to life, I half expected the officer to come running back around the corner of the building. Thankfully, he never did. I was all for informing Detective Morgenstern about this latest incident, but the last thing I wanted was to get quizzed by an officer with no prior knowledge of my situation. That could make for a very long, very frustrating day.

As I put the truck in gear, a strange thought came over me, and I had to shake my head. To the people in the coffee shop, I'd become someone to fear. I was the one who posed the threat. It was absurd, and not a feeling I liked. I couldn't fathom how some people not only enjoyed it, but sought it out.

Crazy.

I needed to put the morning's events behind me for now. Cleanse my pallet, so to speak. I knew exactly where to go, and who I would find there. After looking both ways, I pulled out of the Starbuck's parking lot and headed east.

CHAPTER 22

Dallas's Jeep was parked in its usual spot beside the beat-up green dumpster in the alley behind the garage. Even though I wasn't allowed to work today, I knew Dallas would be. He may have taken the day off from working on customer's vehicles, but not on his own. After all, cars weren't just his business, they were his passion, and Dallas spent much of his free time under their hoods. When I saw the empty Pabst Blue Ribbon carton sitting on top of the trash in the dumpster, I knew his prized Chevy C10 was getting some love.

I entered the building through the storage room in the back, and was immediately met by the psychedelic sounds of 60s rock. Dallas kept a small radio on a shelf in the shop. Judging by the way the music reached the back door, I was willing to bet the volume knob was turned "to eleven." That was the phrase he always used, but I didn't get it. The dial only went to ten. When it came to the radio, I could always count on two things: Dallas living up to the saying, 'if it's too loud, you're too old;' and doing so with the help of WSWO, Dayton's oldies station. I didn't recognize the song or the band, but I recognized that 60s sound.

When I opened the door to the shop, I found Dallas's ass crack staring up at me from above his cut-off shorts. Both his head and arms were down inside the truck's engine compartment. A can of PBR sat balanced on the fender. With the music blasting, I knew he wouldn't hear me coming.

"Knew I'd find you here," I shouted from directly behind him. It wasn't like in the movies. He didn't raise up and hit his head on the hood or anything. Thankfully. He did jump, though.

"Jesus H!"

Above the blaring music, I heard the familiar sound of a dropped wrench inside an engine compartment. It clanked against everything on its way down, finally clattering onto the concrete floor. Since I drop my share of wrenches, I knew the sound all-too well. I don't know why making someone jump is so much fun, but it brought a smile to my face. A much needed smile.

"There goes about three months off my life." Dallas grabbed a nearby red rag and started wiping his greasy hands on it.

"Sorry," I said, but he wasn't fooled by it. Probably because I was having trouble concealing my smile.

"Bullshit." Dallas snatched up his can of beer, but before taking a drink, he jerked the top of the can toward me. A small amount of beer splashed onto my t-shirt. "Aw, look at that. Now you're goin' home to mommy smelling like beer. Might as well make it worthwhile. Cooler's over there."

He nodded toward one of the rear overhead doors and his filthy white cooler on the floor.

"After the morning I've had, I will definitely take you up on that."

I grabbed a beer for myself, and another for Dallas. After turning down the radio, I returned to the truck to find Dallas's legs sticking out from under it. I popped the tab, sucked in the foam, and took a long drink of cold goodness while I waited for him to retrieve his wrench. As soon as he was back on his feet, the interrogation began.

"What do you mean, 'after the morning I've had'? And what the hell you doin' here on your day off?"

I grabbed a seat on a short stack of tires and contemplated whether to bring it up. Who was I kidding? It didn't matter what lie I came up with. Dallas would see right through it. No matter how good it was. Besides, telling him about what happened at the coffee shop was the reason I'd come over.

So, I told him everything.

When I was done, Dallas just leaned against his truck, taking occasional draws from his beer. With his free hand, he stroked the length of his beard. It took a minute or two for him to say anything, and when he did, it wasn't the reaction I was expecting. Nor did he actually *say* anything.

Dallas busted out laughing.

Caught off guard by the response, all I could do was sit and drink my beer and wait for him to be done. It took the last two choruses of The Hollies' "Bus Stop" and a commercial for an assisted living facility before he would speak again.

"Damn, son," Dallas finally said. "I'm sorry, but what in the fuck?"

Still unsure how to respond, I stayed quiet and waited for more. Would this finally be the moment when Dallas would start questioning his involvement? Had it all become too much for him? Was this the point where Dallas concluded I'd finally lost it? Thankfully, he didn't take any of these roads. In fact, it wasn't *my* sanity he questioned at all.

"This guy is grade-A, certified nuts. Wanting to kill you after everything you've told me, I could see. But the extent to which this guy is playing with you, messin' with your head, goes beyond anything I can comprehend. Maybe I'm just one of those guys. When a job needs done, you do it. You don't dick around. But again, maybe that's just me. Maybe it's the military talking. Who the hell knows at this point? I stopped trying to figure this world out a long damn time ago."

Dallas crouched beside the Chevy and slid out the yellow, plastic tub we used to collect a car's used oil. A little of the glossy black stuff slopped onto the floor. Dallas let it go. The small splash of oil was literally a drop in the bucket compared to all the other stains that blackened the concrete.

"Have you asked yourself *why* he isn't just coming after you?" Dallas walked the yellow tub over to a 55-gallon barrel where we kept our used oil until someone came to haul it all away. "I mean, do you think there's a reason? Something other than simply getting his rocks off?"

I thought about it for a moment, then shrugged.

"I don't know," I said. "Could be, he hasn't decided how he wants to do it. How he wants to come after me."

After Dallas slowly poured the oil into the barrel, he clamped the plastic lid back on. When he turned back, an idea shone in his eyes. His eyebrows pointed south in the middle. A valley carved itself down the middle of his forehead, and he looked at me for a moment before speaking.

"Could it be," he asked, "that he's planning something big for you, and he's just not ready yet?"

CHAPTER 23

Could it be he's planning something big?

Dallas's words had been playing over and over in my mind since I left the shop. I spent the afternoon helping him tune up the C10 before taking it for a drive. We stopped for a late lunch, then headed out to the Vietnam Veterans Memorial Park. I walked most of the circle with Dallas, listening to him share stories when we'd come to a name he knew. When he started getting especially sentimental, I returned to the truck and left him alone with his memories. Sitting on the tailgate with my feet swinging, I let the sun warm my face and burn away the events of the morning. I was feeling really good by the time Dallas returned to the truck.

But the good vibes lasted only as long as the sun.

What could Barnes be planning? The question nagged at me as I drove the city streets on my way to the hotel. What could be worse than killing me? Eventually I decided an answer to either of these questions meant bad things for me, so I tried to rid my mind of both.

It was a cool evening. I had the windows down, sharing the new Ice Nine Kills CD with the people of Dayton. Being quite a few years older than most cars on the road, the truck didn't have all the fancy Bluetooth radio options. I had AM, FM and compact disc playability at my fingertips. So yeah, I still bought CDs, and probably would until they either stopped making them, or I somehow came into some money and could buy a newer vehicle. But, I had Garrett's truck, so I was in no hurry for the latter. Hoping to regain the good vibes I'd felt only hours ago, I kicked back in the seat and let the wind and tunes fill the truck's cab. But no matter how hard I tried, I was soon reminded not everything was right with the world.

The headlights mimicked my every move. Hanging a half block behind me, they were there every time I looked in the rearview mirror. When I made a left, they turned left. When I sped up, they did the same. Changing lanes didn't faze them at all, and even when I tried blending in with traffic, the same familiar headlights remained a part of the pack. If the driver wasn't following me, it would have been the mother of all coincidences.

I sat up higher in my seat and tried to determine how to best handle the situation. Not surprisingly, every idea that came to me was something I'd seen in a movie. I decided to start at the top of the list and see what worked.

As the song 'A Grave Mistake" was hitting its halfway point, I jerked the wheel and took a hard right down Sullivan Avenue at the last possible moment. Seconds later, my eyes were glued to the mirror when the headlights followed suit. The vehicle had also made the turn just in time while still maintaining a safe distance. At least the bright lights of an LED billboard provided my first good look at the vehicle. It was a plain white cargo van. There didn't appear to be anything written on its side. Very inconspicuous.

I managed to drive down Sullivan for another half mile before checking my mirror again. It became a balancing act of keeping an eye on the van while still keeping my eyes on the road. There weren't a lot of cars out, but it would only take a close encounter with one to ruin my evening.

It didn't matter whether I sped up or slowed down, the distance between us rarely changed. It was as if there was a length of chain connecting the back of my truck to the van. If the driver was trying to hide the fact he was trailing me, he wasn't doing a very good job, whoever it was. And I had a pretty good idea who.

Another quarter mile and I made my second impulsive move.

The light had just gone from green to yellow. I had plenty of time to make it through the intersection, yet I slammed on my brakes. The truck came to a shrieking stop. The stack of CDs on the seat next to me clattered to the floorboard. There were people pumping gas at the gas station on the corner, and I assumed I'd attracted their undivided attention. But, I didn't care enough to check.

I might have been able to lose the van if I'd gone through the light, but after the events at the coffee shop, I needed to know who was driving; to either identify Barnes once and for all, or find out if some new psycho had set their sights on me for whatever reason. My eyes darted to the rearview mirror. My adrenaline spiked. My foot hovered over the gas pedal in case I felt the need to jump on it. I waited patiently for the van to pull up and give me a good look at the driver, if that was even possible.

Turns out, it wasn't.

The van slowed prematurely, allowing a red Coca-Cola truck to get in between us. Out of sheer frustration, I pounded the steering wheel with both fists. I looked out my side mirror and caught nothing more than a sliver of the white van behind the delivery truck. *Smart move*, I thought, then cursed myself for giving the driver a compliment. Especially since that driver was most likely Barnes.

Drawing on Hollywood again, I checked both side mirrors to make sure no one was approaching from either side. No one was, and for the first time, I felt I was being overly paranoid. Though, not enough to make apologies. With adrenaline coursing through me, I punched the wheel again and watched cars cross through the intersection.

An impulse hit me while I sat there. A move with the potential of righting the wrong that stopping at the light apparently was. I turned right while the light was still red. In doing so, I hoped for one of two things to happen: thanks to the large truck positioned between us, there was a chance my move would go undetected. And if not, the truck might at least block the van from turning long enough for me to slip away.

I pressed hard on the accelerator, eager to get a head start. A newfound confidence straightened my posture. I was finally taking control of the situation, instead of simply driving around and allowing myself to be followed. I was taking actual measures to bring this pursuit to an end.

I looked up in time to see the white van cutting through the corner gas station. My heart sank. My growing confidence wilted like a dead flower. Not only had the driver seen me turn, but he'd countered.

Within seconds, he was again in my rearview.

My pulse quickened. I pressed the gas pedal further toward the floor, my mind and the Chevy's engine both racing. There was no doubt the van was following me. And it didn't appear any mere amateur move was going to lose it.

"Damn it!" My hand smacked the steering wheel again,

causing a slight swerve, but nothing dangerous.

I was quickly working my way out of the familiar part of the city. I had no idea where I was, much less where I was going. I considered reaching for my cell phone and its handy GPS, but buildings were speeding by so fast, I thought better of it.

The steering wheel vibrated beneath my white knuckles. The floorboard trembled beneath my feet.

I took a quick left at another yellow light, a spontaneous decision that didn't allow the truck to slow down as much as it should have. The Chevy stayed on all four wheels, but the tires screeched like a banshee. The van made the left as well. It was closer now than it had ever been.

I pushed the truck down Salem Avenue, a good twenty miles per hour faster than the law suggested. The Chevy's engine roared like a steal beast. As I held the pedal just above the floor, the wind through the open windows drowned out the music I'd forgotten was even playing. When I hit sixty through a busy intersection, I felt fear for the first time. Not for the white van, but my reckless driving.

I let up on the gas just a bit. Not surprisingly, the van did the same. It was at this point I started wondering what would happen if, or when, I could no longer run.

With my heart in my throat, I swerved around a yellow taxi. The cabbie threw me a glare. In this city, when a taxi driver gives you a dirty look for driving too aggressively, that's saying something. Cutting back into my lane, I checked my rearview. The van changed lanes, accelerated passed the yellow cab and fell in behind me. Strobing streetlights flashed by one after the other. Buildings sped by, some lit, some in shadow.

And all the while, the van kept pace.

When I slammed on the brakes and abruptly turned into a McDonald's parking lot, the tires let out another long, anguished cry. The truck hit a yellow-painted speed bump, taking it like a ramp. The jolt bounced me up and out of my seat. I didn't look back this time. I just assumed the van had made the turn as well. It wasn't until I took the curve following the drive thru lane that I cast a glance behind me.

I didn't see the van.

Nor did I get my hopes up. Putting a little distance between us didn't mean I was home free.

Something else I didn't see until it was almost too late were the three teenagers crossing the parking lot. They jumped out of the way, throwing their white bags of food into the air. Golden fries soon covered the pavement. I swerved enough to miss the kids, but was hindered by the row of parked cars lining the lot. I just missed the bumper of a grey sedan with its backing lights on.

I let off the gas, approaching the exit back onto the road. The plan was to double back in the opposite direction. Only the exit wasn't open. The white van was stopped on the street, blocking the lane. It hadn't followed me into the parking lot, after all. Instead, it was trying to box me in.

I jerked the truck to the left. We hit the curb head on, trading pavement for pristine grass and professional landscaping. The wheels temporarily left the ground. The engine raced. The Chevy started a series of bounces, threatening to rip the steering wheel from my hands. Somehow I held on. Just in time, too. The truck was in full-on missile mode, heading right toward the restaurant's plastic and brick roadside sign.

I cut the steering wheel back to the right. The truck didn't respond as I'd hoped. With the wheels on and off the ground, we continued right toward the golden arches. At the last possible second, the truck stopped bouncing, the tires gained their grip, and the truck jerked violently to the right. We'd come so close, I expected at any moment to hear a shriek of sheet metal scraping against brick. The sound never came. The truck couldn't have missed the sign by more than a couple inches.

With only a fleeting glance in either direction, I squeezed between the van and the sign and pulled onto the street. Another hard crank of the steering wheel brought the truck around, heading back in the direction I'd come.

I hit the gas.

I'd come within feet of the white van, as it sat facing the opposite way. I'd been too busy making sure the road was clear to get a look inside. In my rearview mirror, I could see the van trying to make a U-turn. Key word, 'trying.' Cars from both directions were in its way.

I made the most of the opportunity. I took a left at the next intersection, then another immediate left down a darkened alley. The moves brought me directly behind the McDonalds.

My heart pounded as I hurled down the alley. Sweat ran down my face. A tall privacy fence cradling a pair of dumpsters quickly approached on my right. Just passed it, I slammed on my brakes. I threw the truck in reverse, then backed into the shadowy area beside the fence. I immediately cut the lights. It had all been impulse. If this didn't do the trick, I had no idea what my next move would be. If I even had one. If the van came down the alley and stopped right in front of me, I would be trapped.

With my foot on the brake and my hand on the gear shifter, I watched and waited. I stayed ready to take off again if necessary. But that never happened. At least I don't think it did. I honestly don't know.

CHAPTER 24

One minute I was sitting beside the dumpster, waiting to see what the white van would do. Next thing I knew, I was slouched behind the wheel underneath an unlit freeway overpass. The engine was running, but the transmission was in park. The headlights were off.

I straightened with a gasp, panic stricken. Fear had my body in a stranglehold. I scanned all around and found no other vehicles, white vans or otherwise. The Chevy's bed was empty. The mirrors revealed nothing more than the night.

As a semi roared passed, the trucker laid on its horn. The shrill blast echoed off the surrounding concrete. I instantly clamped my hands over my ears. The turbulence from the tractor-trailer's wake sent a violent shimmy through both the Chevy and me. I felt the rocking long after the semi was gone. It was better than any alarm clock. I couldn't be any more awake.

I reached for the knob that turned on the headlights. I was at a loss as to where the time went, or how I'd gotten where I was. Strangely enough, none of that mattered. It was another blackout, pure and simple. It had been awhile since I'd experienced one. Right now, though, getting the hell off the side of the freeway was priority one. Pulling out the knob, the lights came to life.

And my blood turned cold.

The end is near.

The words stared at me from one of the overpass's cement columns. The spray paint still looked wet. Bright yellow streaks ran down the column in thin lines, somewhat blurring the words. The message, however, was clear. I found the phrase more ominous than most people would. It had been so overused in American society that nobody paid attention anymore. But these words were intended specifically for my eyes.

And that wasn't even what frightened me the most.

When the dashboard lights came on, something on the seat beside me shimmered in the dash's soft blue light. It wasn't my collection of compact discs. The ones that had previously fallen to the floor, but were now stacked neatly on the seat. That in itself was perplexing, but would have to wait its turn. It was the four long, curved prongs perched on top of the CDs that nearly sent piss running down my leg. The shiny prongs curled out from a makeshift handle like a claw, something Freddy Krueger would have envied. It was roughly the size of a baseball glove. A murderous glove made of sharpened steel.

I immediately threw open the door and jumped out of the truck. A car whizzed by at the same time, nearly clipping me. I grabbed onto the door and pulled myself back against the truck. All the while, my eyes never left the menacing object. A shiver of fear settled into my lower back. My stomach turned. My chest seized. I took another look around, but saw no one.

What the hell was it?

Where had it come from?

How did it get there?

And just where the fuck did the time go?

The questions came without end. My heart was pounding so fast, I thought I might come unglued. I paced up and down the side of the road, noticing the occasional passing car only when one honked its horn. I grew angrier and more anxious with each one. When I'd returned to the truck for the third time, I suddenly couldn't take it anymore. Enough was enough.

"Barnes!" I shouted, arms extended into the night. Then, to an audience of one, I tilted my head back and let it all out. "Come on, you sick fuck! You sick piece of..."

The rant went on for several seconds. I must have looked like a lunatic pacing the side of the freeway, yelling at the top of my lungs at no one in particular. I didn't care. I was inviting an end to the terror, once and for all.

"Come on!"

I finally dropped my arms. I stopped pacing. My throat was raw from both screaming and failing to breathe. And as far as I could tell, none of it had done any good.

Except for a passing car on the other side of the freeway, nothing filled the night air but silence. Nothing lurked on the hill beside the freeway but un-mowed grass and a few decent-sized rocks. I looked up and down the freeway. No cars were parked beside the road in either direction as far as I could see.

Good or bad, I was still alone.

As my heart rate began to slow, I was torn between two courses of action. Get in the truck, ignore whatever the hell that thing was on the seat, and get my ass to the hotel. Or, I could call Detective Morgenstern and report what happened, get him to meet me out here and let him handle things. While my gut urged the latter, it was the former that won out. In the end, I didn't want to stand beside a dark freeway, waiting around for who knew how long.

With one last glance around, I climbed into the truck. My eyes immediately went to the claw sitting on the seat. There was no way I was driving all the way to the hotel with that thing next to me. With a swipe of my hand, I sent it tumbling onto the passenger side floorboard. I could hear my father's voice in my head, telling me to be careful not to smudge any fingerprints. But I cared about very few things at that point, and tampering with evidence was not one of them.

With the address to the hotel punched into my GPS, I glanced over my shoulder. The freeway was clear. I hit the gas, and the truck shot forward. The large tires gripped the asphalt, taking no time at all to reach eighty miles an hour. And then I backed off a bit, easing down to seventy. I didn't know how I would explain the claw-like instrument if I got pulled over.

The possibilities of what might have happened during that stolen time scared the hell out of me. What worried me even more was knowing Barnes had been so close. That was hard to fathom. It instilled in me a very real, very organic fear. Through it all, one thought both comforted and troubled me to no end.

Somehow, some way, I was still alive.

CHAPTER 25

"It's called a Spanish Tickler," Detective Morgenstern said. "Sometimes referred to as a Cat's Paw, but unlike this one with its four prongs, those traditionally only have three."

We stood beside my truck under a light in the hotel's parking lot. As I knew he would, the first thing my father did when I got to the hotel was call up Morgenstern. Because I didn't want to freak out my mother any more than I had to, I'd left my shiny new gift in the truck. The detective had pulled it out and set it on the Chevy's hood, and was now in the process of giving my dad and me a quick lesson in brutality.

"It's an instrument of torture developed during the Spanish Inquisition," he continued, turning the thing over with his pen. "Basically, they would string someone up by their wrists and use one of these on their back, tearing right through the flesh. Sometimes even the bone. Really nasty stuff. Almost always lethal."

"And how do you know all this?" my father asked.

"Studied Criminal Justice at the University of Cincinnati. One of the courses was a history of crime and justice. Interesting class, but made me shake my head in disbelief more than a few times. The levels of brutality humans inflicted on one another back then was hard to comprehend."

"Not just back then," I said, receiving two nods of solemn

agreement in response.

We took a break from the conversation and watched a maroon Toyota roll slowly through the parking lot. After creeping up and down two different rows, the sedan eventually pulled into a nearby spot. A minute later, with three pairs of eyes scrutinizing them, an elderly couple eventually climbed out.

I let out an exhaustive breath. I didn't even realize I'd been holding it, but that's what happens when you're wound too tight. Suddenly, Darth Vader was in my head: 'The paranoia is strong with this one.'

"So, a white cargo van," Morgenstern said, ending our fascination with someone's grandparents.

I nodded.

"But you can't say for sure it was definitely trailing you."

"Pretty sure, but not positive." I kept my head down, like I was inspecting my shoes. I hadn't told the detective or my father about the blackout. I'd actually lied and said I'd stopped at a drug store for gum and a bottle of water after losing the van, and the pronged instrument was on the seat when I came out. That led to Morgenstern wondering out loud if the drug store might have a security camera trained on its parking lot. He assured me that if it did, then he would be able to pull the video footage. Which then led me to another lie. I told them I felt safer parking in the shadow of the building on the side, rather than out in the open. The lie was as thin as the edge of a finely honed bolo knife. I'm not sure the detective bought it. I know my father didn't, and I flinched at the look of concern in his eyes.

But that was the lesser of two evils at the moment.

My bigger worry was that either of them would start to

question whether Corwin Barnes was involved in any of this. Start wondering if it wasn't my PTSD causing these issues. It was an ever-present risk, and telling them I couldn't explain my whereabouts for part of the evening would ease them toward that conclusion. Especially when one of them was a veteran detective trained to be objective and consider all angles of a case. I couldn't trust they would take into account it was probably the stress Barnes was causing me that had reawakened the effects.

"Okay, well, I'll make note of it. At the very least, it's a good piece of information to have. If it turns out later that a white van doesn't factor in, then no harm no foul."

I nodded and glanced over at my father. He couldn't have heard a word Morgenstern had said. His eyes were too busy questioning me. I didn't know if this latest incident had heightened his concern for my safety, or if the bold-faced lies had him questioning my mental wellbeing. Regardless, I didn't like the look in his eyes, and I turned away.

"So," Morgenstern said, picking the Spanish Tickler up with his pen and carefully sliding a large evidence bag over it, "I'll get this looked at. See if we can lift any prints off it."

"Any word yet on the other evidence we've given you?" my father asked.

"Not yet. Should know something in a day or two."

My father offered his hand to the detective. "Thanks for coming by, Detective. We appreciate it."

"No problem." Morgenstern grasped my father's hand with a firm shake. "Whatever will help catch this guy. Luke," he said, extending his hand toward me, "sorry you had another scare tonight. But, this may be enough to justify posting a security detail at your house. So if anything good came from someone giving you this thing, it's that you'll probably get to go home soon."

"That would be great," I said, shaking his hand. I expected him to hold on to my hand longer than necessary, to look deep into my eyes and search for the truth. He didn't. He simply gave my hand a quick shake and let go. Then he turned toward his car parked a couple spots down.

We stood under the lamppost long enough to watch Morgenstern pull out of the parking lot. When he was gone, my father put his hand on my shoulder and we walked toward the hotel's main entrance. I took a deep breath, bracing myself for a second line of questioning that surprisingly never came. It was an uneventful finish to a very eventful day; one that started so innocently enough at a coffee shop and spiraled downhill from there.

As I stripped off my clothes and crawled into bed, I was already dreading what tomorrow might have in store.

CHAPTER 26

I didn't sleep at all, and it wasn't because of my father's snoring. When my PTSD was in full swing a year ago, my nights were marked with either chronic insomnia or nightmares. There was no in between. At least with the insomnia, I had coffee to help get me through the next day. For that fact alone, I gladly would have traded the nightmares. My opinion since then hadn't changed.

My life was enough of a nightmare, thank you.

I spent most of the night standing at my hotel room window, looking out over the parking lot. I wondered if Corwin Barnes was in one of the shadowy cars parked below, hidden from view. *Can he see me?* It was for that very reason I kept the lights off in the room. I didn't even turn on the television.

Something else keeping me from dreamland was wondering how he was making all of these deliveries without anyone catching a glimpse of him. Not that my parents, or Claire, or even Dallas, had any idea what Barnes looked like. That hardly mattered. They would have seen *somebody* leaving these gifts for me, whether they recognized him or not. Maybe next time. If there was a next time. How long did he plan on dragging this thing out, anyway?

The end is near.

The words came back to me, keeping any and all thoughts of sleep at bay.

It was just after five and still an hour from sunrise when I determined two things: I couldn't remain in my room a minute longer; and it wasn't too early to start the caffeine intake. I'd paced a path in the carpet, and was in dire need of a change of scenery.

I pulled on a pair of jeans and my tennis shoes and crept out of the room, taking extra care as I quietly closed the door behind me.

In contrast to the darkened room, the hallway was brightly lit, which did it no favors. It only allowed a better look at the God-awful carpeting. With more colors running through it than a standard box of crayons, the fact the carpet's design didn't continue into the rooms was the only good thing about it. The corridor was quiet as I made my way down to the elevators. I imagined everyone else in the hotel sleeping soundly in their beds, and I had to admit to a touch of jealousy. Imagine, being the focus of envy simply for the ability to sleep.

It didn't take long for the elevator to arrive. It took even less time for me to reach the first floor. The elevator car came to a halt with a slight shimmy and the sound of a bell. As soon as the doors slid open, the quiet of the last few hours was shattered.

Somewhere in the lobby, a television raged. The volume was surprisingly loud for the early hour. From the intensity of the voices going back and forth, I knew right away it was tuned to one of those twenty-four-hour news channels my father seemed to never tire of. Between the television and the bright lights, you would have thought it was the middle of the day.

The news anchors were in mid-debate. The subject, the merits and drawbacks of a two-party system. Unfortunately for them, nobody was listening. The lobby was completely empty. I looked to the front desk, expecting to see a dreary-eyed night attendant with elbows on the counter and head in their hands staring blindly at the screen from across the room. No one was at the desk, either. In fact, there was nobody anywhere. It all felt a little eerie, yet because of the television, too lively to feel alone.

The eeriness fell by the wayside once I saw that fresh coffee awaited me in the breakfast area. As I poured the rich, black java into my paper cup, a gratifying steam rose from the pot. I tried not to think about what happened at the coffee shop less than twenty-four hours earlier, but I failed. The incident was too new, too fresh. I was successful, however, in still looking forward to the cup I was about to drink.

Which I would have enjoyed had there been any creamer around. The little wicker caddie that usually displayed those little cups of creamer sat empty beside the coffee pot. This posed a problem. I literally felt my shoulders deflate. Coffee without creamer wasn't something I cared for. Like burgers without cheese, or hot wings without celery and bleu cheese dressing.

I searched all through the breakfast area, even looking in a couple of storage cabinets. If there was a single little cup of creamer anywhere in the hotel, it was a heavily guarded secret. I wondered what time someone showed up to start setting up breakfast. It didn't look like it would be anytime soon, and I didn't feel like waiting. The lack of both sleep and caffeine was awakening the cranky monster in me. One without the other was fine, but having neither? Someone might get hurt.

I tapped the bell on the front desk a couple of times. Someone had to be around, I was sure of it. They had to be somewhere. Hotels don't just run themselves. What if there was an emergency? What if someone showed up late? What if someone had an early flight to catch and found they had no hot water in their shower? After what should have been enough time for someone to emerge from the back room, I tapped on the bell a third time.

"Hello?"

Another thirty seconds passed, and still I saw no one. The television was showing commercials now, and it seemed to be even louder than before. Giving up on the front desk clerk, I headed back to the breakfast area. I swiped the paper cup from the counter and tossed it into a nearby trashcan.

The hotel's entrance, the pair of sliding glass doors beckoned me. Was it worth the effort to leave and grab a cup of joe at the gas station across the street? Or, should I head back up to the room, crawl back in bed and hang out for another hour or so until the rest of the world awakened? It was a close competition, but coffee won out over waiting.

Cool, pre-dawn air greeted me as the sliding glass doors slid open. As I passed through the entrance, I took a deep breath and let the air soothe my insides. The doors closed behind me, and I stopped abruptly. *Was that...*

My need for caffeine vanished.

CHAPTER 27

I cautiously approached the white van. I wasn't sure how I hadn't noticed it from the window in my room, but somehow its presence had slipped by me. Because, it wasn't just parked near the Chevy; it sat *right beside* it. I'd purposefully parked under a light the night before, and now that light illuminated the van's interior like a spotlight. Even from the hotel's entrance, I could see there was no one behind the wheel. My pace slowed as I drew nearer. Soon I could reach out and touch the driver's side door.

A chill ran through me, and it wasn't from the weather.

I didn't know if the doors were locked, and I wasn't prepared to find out. The van probably had an alarm system, anyway. The last thing I needed was to draw that kind of attention. I could see some guy coming out with muscles busting out of his Joe's Plumbing t-shirt, pissed not only that I was trying to get inside his work van, but that I'd been so rude as to have awoken him. Besides, I couldn't be sure this was the same van that had followed me. Ignoring the door handle, I cupped my hands around my eyes and leaned against the window.

Empty Mountain Dew cans littered the passenger side floorboard. Covering the passenger seat and center console were wrappers from various energy bars. I stopped counting at six. With all the trash, there was no place for a passenger to sit. Whoever drove that particular van, worked alone. I tried to look deeper into the interior, but couldn't see much beyond the seats. The light coming through the windshield only penetrated so far.

I shot a glance up at a random third-floor window, one I thought could be mine. I fought off the urge to run and get my father. It seemed premature. There were at least a thousand white cargo vans in a city this size. Still, it certainly looked like the one that had been following me. Coincidence? Hopefully time would tell.

I turned toward the rear of the van.

Each of the rear doors possessed a window. The way the van sat, the doors pointed away from the overhead light. I could still make out a few objects among the shadows in the back. A beat up black toolbox sat near the back door. A pair of kneepads rested on top. They looked similar to the ones my father had used when we laid new tile in the kitchen of our old house. Next to the toolbox, a lumpy roll of grey carpeting ran most of the length of the van. And next to that, a roll of padding. I deduced the van must have belonged to a carpet layer. Unless Barnes had taken up a new profession, the van itself was looking less and less threatening.

It all changed when I got around to the passenger side.

Looking in through the window, the first thing I noticed, besides the trash, was a clipboard. It stood upright, tucked in the space between the seats. Clamped to it was a sizeable stack of papers. Thanks to the light coming through the windshield, I was able to see the top sheet clearly.

It was a map. A simplistically drawn map. When I squinted to make out more of the details, I realized it wasn't a map after all. Maps don't show elevator shafts and stairwells. This was a photocopied section of a floor plan.

I looked up at the hotel for a moment, then back at the floor plan. Over the last few days, I'd explored every square inch of the hotel out of sheer boredom. The visible section of the floor plan matched the easternmost part of the hotel, including the small workout room. I exhaled deeply. The work van, the tools, the carpeting, even the floor plan. It all made perfect sense, really. The whole situation seemed completely logical.

Until I noticed what was written at the top of the page.

3227

The numbers were circled in red ink.

My stomach dropped. My jaw did the same. It couldn't have been a mere coincidence. A coincidence of that magnitude had an entirely different name. It's called a certainty.

3227 wasn't just a number. It was a room number. And not just any room number. It was the room I'd been sleeping in for the last three nights.

CHAPTER 28

I pressed the button like Woody pecking at a dead pine, like it would somehow make the elevator move faster. What was probably only a few seconds seemed like hours. The very act of standing there was costing me time I didn't have. I briefly considered using the stairs. But a darkened stairwell wasn't exactly where I wanted to be at the moment. I filed the option in my back pocket, just in case the elevator took too much longer.

Where had it gone?

I'd just gotten off of it five minutes ago. Why wasn't the elevator car where I left it? There still wasn't anyone else around. The lobby and front desk remained a ghost town. I didn't waste too much time worrying about what it all meant. I had much bigger things on my mind.

I was reconsidering the stairs when the elevator bell chimed. After a brief pause, the doors split in the middle. Like the rest of the place, the elevator car was empty, and I walked right in.

I pressed the button for the third floor only once, but I replayed my woodpecker impression on the 'close doors' button for several seconds. Eventually, the doors started their slow journey toward each other. I held my breath. I waited for a hand to reach in and stop the doors at the last second. It didn't happen. Once the doors had closed and the elevator started its ascent, I could finally release the breath I'd held captive.

As if it were the theme of the day, the elevator ride took much longer than it should have. Days longer than the ride down. As I stared at the large, red numbers above the doors, I felt like I should be whistling or something. But my heart was beating so fast, it would have thrown off my tempo. I chose to stand there in silence and bite my lower lip instead.

The red number finally changed from a one to a two. I started thinking about my parents sleeping in the room next to mine. Claire wasn't staying with us any longer, so the door connecting the rooms was being kept shut, despite my mother's protests. She wanted it open, but I wouldn't have it. I needed *some* privacy. We'd compromised and agreed to keep the door closed, but unlocked. In hindsight, it may have been a bad idea. Whoever had access to my room, subsequently had access to theirs. All anyone would have to do was turn a knob. This bothered me the most as I waited for the world's longest elevator ride to be over.

When the red number finally changed to a three, I took a step toward the door and started bouncing. The bell chimed. The doors split apart. Once the opening was wide enough for me to squeeze through, I bolted.

And rammed an older woman in a light blue dress, white apron and hairnet.

"Shit," I said, gaining my footing. I towered over the woman, holding her up by her frail arm. She was seventy if she was a day. "I'm really sorry."

"It's quite alright," she said in a startled voice. Her free hand went to her chest, where she took rapid breaths, and I helped her gain her footing.

"Are you okay?"

"I'm fine," she said, but not until her breathing had slowed a bit. "Just scared me is all."

"Again, I'm really, really sorry. Didn't expect anyone else to be up this early."

She nodded her head and smiled weakly, but if she said anything at that point, I didn't hear it. The hollow sound of a closing door echoed down the hall. I shot it a quick glance. I didn't see anyone, but that didn't mean anything. My heart was still thumping my chest when the elderly woman regained my attention.

"Oh, I'm an early riser," she said. "And breakfast doesn't make itself." She pushed the button to summon the elevator. In all the commotion, the doors had closed. Thankfully, the elevator hadn't moved, and the doors opened almost immediately. "Have a nice day, dear."

"You, too," I said, and watched her enter the elevator. As the doors started to slide together, I offered her the best smile I could muster. With the doors closed, the elevator started its descent. I dropped the smile and turned up the hallway. As best I could with my bad ankle, I sprinted to the room circled in red on the van's clipboard.

My heart seized.

The door was open.

No more than a half-inch, but a half-inch more than I'd left it. Without so much as a cell phone on me, I stood in the hallway staring at the black sliver of space between the door and the doorjamb. My feet had grown roots. Shock had me at a loss for a plan. I had to do something. Every second I waited, the more danger I put my parents in.

I considered banging on my parents' door but didn't know if it was the best thing to do. Waking them definitely seemed like a good idea. Question was, what kind of trap might I be thrusting them into? I considered going to get help, but that could take forever, given the hotel's lack of warm bodies. I doubted the elderly woman would be much help in a fight. She'd gone down pretty easy when I ran into her.

Ultimately, I had only one real option.

With a final look up and down the hallway, I placed both hands on the door and gave it a slight push. And I do mean slight. I gave myself just enough room to slide my hand in. Once I found the light switch located just inside the room, I flipped it on. I leaned in and listened for sudden movement. When it was clear the burst of light hadn't triggered a reaction, I slowly opened the door all the way.

The bathroom was directly to my right. A short hallway invited me further. I had to accept the invitation in order to see into the actual room. It took both a deep breath and a moment to psych myself up before I could approach the corner. Once there, I got my first look at the entire room.

There was no one there. At least not at first glance.

Picking up the ice bucket from the refrigerator cabinet, I decided to poke my head into the bathroom before going any further. I didn't want anyone sneaking up behind me. As I flipped on the light, I braced myself for combat. Turns out, I didn't have a fight on my hands just yet. After looking behind the door and opening the shower curtain, it was clear no one would be jumping me from behind.

I turned my attention back to the main room. No one had magically appeared in the last thirty seconds. I checked between the bed and the wall, behind the sitting chair. I even looked underneath the writing desk, though if anyone had been hiding under there, it would have been fairly obvious.

I was alone.

After unplugging my cell phone and sliding it into my pocket, I turned my attention to the door connecting the two rooms.

I still clutched the bucket, poised to do someone bodily harm if need be. I put my ear to the wooded door. For close to a minute, I listened for any sounds coming from the other room. When I didn't hear anything except the rapid beating of my heart, I turned the knob and opened the door.

My parents' room was like a cave. The under-window air conditioner hummed away, keeping the room cooler than I liked. The only light filtering in was the light I'd introduced by opening the door. The drapes were pulled tight. A folded pair of boxers probably covered the clock on the nightstand. My mother couldn't sleep if she was too warm. My father couldn't sleep unless the room was pitch black. To me, they both seemed high maintenance, but it apparently worked. Though the darkness wasn't helping me in my pursuit.

"Dad."

It was one of those forced whispers; the kind where you're trying to keep your voice low, but still needing to project across a room. I sounded like a sick goat.

No answer. No response of any kind. It was so quiet, I didn't even hear the soft, nasally breathing that usually accompanied my mother's sleep.

"Dad." This time, I said it louder while searching the wall for a light switch. My heart was pounding like a frightened, caged animal. I expected a loud crash, maybe a swift and heavy blow to the face at any moment. It could've been my overactive imagination. It also could've been the fact that being attacked was a very real possibility, given the situation. Because there really was no telling what the darkness held, the adrenaline pumping through me showed no signs of letting up.

After failing to garner a response a second time, and unable to find a light switch on the wall, I had a decision to make. I left the safety of the doorway light and made my way through my parents' room and toward their front door. I moved as swiftly as the dark allowed, with every step bringing renewed fear. Fear of both a phantom attacker, and of an errant suitcase or cooler in my path. The air inside my lungs begged for release. The skin on the back of my neck grew damp with sweat. My body was trying to tell me how stupid this decision was. I just hoped it wasn't a costly one.

I found the bank of light switches just inside the entryway. I spun around just as I flipped the switch, instinctively cowering against anyone or anything that might have been using the dark for cover.

The room erupted into a sudden and brilliant light.

My father shot upright in bed.

"What the hell?" he mumbled, shielding squinting eyes. His face was a mass of scrunched up creases as he fought the sting from the light. I almost felt sorry for waking him in such a manor, but my attention was quickly drawn to something else.

"Where's mom?"

"What?" he asked, his hand blindly searching the nightstand for his glasses.

The space in the bed beside my father was vacant. The covers were tossed aside, and the pillow supported nothing but a dent. A quick glance around revealed no sign of my mother anywhere in the room.

As much as it seemed impossible, my heart started pounding even harder. I tried to block out the fact Barnes had an affinity for females. Key word: *tried*. I shook my head free of an image of my mother lying beside my father in bed, her entire side soaked in red. That's when I noticed the bathroom door. It was closed. A thin sliver of light ran along the floor beneath it.

Hoping for the best, I couldn't help but fear the worst.

I looked at my father and gave him the universal 'shush' sign: a finger to my lips. My grip on the ice bucket tightened as I raised it like a hammer. I reached for the door handle and paused. My trembling hand hovered over the knob.

The sound of a toilet flushing broke the tension from the other side of the door. A moment later, the faucet came on, ran for a few seconds, then shut off. About the time I was pulling my hand away from the handle, the door opened.

My mother gasped and clutched the top of her robe.

"Luke!"

I took a step back. I dropped the bucket to my side, imagining how things must've looked as my mother opened the door. She was lucky it was only me standing there, even if she didn't know it.

"What is it, Luke?" my father asked, getting to his feet. His eyes were still adjusting to the light as he put on his glasses.

Ignoring the question, I returned to my room. By the time I'd shut my front door and thrown the lock into place, my father stood in the doorway between the rooms. My mother hung behind him, looking over his shoulder.

"Luke?"

"I'm not sure." I took a deep breath, then sat on the corner of the bed. "Something's not right."

Where the hell should I start? So much had transpired in the last few minutes. But with nothing to show for any of it, a tentacle of self-doubt started polluting my mind. *The van.* Did I really see what I thought I saw? *My door.* Could I have simply not shut it all the way? Could it all just be one big string of coincidences?

I hunched forward and began rubbing my temples.

It was all very possible and improbable at the same time. I wanted to believe everything was just as I'd perceived. I wanted to believe in myself. More importantly, I wanted my parents to believe it.

For that reason alone, not telling my father wasn't an option. Especially after the look in his eyes while we spoke with the detective. There could be no more lies or half-truths. So, I did what was both the easiest and most difficult at the same time. I started from the beginning and told them everything I knew to be true.

CHAPTER 29

It was nearly six o'clock by the time I finished telling my side of things. The sun wasn't yet peeking through the glass doors, but it was warming up to it. The sky appeared a shade lighter than before as we made our way through the lobby.

"Maybe I should call Detective Morgenstern," my father suggested.

I didn't respond. I was still processing the last forty-five minutes of my life, trying to differentiate fact from fiction. I figured he was capable of making the decision.

The lobby was less like a ghost town this time around. There was a shiny, smiling face at the front desk, her dark brown hair pulled up into a bun. A trio of business executives in pressed suits milled around the breakfast stations, their plates full of fruit and fresh-made waffles. One man drew my attention, standing to the side, waiting on his toast. At first, I thought he was talking to himself. Then he turned, revealing a Bluetooth headset clipped to his ear. The woman I'd met at the elevator poured apple juice from a large bag into the dispenser.

What a difference forty-five minutes can make.

The sliding glass doors parted as we approached. My father had his cell phone out, scrolling through his contacts. I just hoped it wouldn't be a wasted call. And a wasted trip for Morgenstern. While my father put on pants and shoes in the room, it gave me more time to think. And more time to doubt myself, which wasn't surprising considering the apparent return of my PTSD. Doubting myself was something I'd gotten all too comfortable with after the events of a year ago.

The only part I was absolutely certain of was the van. I knew I hadn't imagined it. It was very real. Maybe it was just one of a thousand in the city. Maybe it was a coincidence one would be parked beside me. Maybe it wasn't even the van that had followed me the night before.

But it could be.

Unfortunately, we would never find out.

"You can put your phone away," I mumbled, my pace slowing, my heart falling.

Standing there looking at the empty spot beside my truck, my hope for the first real clue died. Not even a fresh oil stain remained to prove the van, or any other vehicle, had parked there recently.

I knew what was coming before he even asked.

"Did you happen to get the license--"

"No," I snapped. "I didn't." Then I cursed aloud before turning back toward the hotel.

Dad ended up not calling Morgenstern. He did, however, offer to trade me vehicles for the day. Knowing how much he hated driving the truck, I turned down his gracious offer. I'm not sure if he was relieved or not. I'm sure the part of him that wasn't a selfless parent couldn't have been too disappointed.

By the time I arrived at work an hour and a half later, I had probably checked my rearview mirror a total of a hundred and sixty-seven times. Hell, before I'd even started up the truck, I performed a thorough inspection, making sure there was nothing out of the ordinary. I was slowly perfecting the art of paranoia.

"Long time, no see," Dallas said, as I entered through the back door.

"I know, right? What's it been, like twelve hours?"

"Something like that." Dallas sat at his rickety, wooden desk, smiling too broadly so early in the morning. But then, he didn't always need coffee to get him going. Sometimes the smell of motor oil and antifreeze did the trick. He appeared to be sorting through a disheveled stack of receipts, so I was more than happy to leave him to it.

I continued into the office where the coffee maker sat waiting. I'd been in such a hurry to get out of the hotel, I didn't bother getting a cup on my way out. And I definitely wasn't stopping anywhere after what happened at the Starbucks the day before. For all I knew, there was a sign now posted at every location with my photo on it: 'do not serve this person.'

With a fresh cup of steaming fuel, I headed in the direction of the shop, eager to get to work. I hoped it would take my mind off of the events of the last twenty-four hours. Just as I got to the doorway, Dallas entered the office behind me. I wasn't in a talkative mood, so I was hoping he wasn't, either.

"So," he said innocently, "do anything exciting last night?"

I just looked at him. It was all I could do not to roll my eyes. But, knowing he meant nothing by it, I somehow found the restraint.

"You have no idea," I said, and walked out into the shop.

CHAPTER 30

It was sometime after lunch when I felt my mood finally improve. Maybe it was the work taking my mind off of things. Maybe it was the soulful sounds of Motown the radio station seemed stuck on that day. Hell, I'd spent so much time around Dallas, maybe it was the smell of grease, brake fluid, and hydraulic oil cheering me up.

Whatever it was, I went with it.

I had just struck the tip of the acetylene torch and was about to cut off the rusty muffler bolts from an older model Oldsmobile when I first noticed the boots. The cuffs of dark grey uniform pants covered most of the black work boots. It was all I could see of the person from underneath the car. I had no idea who they belonged to. Since I hadn't heard anyone say my name, I continued with the task at hand. With the casual way Dallas did business, customers coming into the shop were a frequent occurrence. Safety protocols be damned.

By the time I wiggled the muffler loose and rolled the creeper out from under the car, I figured Dallas had taken care of the wandering customer.

But he hadn't. And it wasn't a customer.

"What's up, man?" a smiling Arashk asked, looking down at me as I laid on my back looking up at his crotch.

"Hey," I said, and because it's difficult to hold a conversation looking up at someone's crotch, I rolled off the creeper. My anger and frustration had subsided, but I was still a little on edge. And I felt a little vulnerable lying there with this tall man standing over me, even if it was someone I knew. Arashk drove for NAPA, delivering parts and such to garages. He stopped in Tipsword's at least once a week to drop off something we'd ordered. "What do you have for me today?" I asked as I stood up.

"*Nimic.*"

"Sorry?"

Arashk chuckled to himself.

"*Nimic*," he repeated. "Is Romanian for 'nothing.' I have nothing for you today, my friend."

"Oh, okay," I said, shutting off the acetylene and oxygen tanks. I tossed the green-tinted goggles onto the roof of the Oldsmobile and leaned against it. If Arashk wasn't dropping something off, I was more than a little curious as to what I owed this visit. "So what's up? Need your truck fixed?"

"Nah," he said. "Boss gave me a pair of Reds tickets for the game Saturday. I'm not too much into baseball. Thought I'd see if you wanted them. Seems nobody else can use them. Didn't know if you were into baseball or not, but thought maybe. It is your national pastime, correct?"

It was, but I wasn't. I wasn't really into sports at all, but my father was. He was actually a big Cincinnati Reds fan. And that was enough to pique my interest.

"Yeah, maybe," I said, thinking if nothing else, it might be a good distraction for the two of us. "How much are they?"

"No cost, my friend. Just don't want them to go to waste."

"Well, in that case," I said, "I'll definitely take 'em.

Thanks."

"No problem, except I don't have the tickets with me. I'll bring them next time," he said with his normal broad smile. His teeth were a little off color, and his long black hair sometimes looked like it needed introduced to shampoo, but Arashk always seemed to be in a good mood. I had to hand it to him. "Oh wait," he continued, his smile wilting just a bit. "I don't know if you guys have any parts on order. No. Right now, *nimic*. How about you give me your number, and I'll catch up with you sometime before Saturday?"

I rattled off the first three numbers before the fourth caught in my throat. I barely knew Arashk. He was just the parts delivery guy, not necessarily a friend. Passing my phone number around to just anyone didn't sound like something I should be doing. Especially with everything going on.

"Is something a problem?" Arashk asked, wiping a wisp of dark hair out of his eyes.

I cleared my throat and coughed. "Must have breathed in some dust," I lied. What was I afraid of? Arashk wasn't Barnes, and I didn't want to look like an idiot. It's not like I didn't know him at all. What excuse could I possibly use for not wanting to give him my number that wouldn't sound utterly lame? I decided to give him my number, but just couldn't make a habit of giving out personal information.

I started over, rattling off the numbers as he typed them directly into his phone.

"Cool," he said, dropping his phone into the pocket of his uniform shirt, right behind the patch with his name on it. "I'll call you in the next day or two. We can meet up somewhere to exchange."

"Sounds good," I said. "It'll be a nice break from

everything for me and my old man."

"Old man?" Arashk asked, his eyes narrowing.

"My dad," I clarified.

"Oh," he said, with a nod of understanding. "I see. And, break from everything? Are you having a rough time?"

"It's nothing," I said, trying to steer the conversation away from the growing inquisition. "Just been really busy lately. It'll just be nice to do something fun for a change."

"Oh. Alright, then. See ya."

With a wave, he turned and walked away. When he got to the shop door, he stopped and turned back.

"By the way," Arashk said, "Boss sometimes gives me concert tickets, too. You're into the hard stuff, right? Metalcore and stuff? I'll keep you in mind."

"Yeah, thanks," I said, picking the creeper up and stowing it against a wall so Dallas wouldn't trip over it. When I turned back around, Arashk was gone.

When I got home from work, a dark blue sedan sat across the street from our house. It had no markings or visible connection to the Dayton Police Department, but it didn't take a character from *The Big Bang Theory* to recognize who it was and why it was there. I nodded at the plainclothes officer behind the wheel and he nodded back.

"His name's Courtney," my father said, as I shut the front door behind me. He stood in the living room, looking out the front window and shaking his head. "And that's his first name. Officer Courtney Stine. Can't imagine what his parents were thinking giving him a name like that."

"Maybe it's a family name." I shrugged and dropped my keys onto the table beside the door.

"Maybe," my father said. "Still..." but he let his thought

die then and there, and I chose not to resurrect it. "Your mother's making dinner tonight," he continued. "I assume you're going to be here?"

He gave me one of those looks that parents are so good at. The one telling me what my answer had better be.

"Yeah," I said. The thought of my mother's cooking actually perked me up. I'm usually happy to eat my share of pizza, burritos and take out Chinese, but even I was getting tired of eating at the hotel. "I'm here for the night. Probably gonna crash early. I'm wiped."

"I can imagine." Then a look of fatherly concern narrowed his eyes. "Anything out of the ordinary happen today?"

I shook my head, even though he already knew nothing had. Both he and my mother had texted me a hundred times over the course of the day.

"Well, with our new watchdog out there, you can sleep easy tonight. I know I'm looking forward to sleeping in my own bed for a change."

I nodded. "And I'm looking forward to a home cooked meal."

"Guess we both win!" Then my father sprouted the first smile I'd seen in a couple days. "I'm gonna see if she needs any help."

He turned in the direction of the kitchen, but not before looking out the window one more time.

CHAPTER 31

Claire had never sent me a photo quite like it before. She was always texting me playful selfies, or photos of her and her college friends doing something funny. Usually whenever she thought I could use a pick me up. One time, during what has become known as my 'dark days,' she sent me a photo from a salon where she was getting her hair cut. She'd taken the hair her stylist had just cut off and stuck it to her upper lip and chin with styling gel. Her deep, reddish-brown goatee matched her hair perfectly. After posing with a scowl like a ginger Charlie Hunnam, she snapped a selfie and texted it to me, hoping to make me laugh. It did, and it chased the storm clouds away for one day, at least.

The photo she sent me that night after dinner was tastefully done and completely obliterated the day's storm clouds. The red lace stood out against her soft, pale skin. The top of the bra was cut low, the bottoms of the panties were cut high, and I was forced to walk over and shut my bedroom door.

'well?'

The text followed minutes after the photo. Still recovering from my initial reaction, I could only reply with a single word of my own.

'wow'

I figured that was okay, because it summed up my thoughts perfectly.

'hope that's a good wow'

It was, I assured her. Propping my pillows up against my headboard, I laid back to settle in for a relaxing text swap with my girl.

'whats the occasion'

While I waited for her response, I found myself in the mood for something slightly more mellow than my usual heavy metal fare. Scrolling through the playlists on my phone, I stopped at 3 Doors Down. Cueing up their *Away from the Sun* release, I hit play. By the time the slinking guitar opening of "When I'm Gone" started curling through the speaker, my attention had returned to Claire.

'Just loving you' was the text I received back, and just like that, the stress of the last twenty-four hours was washed away. I can't lie, the photo started the process. Seeing those words just finished it off. The job at Tipsword's was going well, and my family was healthy, but there were still times when I felt like Claire was the one really good thing I had going for me. Sometimes, nothing and no one else seemed to matter.

Even though the photo was still fresh in my mind, I found myself needing to see it again. Exiting the screen showing our chain of texts, I swiped over to the photo gallery where I'd downloaded the red lace. The gallery menu popped up displaying all the photos on my cell arranged by date.

And that's when I first noticed something might be wrong.

There were six tiny thumbnail photos grouped together for that day. And therein laid the confusion. Not only had I downloaded only the one photo from Claire, I hadn't taken any photos myself. I couldn't remember the last time I had. Taking selfies wasn't really my thing.

My phone buzzed. That tiny envelope appeared at the top of the screen, notifying me of a new text. *Claire.* I ignored it for the time being. I chose instead to investigate the five mystery photos.

The familiar interior of room 3227 filled the screen. The photo showed both the nightstand beside the bed and the bed itself, taken from the foot of it. The bed looked rumpled; the comforter tossed aside. All four pillows lay scrunched up against the headboard. The bed looked pretty much how I'd left it that morning.

The second and third photos were more of the same; the vanity and sink area where my deodorant and toothbrush sat; the cabinet that hid the mini fridge with the flat screen perched on top. They were simple, unartistic photos taken inside the room, very much like the photos people take to inventory their things for insurance purposes. The only problem was I didn't remember taking any of these.

The phone buzzed again. This time, I didn't have to ignore the notification. It got run over by the thoughts racing through my mind. My heart started beating a little faster. Possibilities started to form. Dark, frightening possibilities.

The fourth photo was difficult to make out, and it took me a few seconds to realize what it was: my parents' bed in the adjoining room. The room was dark, the shared doorway introducing just enough light to create shadows around the folds in my parents' comforter. I could make out my father's silhouette. He had his back to the photographer with his arm draping my mother's hip.

The fifth and final photo concluded the story.

The photo was of something personal. The shot framed

only my small, dark green suitcase sitting on the floor in the hotel room. My focus narrowed. I looked over to where the suitcase leaned against my closet door, still waiting to be unpacked. And then I realized; it had to be a clue, an invitation to take a closer look. Why else take the photo?

Dropping the phone onto the bed, I swung my legs off the side and stood up.

I stared at the suitcase for a moment, a suitcase I was wholly familiar with, yet suddenly felt detached from. Dragging it over to the bed, I hefted the suitcase up. It bounced when I tossed it onto my bed. Without pause, I yanked the shiny gold zipper around the perimeter of the case and threw open the lid.

Nothing but clothes stared back at me, mocking my elevated heart rate. Everything appeared just as I packed it. Folded jeans and t-shirts took up the bulk of the space. Sitting on top were several pairs of socks and underwear, some clean, some not so much.

I started pulling everything out of the suitcase, one article at a time. I dumped it all in a pile on the floor. Within the space of a minute, the suitcase was empty. A hollow cavity stared back at me, questioning not only what I might be looking for, but my intentions. I was clueless on both accounts.

Maybe I was looking in the wrong place. I grabbed ahold of the suitcase lid and flipped it back over. Starting at the top, I checked the zippered pockets; pockets I rarely used.

It was in the third pocket, the largest of the three, where my hand brushed against something.

"Shit."

I pulled out a folded sheet of paper. Even though it was a different type of paper than the previous notes, I knew it was from the same author. Like a love note passed around a classroom, the paper was crudely folded into quarters. The hotel's logo taunted me from one side. My heart knocked against my chest as I unfolded the paper...

'SORRY I MISSED YOU. WILL TRY AGAIN SOON.'

I dropped the note and stumbled backward, settling into the chair beside my desk. And that's when I knew: I wasn't losing it. Someone truly had been in my hotel room that morning. I wasn't crazy, I was being stalked. Strangely, I didn't know which was worse.

CHAPTER 32

It was finally Friday. Which meant it had been a week since I'd received the first package with the bones and Garrett's class ring. Since then, so much had happened. And when I say 'so much,' I mean 'almost too much.' Once we'd checked out of the hotel and returned home, however, the days had come and gone without incident. And if I didn't know better, I'd say Dallas was actually disappointed about it. I don't know if our little trip to the church had reawakened the soldier in him or what, but he seemed alert and ready to go if something were to ever happen. Something like, Corwin Barnes deciding to show his face.

I, on the other hand, wasn't quite as eager. I was enjoying the break from the terror very much, thank you. Enjoying it, because I wasn't naïve enough to think it was over. Barnes hadn't simply gotten bored. He hadn't said 'screw it' and left town. Having been burned there permanently, his shadow lingered, never far from my mind. The threat was as real as ever.

When I asked Dallas his thoughts on why Barnes was taking a break, he did something I didn't know he could. He quoted a book. *The Art of War* by Sun Tzu to be exact.

"Rouse him, and learn the principle of his activity or inactivity," Dallas said. "Force him to reveal himself, to find out his vulnerable spots."

"Great," I'd said. "And here I was hoping to keep my vulnerable spots to myself."

Claire's parents were home from their trip, so I hadn't seen her at all that week. It didn't help my mother had called hers their first night back and spent forty-five minutes on the phone going over the entire situation. She felt it was the right thing to do, and honestly, I couldn't muster much of an argument. I was just worried about the blowback. After their conversation, my only contact with Claire had been by cell. Perhaps her parents were urging her to keep her distance for a while. Perhaps they were right.

Today, however, she was swinging by the shop to have lunch with me. And by 'having lunch,' I meant we were going to the police station to visit Detective Morgenstern. We hadn't heard a word since that Monday night in the hotel parking lot. I found it strange, not to mention a little concerning, he wouldn't have kept better in touch. But then, my only knowledge about how situations like this are handled stemmed from police shows on television. Who knows how accurately these things are portrayed for prime time.

I was under the hood of an import sedan when I heard the car horn out front. It lit a flicker of excitement inside me, and I immediately dropped what I was doing. It had been a few days, and I was eager to see Claire. Red lace or not.

I grabbed a nearby rag and started wiping my grubby hands as I made my way to the nearest overhead door. When I'd come into work on Tuesday, large white tarps covered all the glass overheads. Dallas had stayed late Monday night, fastening them to prevent anyone from seeing in. The only downside was it also kept us from seeing out. I pulled one of the sheets to the side about an inch, just enough to view the parking lot. Claire's silver Prius sat out front, pulled directly in front of the door as always. I tossed the rag onto a nearby toolbox and headed toward the sink. As I scrubbed my hands, I tried to keep my goofy smile under control. I never did possess much of a poker face. Today was no exception.

By the time I had dried my hands and changed my shirt, Claire stood outside her car, leaning against the driver's side door. With her cell phone in hand, her thumbs were executing an all-out assault on the screen. I wondered if she was texting me, asking where the hell I was. For all her good points, Claire could be a tad impatient.

"About time," she said, as I approached. "Didn't your father ever teach you not to keep a lady waiting?"

"Sorry." I slid my hands around Claire's hips and leaned in. "Forgive me?" The kiss was a short one, and I was left wanting more. But, like I said, she could be impatient. Especially when there was somewhere she wanted to be. Still, she couldn't entirely conceal her own smile, so I knew she was just as happy to see me. It seemed like it had been weeks, not just days.

As I was letting go, the NAPA delivery truck pulled in next to Claire's Prius. Arashk climbed out of the driver's side and disappeared around the back of the truck. A moment later, he emerged with a cardboard box. I assumed it was the alternator I would be installing in the import after lunch.

"Hey, Luke," he said, tossing me a smile and gesturing with the box. "Got your alternator."

"Thanks, Arashk." I nodded toward the office. "Dallas is in there. He'll sign for it."

"Alright, man. Thanks." Arashk flashed a smile in Claire's

direction. "Have a good lunch!"

Once we were in the car, I leaned over and nuzzled my nose against Claire's bare shoulder. Her skin was soft and warm from its short time in the sun. I couldn't be more thrilled summer was finally here. That meant I'd be seeing more of Claire's skin. And seeing more of Claire's anything was a good thing.

"That's an interesting accent," she said, starting up the car.

"What? That guy?" I asked, pulling away and fastening my seatbelt. "Said he's from Romania, or something. Why, do you like it? Do I need to be worried about Arashk?"

She knew I was joking, but slapped my leg anyway. As we pulled out of the parking lot, I glanced back at the NAPA truck. Arashk hadn't mentioned the Reds tickets, and I'd been too consumed with Claire to ask.

CHAPTER 33

The officer working the front desk issued us visitor passes and told us to have a seat. She said Detective Morgenstern would be with us shortly. Twenty minutes later, we were still waiting. And I was getting antsy. This wasn't like a dentist or doctor's office. The only reading materials the station provided were two public service posters hanging on the wall. If the plan was to leave us in the lobby long enough for the posted information to sink in, the officer was wasting her time. I wouldn't be joining the police force anytime soon, nor was I involved in gang activity. The irony that one poster was offering assistance in escaping a gang, while the other was basically recruiting us for one, was not lost on either of us.

"I could take a nap," Claire said, after one of her many yawns.

I nodded and agreed I could do the same. For me at least, it wasn't so much I was tired, just bored.

About the time I stood up to stretch my legs and make sure they hadn't forgotten about us, a buzzing sound interrupted the quiet. A door beside the glass window opened, and the officer from the front desk called us back.

Claire and I were shown to a makeshift office where Morgenstern sat behind a metal desk situated in the middle of the room. He was talking on his cell phone and doodling in an open notebook as we entered. When he looked up and saw the two of us, he used the ink pen to point us in the direction of two uncomfortable chairs across the desk from him. I knew they were uncomfortable because they were the same as the ones in the lobby.

"I don't give a Goddamn if he's a city councilman or not," Morgenstern said, slamming his pen onto the desk. There was an edge to his voice I hadn't heard before; an authority I'd never seen. "I want that address! I don't care if you have to bend the son of a bitch over your knee, reach your hand up his ass and grab him by the throat to make him understand just how bad I want it!"

I looked at Claire and she looked at me. She raised her eyebrows in a show of solidarity. We were both happy not to be on the receiving end of that conversation, and I tried not to appear as impatient as I was.

I took in my surroundings, assessing the space like an amateur interior designer. The tiny area looked more like a storage room than an office. It was about as drab a room as any you would ever find. I wondered if it was a temporary workspace for Morgenstern, or if he was just that boring. Except for a scattering of manila folders and a single picture frame showing a woman and child in a beach scene, the desktop was empty, too. The walls were grey and bare. Not even a wall calendar hung precariously by a thumbtack.

"I guess you're here to see if I've found out anything."

It took a few seconds to realize Morgenstern was talking to us. I didn't know he'd ended his phone call. I hadn't heard him say goodbye.

"Uh, yeah," I said, catching up with the conversation. "It's been a few days, and we haven't heard anything. Thought I'd touch base."

With an audible huff, the detective started sorting through the stack of folders on his desk.

I looked to Claire for moral support. Maybe we'd picked a bad time to drop in on the guy. He was already pissed. The last thing I wanted was to push any more buttons. Claire's assuring nod told me to stand my ground. Besides, it was too late to reverse course. Our asses were already in the seats.

"Alright," he said, opening a folder. "Let's start from the beginning. The bones. First of all, a person's identity can't be determined from bones alone. What they can pinpoint, however, is an approximate age and gender. Now, you say you think these particular bones are your friend's. A finger?"

I nodded.

"Well, unless he had unusually small, dainty hands, I would say they're not. Forensics tells me the bones are most likely those of a young female. Roughly the same age, but definitely not the right gender."

I exchanged another look with Claire. I wasn't sure if I was happy it wasn't Garrett's finger or not, and was looking for some indication as to how I should feel. For the first time I can remember, she wasn't any help. The blank look on her face told me she was trying to sort out her own feelings.

"The ring, however, is your friend's, which gives credibility to the idea this Corwin Barnes fellow is involved. We reached out to your friend's parents. They affirmed his class ring had been missing when they identified the body. I sent them photos of the ring, and they confirmed it was his."

I took in a deep breath and let it right back out. "Okay."

At the moment, it was all I could summon, and even that was a struggle. The information so far had me at a momentary loss for words. *The ring was Garrett's; the bones were not.* It was the mention of Garrett's parents, however, that derailed all other trains of thought. I immediately wondered how they were coping. I felt bad that Morgenstern had forced them to dredge up painful memories.

"Moving on," the detective said, pulling out the folded pieces of paper I'd given him over the past week. No break in the action, no giving me time to further process the information. All business, this guy. "The notes. All the sheets of paper were the same size, the same weight and most likely pulled from the same package. Common. Nothing special about them. The block lettering on the notes is consistent across the board. It's relatively safe to say they were done by the same hand. However, since the large block letters were drawn as opposed to handwritten, that's about all we can determine from those."

"Okay," I said, raising my hand like I was back in school. "Can we back up a second? You said the ring in the box was Garrett's, but you're pretty sure the bones are not."

Claire's hand reached over and took hold of mine.

"That's correct," Morgenstern said. I was a little surprised there wasn't more attitude in his voice since I'd interrupted his flow. His temperament seemed to be mellowing some.

"And you're saying this lends *some* credibility to Barnes being involved?" Claire chimed in. As usual, she knew exactly where I was heading. "Sounds to me, that's what guys like you would call a smoking gun."

"It's possible," the detective said, leaning back in his chair. He looked at Claire for a moment, then back to me. I could see in his eyes he was processing something. I just didn't know what. More than likely, he was deciding how much he should share. "Problem is, we don't know for sure Barnes was in possession of the ring to begin with? Could have gotten misplaced at the morgue. Maybe some flunky janitor at the coroner's office lifted it. Honestly, ma'am, we're just not sure."

Morgenstern's demeanor softened even more. I would have thought this would have put me more at ease. It didn't.

"That brings me to what we do know," he continued, his voice less edgy and abrupt. "The fingerprints."

"Are they Barnes's?" Claire asked, and I was glad she had. The anticipation was killing me.

Morgenstern shook his head.

"No," he said, then paused to gauge my reaction. When I didn't offer one, he continued. "But, they are all the same. And they're on everything. The notes, the boxes, even the Spanish Tickler. Whoever those prints belonged to couldn't have cared less if we lifted them."

I kept my focus forward. I could see Claire giving me a look out of the corner of my eye, but I ignored it. I never told her about the instrument of torture I found on my truck seat, and I'd be catching hell for it when we were done here.

"And you're sure they're not Barnes'?" I reiterated.

"Not according to the state. Those fingerprints don't match the ones we have in the system for Barnes."

"So who's are they?" Claire asked.

Morgenstern looked at us both for a few seconds. When he finally answered, the payoff wasn't worth the wait.

"That's the million dollar question," he said. "We don't know."

CHAPTER 34

"Well, that was a waste of time," Claire said, giving voice to my initial thoughts. Only it wasn't a complete waste. We did find out the bones didn't belong to Garrett, and at some point while sitting in Morgenstern's office, I'd determined that was a positive development. The ring was one thing. Imagining that Barnes had not only cut off Garrett's finger, but had kept it as a souvenir all this time was like grinding salt into an old, festering wound. I could finally let go of that notion.

Compared to the dismal lighting in Morgenstern's dungeon-like office, the harsh sun was an intolerable shock. Exiting the station, I had to use my hand to shield my eyes. Taking Claire's hand with my other, we walked down the concrete steps and turned up the sidewalk that lead to the parking lot and her awaiting Prius.

Other than the news about the bones, I was disappointed in the lack of information the police had uncovered so far. They were working the case, but how hard, I wondered? My mind flashed to the stack of manila envelopes on the detective's desk, my case just one among many. Either way, the information didn't seem to be coming very quickly. I felt like a baby bird whose mother only feeds it small bites at a time. I was hungry for much more. Not to mention the fact I was growing irritated with the lethargy of the entire process. Did the police not understand my life, and those of the people around me, was in danger?

You hear about it all the time in the news. A frightened woman complains to the police about an abusive ex-boyfriend who won't leave her alone. Only the police tell her they can't do anything until an actual crime is committed. Usually by then, though, it's too late. In my case, other than a couple of veiled threats that hadn't yet materialized, what reason did the police really have to move with more urgency? What reason did they have to take any of it seriously?

As we reached the car, my cell phone rang. I pulled it out and answered while waiting for Claire to unlock the doors. It was as if the universe had heard my questions. Because, just that quick, the voice on the other end offered a reason.

The patrol car sat in front of Tipsword's Automotive. Its lights were off, but the motor was running. On the way there, I'd filled Claire in on what I knew. It wasn't much. We would find the rest of it out together.

"Do you have any idea what they might have been looking for?" the officer was asking as we entered the office. Hearing the bells above the door, the officer turned and gave us the once over. She didn't, however, turn far enough towards us for me to catch her name. Nor did she give me much time. She must have decided we weren't a threat, because she dismissed us just as quickly.

"Damned if I know," Dallas said. "But they made one hell of a mess, as you can see."

The officer stopped writing in her spiral notepad long enough to take a look around. I knew what she was thinking, and she was right. The office was always a mess. Wrinkled magazines, some more than a year old, lay on every flat surface in the room. More than one greasy rag had found its way in between the mismatched chairs sitting in front of the large, plate-glass window. Plastic cups from the water fountain, and Styrofoam cups from the coffee maker, spilled out of the small, overflowing trashcan. Basically, it was everything you would expect an automotive repair shop's office to look like. Especially one run by a recently divorced sixty-something.

Adding to the usual mess were the contents of Dallas's desk. Dingy manila folders with black fingerprint smudges spewed sheets of yellowed paper-like vomit. A handful of old metal keys, whose purpose had long been forgotten, lay scattered across the grimy linoleum floor. In the middle of it all, sat one of the wooden desk drawers lying upside down, cast aside in haste.

The scene brought on a sense of wariness. I reached over and slid my hand around Claire's hip.

"And where were you at the time, Mr. Tipsword?" The officer's voice remained rigid, more deadpan than stern.

"Out there," Dallas said, gesturing toward the garage. "Under a truck."

"And you were the only one here?"

"Yes. My employee here was out to lunch."

Something about that statement piqued the officer's interest. She turned my way, but still not enough for me to read her nameplate. She gave me another once over, this time with eyebrows raised.

"And where were you?" she asked.

"Ironically enough, my girlfriend and I were just at the station over on Washington. Talking to Detective

Morgenstern."

"Hmm, now that's interesting," said the officer, who then turned her eyes on Claire. "I assume you can corroborate that?"

"Absolutely."

After looking us up and down a second time, Claire more than me, we were once again dismissed as the officer returned her attention to Dallas.

I looked to Claire, confused. She shrugged. She didn't know what was so interesting about us being at the police station, either.

"And what, if anything was taken, Mr. Tipsword?" the officer continued. "Money? Receipts? Other important documents?"

"That's just it," Dallas said, plopping down in the worn leather chair behind the desk. "Ain't nothin' in there worth taking. I don't keep cash or even a checkbook on the premises. Most of the papers in these drawers are old and probably shoulda been pitched years ago. Any information on 'em is outdated. I seriously doubt whoever did this found what they were looking for. Whatever it was."

The officer busied herself jotting more notes in her notepad, while the three of us fell silent and exchanged anxious looks. Things stayed that way for several minutes while the officer worked the pen. I don't know whether we were afraid to speak in front of her, or if all our minds were just racing, and probably in the same direction. *Barnes.* I looked around at the disarray, wondering if we should start picking up. The way Dallas sat in the chair with his hands folded in his lap, he didn't seem to be in a hurry, so I let the thought pass.

"Alright," the officer said, his flighty tone letting us know she was wrapping things up, "let me see if I've got everything straight. You've had no problems with neighboring business owners or unsatisfied customers, and you haven't seen anyone suspicious milling around lately. Point of entry is hard to determine since both the front and back doors were unlocked. Which, also rules out forced entry. And nothing, as far as you can tell, Mr. Tipsword, was taken."

Dallas nodded. "The tall and short of it."

"Okay, then. Looks like I'm done here." The officer closed her notepad and pulled a business card from her chest pocket. "You can come down to the station if you want a copy of the report for insurance purposes. Though I'm not sure you have much of a claim if nothing was stolen and no property damaged. You discover something's missing, come on down or give me a call. We can update the report."

The officer looked around the office again, letting her words hang in the air, giving Dallas a chance to claim at least some of this disaster area as the result of the break in. When he didn't bite, she shrugged and told him to have a nice day. She offered a nod to Claire and me before excusing herself and exiting to her patrol car out front.

"Okay," I said when the bell had chimed, marking the closing of the glass door, "are you going to say it or should I? We're all thinking the same thing." Maybe I was on to something; maybe I was being paranoid. But anything out of the ordinary lately I attributed to Corwin Barnes. If the phone rang at the house or here at work, and nobody spoke when I answered, it was Barnes. If my father couldn't find the newspaper on the front porch in the morning, Barnes had obviously taken it and was perusing the classifieds for whatever the hell psychos perused the classifieds for. Like I said, anything out of the ordinary.

And this had Barnes written all over it.

"You really think so?" Dallas asked, looking passed me and out the window to where the officer still sat in her cruiser.

"Who else?"

"What would he be looking for?" Claire asked.

"I don't know," I said. "An address?"

"Whose? He already knows where you live," Dallas said. "Remember the box he left on your door step?"

"Like I could forget?"

Dallas stroked his beard and stared out the front window. He was either lost in thought, or he had a thing for the officer whose name I never caught.

"I don't know," he said. "Might've been him, but that sure as hell doesn't sit well. Knowing he was right here in the office while I was out there under a Dodge? Fuck. Imagine if he'd been looking for payback instead of information."

The three of us grew quiet again. I don't know about Dallas and Claire, but several scenarios of what might have happened played through my mind. None of them ended well.

"Maybe we should start locking the doors when either of us is here alone," I suggested.

Dallas turned away from the window as the patrol car pulled out of the parking lot. "Maybe I should start bringing Prudence to work with me."

I don't know if he meant it as a joke, but none of us laughed.

CHAPTER 35

What happened at the shop that afternoon was unsettling, kind of like eating most of a burrito before finding a band aid in it. And I wasn't even sure what the worst part was. The fact Barnes had the balls to search through Dallas's office in broad daylight, or the fact Dallas had been right there and so vulnerably unaware of it. The only thing I was completely sure of was I was getting sick and tired of dealing with cops. Nothing was coming from it, and yet we kept calling them. 'Report takers' is what they should be called.

I didn't stress over the break-in for long before something else came along to occupy my thoughts. Claire announced she had plans for us that evening. I immediately declined whatever she had in mind. I wasn't sure she was getting the whole, "being stalked by a psychotic killer" thing I had going on at the moment. But she countered. It would be good for me, she said. A nice distraction, she said. All of this without even telling me what the plans were. I was instantly wary.

Turns out, I had every reason to be.

The guy's name was Raun, pronounced 'Ron', last name Stiletto. I was pretty sure the last name was a fake. The jury was still out on the first. He was the singer in a Goth metal band and the boyfriend of one of Claire's college roommates. Raun's band, Shadows of Misery, was playing that night in a small, unnamed club somewhere downtown. Claire's friend, Mackenzie would be riding with us, and Raun had all but guaranteed he could get us in. 'Lucky for us,' is how Claire put it, the eternal spin-doctor. Admittedly, I viewed it differently. His guarantee only meant I couldn't use our underage status as a way out. Neither was my argument that three didn't ride comfortably in a pickup truck. Claire had thought of a way around that as well.

A little after nine o'clock, the silver Prius pulled into the driveway. Personally, I was finding the more I rode in Claire's car, the less of a fan I was. It was hard going from the height and size of Garrett's pickup down to the Prius. Not to mention the truck was a hell of a lot more manly than riding shotgun in my girlfriend's shiny sub-compact. Claire insisted there was nothing emasculating about it, but I had my doubts. Not to mention the fact I wouldn't even be riding shotgun this time around. I'd be sitting in the back. Which promised an even greater constriction of blood flow to my legs than usual.

I let the ladies get out of the car, before heading down the sidewalk to greet them. Both were dressed for a night on the town. Claire wore dark skinny jeans tucked into her distressed brown leather engineer boots. Her rust-colored blouse hung loose, its plunging neckline showing off more cleavage than I was used to. She looked amazing, and I didn't even bother trying to conceal my smile. I figured I needed to save my energy. I had a long night of fighting off better looking guys ahead of me.

Mackenzie wasn't at all what I expected of a friend of Claire's. From first impressions, she looked to be taking the whole Goth scene to heart; much different from Claire, whose musical tastes leaned more toward Top 40 or country. But that's the thing about college roommates: you meet up with individuals you wouldn't ordinarily meet up with.

Mackenzie's long, wavy hair was the unnatural color of black ink, befitting a woman dating a guy in a Goth band. Her studded leather top, short leather skirt, and heeled boots that rose to her knees spoke the same Goth language. Apparently, black was on the menu for the evening, and not just in her clothing. Her eyes looked sallow and sunken thanks to the heavy makeup. And accentuating her not so modest cleavage was the biggest silver cross I'd ever seen. The points were pointy, the edges edgy, and I immediately shuttered at the damage it might cause to her ample bosom if she wasn't careful.

"Hey, baby," Claire sang, throwing her arms around my neck.

I said hey back and pulled her in. We embraced long and hard, like we hadn't just seen each other earlier in the day. As I held her, I could see the unmarked sedan over her shoulder, parked a little ways down the street. Officer Stine's eyes were on us. I assumed Claire's car pulling into our driveway had piqued his attention. It was comforting having him around, though it was a constant reminder of Corwin Barnes and his threats. Heaven forbid I do anything without that son of a bitch hovering in the back of my mind.

"This is Mackenzie," Claire said, breaking free.

Mackenzie and I exchanged pleasantries, which included her drawing me in for a hug. I could feel the silver cross poking into my chest, and I cringed at what it might be doing to hers.

"You ready for this?" Mackenzie asked as we broke our little huddle.

"I think so," I said with a smile. "Not sure if Claire told you or not, but this'll be my first Goth experience."

"Well, I hope you have your fun pants on," she said, a sly smile carving shallow dimples in her cheeks. "After tonight, your life'll never be the same."

As if it hadn't been inconvenient enough spending thirty minutes cooped up in the Prius's sad excuse for a back seat, when Mackenzie texted her boyfriend to let him know we'd arrived, he greeted her with both good news and bad. The good news was he had kept his promise. Raun had talked to the manager of the club, and the guy was going to let us in as guests of the band. No cover charge, no I.D. check.

The bad news was we were going to have to enter through the back door to avoid some of Dayton's finest providing security at the front. I hadn't been to a lot of clubs in my life, but I had to think enlisting the services of actual police officers to work security instead of bouncers was enough to raise a red flag on this place. But then, what did I know?

The alley was your usual narrow corridor running behind the deteriorating brick buildings. If anything, it was probably narrower than most. It was barely wide enough for a garbage truck to pull through. And when it did, the driver had better know what he or she was doing. A couple of the buildings had floodlights mounted above their rear entry doors. They illuminated the back steps, but not much else. I counted three street lamps running the length of the alley, spaced much too far apart. Where there was light, shadows spilled out from crippled grocery carts, old tires, and battered dumpsters overflowing with cardboard liquor boxes. In the gaps between the light, the night was as dark as you'd ever want to see.

The scattering of industrial-sized black trash bags sitting around only upped the creepiness factor. I didn't have a guess as to what might be in them, but they would have looked ominous even in the daylight. Mostly because they were the perfect size for transporting dismembered bodies. I tried to convince myself a community cleanup had taken place, and with all the dumpsters full, the bags were just waiting to be hauled away.

The explanation was thin, I know, but I clung to it like a life preserver in a storm.

The overwhelming stench of urine and stale beer, along with the low, rhythmic thumping of a bass coming from somewhere inside the buildings, rounded out the alley's unwelcoming atmosphere. The only things missing were a mumbling homeless guy huddled inside a makeshift lean-to, or a too-thin prostitute giving some low-life dealer a hummer in exchange for her evening fix. As much as I'd been dreading spending my evening at the Goth club, I found myself suddenly eager as hell to get inside.

"Well," Claire whispered, as we started down the dark passage in a tight bunch, "this isn't creepy at all."

"Nothing to be afraid of here," Mackenzie said, matching Claire's level of sarcasm.

Other than that brief exchange, we remained silent. I don't think any of us wanted to draw attention to our presence. There was no telling what, or who might be lurking in the darkness.

After what seemed like an hour-long hike, but had probably taken only a few minutes, we came upon the dirty red door we'd been instructed to look for. The door was dented with its paint scuffed and chipped in places. Rusty hinges showed no more signs of the shiny metal they once were. It looked very much the way you would expect an underground club's back door to look.

I took a moment to glance around, searching for anything that might go bump in the night, before climbing the two crumbling concrete steps. The low muffle of music eked its way through the steel slab. I raised my hand and pounded on the door with my fist. I looked back at Claire and Mackenzie while I waited. They both looked up at me with arms wrapped around themselves, despite the fact it was a warm evening.

A sudden crash of empty bottles clattered from the shadow of a dumpster further down the alley. With an offsetting click-clack sound, a brown beer bottle slowly rolled out into the light cast by the middle of the three streetlamps.

Claire and Mackenzie both took an instinctive step in my direction just as the thumping bass exploded from the doorway.

The dingy red door opened up and invited us in.

CHAPTER 36

A female server, wearing nearly the same outfit as Mackenzie's, only with a little more fishnet covering her arms, escorted us into a small room where the members of Shadows of Misery were hanging out. Raun rose from his metal folding chair and greeted Mackenzie with a hug. A hug that turned into an uncomfortably long make-out session. Uncomfortable for me, but obviously not them. It did, however, give me a moment to inventory their attire. It was nearly identical. Only Raun, had replaced the skirt with black skinny jeans that looked like they would have fit a twelve-year-old if not for the rips across the thighs.

And none of the many chains around Raun's neck supported a large cross.

Half an hour later, after we'd had a beer with the band and listened to Raun pontificate on how commercial acts like Marilyn Manson gave the culture a bad name, the ladies and I found ourselves an arms-length away from the stage, swept up in what could only be described as a sea of teenage angst all grown up. As a guy from a small Midwestern town, it wasn't my crowd. With the loud synth music and blinding strobe lights of the pre-show, the queasiness in my stomach that started while out in the alley continued to worsen. Then, when I thought my uneasiness had reached its pinnacle, I was proven wrong.

"I'm gonna use the little girls room before the show starts."

Mackenzie had screamed the words from the other side of Claire. I barely heard them, and was hoping I'd heard wrong. Considering Mackenzie was already on her third beer, it wasn't surprising. Claire had heard her friend just fine, though, and nodded to her before turning to me.

"We'll be right back," Claire shouted into my ear. And suddenly, I was alone in a mass of black leather, fishnet and chains; a true stranger in a strange land in my jeans and faded blue t-shirt.

The ladies had only been gone a few minutes when the frenetic bass thumping from the house sound system came to an abrupt halt. As the echo from the music faded, the black, windowless walls seemed to absorb the strobing lights. The already darkened room plunged itself into near pitch. The only means of light came from a red exit sign mounted above a door in the back, and a couple of small flashlights snaking around onstage.

The flashlights soon picked up on a slowly erupting, hazy white fog seconds before the crowd did. When everything was apparently set, and the flashlights scurried off the stage, the crowd erupted into cheers and whistles. The energy level in the otherwise silent and darkened room went through the proverbial roof. Bodies all around me jumped up and down. The escalating frenzy took my anxiety along with it.

My personal space shrank to hardly enough to scratch myself.

Claustrophobia set in.

My chest constricted.

It was a mistake. I shouldn't have been there. A situation like that was the last place I should have put myself. Unfortunately, it was too late to do anything about it. I'd have to wait until Claire and Mackenzie returned. I couldn't very well leave without them.

Or, at least without Claire.

Purple and green lights converged on the stage. Eerie keyboards started creeping from the overhead speakers. Drawing the attention of everyone in the room, including my own, the mesmerizing lights began a seductive dance with the growing fog. Slowly, the two intertwined. They took on a life all its own, silhouetting the five men taking the stage.

One by one, the fans took notice. Somehow, the cheers climbed to new heights. Not wanting to be overshadowed, the music grew with the cheers. The keyboards embraced the crowd. The notes pulled it tighter, closer to the stage. Within seconds, there were no individuals left, only one solid being.

And I wanted no part of it.

I turned and took a few steps, testing the crowd's willingness to give up one of its one. The sea of revelers parted, then blended seamlessly back together to fill my void. The crowd was too enthralled with what was happening onstage to care. For them, my exit meant they could inch another step closer. I kept retreating, excusing myself left and right, working through the melee. I found myself on the outskirts of the throbbing horde.

Free to breathe, I watched the stage come alive from the back of the room.

Despite the fact I neither fit in with the crowd, nor would ever consider frequenting this kind of place on my own, I did find one thing to my liking: the music. When the drums and guitar started slithering their way into the fold, my head started bobbing up and down. When all the instruments landed on a groove that sounded like a chugging freight train, I let go of all my troubles and immersed myself in the shredding. It wasn't until Raun approached the front of the stage, and a narrow shaft of light spotlighted him, that I stopped banging.

I lost focus on the music altogether.

Bones.

Long and thin. sleek and white. An entire string of bones made up the roughly five-foot tall microphone stand that Raun grabbed and began swinging within the tight space. Whether they were bones from an arm or a leg, I didn't know. Hell, I didn't even know if they were animal or—*God forbid*—human.

The sight of them sent a shiver up my spine. The queasiness in my stomach returned tenfold. The tuna casserole I'd thrown down for dinner threatened to make a reappearance. Maybe to Raun and his fans, a mic stand made entirely of bones was just a cool piece of craftsmanship, one small decorative piece that added to the overall theme they were trying to convey.

But, for me, it was something else altogether.

I was suddenly wound so tight, when someone tugged on my shirt, I spun around and cocked my arm. In doing so, I nearly clocked Claire in the face with my elbow. She wore a strange expression. Even in the disorienting strobe of darkness and colored lights, I could see her look of concern. Were her and Mackenzie just as disturbed by Raun's mic stand as I was?

When Claire spoke, her words made me wish it was something that simple, and took my mind off the bones entirely.

"Mackenzie's gone."

CHAPTER 37

Cutting our way through the throng of bouncing people, logic told me, most likely, Claire's roommate had probably just wandered off. Maybe she'd run into someone she knew. Maybe she'd made their way backstage again. Maybe the three beers she'd had in less than an hour had simply caused her to forget about Claire and me. I'd just met the woman. I had no idea how well she held her alcohol. That much beer in such little time would affect some men who weighed considerably more. Either way, I was sure there was a reasonable explanation.

Still, I couldn't silence the nagging voice in the back of my mind that whispered a name: Corwin Barnes.

It seemed like a ridiculous notion, like the voice was making a mountain-sized assumption out of a molehill. But it also couldn't be discounted. Especially since, if there was one thing I'd learned over the last couple weeks, it was Barnes could be following me at any given time. He had proven this fact more than once. It didn't help Mackenzie fit the profile of the missing New Paris girls of a year ago. The ones Barnes kidnapped and brutally slaughtered. The ones like Becca.

Holding Claire's hand, I lead the search with renewed enthusiasm.

"Where'd you see her last?" I shouted over the music. I

scanned the crowd, searching the sea of nameless faces for one in particular. Maybe two. I reminded myself to not lose sight of things and keep an eye out for Mackenzie as well.

"Right around here," Claire said, herself looking out over the crowd.

We could have covered more ground if we'd separated, but I wasn't about to let Claire out of my sight again. I was already wracked with anxiety. My level of alertness had red-lined in the last few minutes, and not just for Mackenzie's well-being. If Barnes was coming after Claire, he'd have to kill me to get to her.

The crowd erupted as Shadows of Misery wrapped up a song. I couldn't decide which was more deafening, the music or their fans' reaction to it. I just knew my ears would ring for the foreseeable future.

"Did you try texting her?" I asked, as the band launched into another song.

Claire was up on her toes looking around, I wasn't sure she heard me. I was about to ask again when I took a hard shove from behind. The force nearly knocked me off my feet. I had to take a step forward to maintain my balance, and once I had, I spun around with both fear and anger at the helm.

"What the—"

"Hey, man," the guy interrupted. "Sorry. Girlfriend's passed out. What are ya gonna do, right?" Then he laughed it off. Which seemed odd, but at least he wasn't lying. Not only was his date draped over him like a lifeless corpse, but she had the makeup to match.

Standing there with my heart racing and my fists balled, I felt Claire's hand go to my chest. It was her signature move, the one she resorted to when wanting to calm me without using words. My guard was certainly up. My clenched jaw ached. Ultimately, it was the warmth of Claire's touch that helped me dial it back just a little. I took a deep breath and watched the guy dressed head to toe in black practically drag his girlfriend through the crowd toward the stage. It was the exact opposite direction he should have been heading, and I could only shake my head.

"Baby, let it go," Claire whispered, her lips brushing my ear. "He's drunk."

With more resignation than anything, I turned to her. I still didn't like the look on her face. Her eyes held a wariness in them; her brow was creased in a place I wasn't used to seeing. The last time I'd seen concern of that magnitude from Claire was when my parents checked me into the nuthouse. That was a year ago.

"She probably just hooked up with another friend," Claire said, her eyes still scanning the crowd, but with less eagerness and more reconciliation. Then she turned back to me and leaned in close. "The other girlfriends. They're always hanging out."

"Maybe. But, aren't you worried? I mean, in a place like this…"

"The look in your eyes has me more worried than anything," she said, hand once again on my chest. "I know what you're thinking, but I don't think it has anything to do with him, Luke."

I looked at her warily.

"This isn't about Barnes," she continued. "It's about my drunk roommate who's not being very considerate at the moment. And right now, the way this is all affecting you is worrying me more than not being able to find Mackenzie."

"How do you know he's not involved?" I asked, my attention drawn to the faces of two young ladies walking by. Neither of them was Mackenzie, and they sure as hell weren't Barnes.

It didn't matter. The discussion was over. Claire didn't have to say another word. Her face did the pleading for her, and for the first time since she told me she'd lost Mackenzie, I saw how much I was overreacting. Maybe it was the music and the chaotic flashing lights. Maybe the shop break-in was the final straw. Maybe I was just losing it, letting this whole Barnes situation get the best of me. I felt like a nuclear reactor on the verge of meltdown. Between my heart racing and my adrenalin pumping, I was surprised I hadn't turned around and punched that guy in the face, no questions asked. The fact it would have been a hell of a release didn't even matter. Fighting wasn't in my nature.

"So, what about Mackenzie?" I asked with as much calm as possible. I didn't want to worry Claire any more than I already had. It wasn't one of my favorite things to do.

Claire shrugged. "She was planning on going home with Raun anyway," she said. "I'll touch base with her later. I'm sure she's fine."

"Okay," I said, but only after thinking on it for another minute. I had to defer to Claire on this one, my own brain being unreliable at the moment. Mackenzie's disappearance probably had nothing to do with Barnes. Still, I hated taking the chance. If Claire wanted to leave, though, I wasn't going to object. But, we sure as hell weren't going out the same way we came in.

I took her hand and started cutting through the crowd in the direction of the front door, MC Ren's voice in my head.

Fuck tha Police.

Fifteen minutes later, we were parked at a bus stop parking lot beside the river making love in the back seat of the Prius, which was a feat in and of itself, considering the tight quarters. Like a craving that consumes you and becomes all you can think about, it was just something we both needed, right then and there.

CHAPTER 38

I must have gotten the first text when Claire and I were in my driveway, leaning against her car. I was basking in the afterglow and probably too engaged to notice. With her safely in my arms, head on my chest, I was dreading letting her go. At one point, my nose was nuzzled so deeply in her soft hair, I could have survived off the scent of her alone. But it was getting late, and she still had almost an hour-long drive back to her parent's house in New Paris.

I hated she had to make the drive by herself. I'd been thinking about getting an apartment and asking Claire to move in with me, but I hadn't yet broached the subject. Partly because she was still in school, which meant she lived three hours away eight months out of the year. The other part of it was I wasn't sure I could afford an apartment on my own while she was on campus. In the meantime, we'd worked out a system. She always either texted or called when she got home so I knew she was safe.

Already anticipating talking to her later, I said goodbye and watched her pull onto the road.

Later that evening, I was lying on my bed, looking through one of Dallas's car catalogs at overpriced rims, when my cell phone vibrated on the nightstand. Relieved Claire had made it home safely, I snatched up the phone. And paused. Not only did I not recognize the number, but I already had a text waiting on me from whoever it belonged to. Both messages were short and simple.

'hey man.'

A tiny alarm went off in my head, but it wasn't very loud. At least not yet. Ordinarily, receiving a text from an unknown number isn't cause for concern. But, my life was far from ordinary, and the night's earlier tension peaked out from the shadows.

With just a hint of apprehension, I responded with my own text asking who it was. A moment later, I got my answer. The tension already building in my shoulders backed off just as quickly.

"hey, Arashk." I spoke the words as I typed them, a habit of mine. "how's it going?"

Like with my previous question, his answer was immediate.

'got the tickets. can we meet?'

Sitting up in bed, I considered the question. The stress from the situation at the club, not to mention the lovemaking, had physically drained me of energy. Mentally, however, I was still alert and wouldn't be able to sleep anytime soon. Besides, I was still waiting to hear from Claire, and I'd already told my father about the tickets.

'where. when,' I typed.

'I'm actually at an elementary school. think it's by your house?'

I looked up at my window, but I sat too low to see the school beyond the backyard. There probably thirty elementary schools in a city this size, how did Arashk know he was at the one by me? More importantly, how did he know where I lived? Had I mentioned it at some point? I didn't know. Maybe.

'if your nearby, how about dropping off?'

It took a minute or two for the answer to hit my phone. His last response wasn't coming as quickly as his previous texts.

'supposed to meet a buddy here. can you just head this way?'

I exhaled until my lungs were spent.

The entire conversation felt a little strange, and it revived that same prickly apprehension I'd been feeling a lot lately. It was getting more difficult to sort things out in my head, and I'd been doing more than my share of jumping to paranoid conclusions. Despite my reservations, I vowed not to read too much into things this time. Being continually paranoid of everything and everyone was no way to live, I told myself.

'be there in 5'

CHAPTER 39

None of the houses in my neighborhood had fences around their back yards. It was some sort of homeowner's association bylaw or something. A couple of properties had a line of shrubs along the edge or in the corners to help separate theirs from their neighbors, but most of the backyards simply blended into one another. Generally, the only way to tell where one property ended and the other started was by the different patterns in the way the homeowners mowed.

As for my father, he liked it that way. He said fences only chopped up the landscape, and people shouldn't be so quick to separate themselves from one another, anyway. For me, I didn't really have an opinion. Other than the fact it made it a hell of a lot easier to get from my house to the school, even in the dark.

By the faint light of a quarter moon, I made my way around the Richter's clump of boxwoods and down the embankment of the narrow creek that served as the boundary separating the school grounds from the housing development. Luckily, we hadn't had rain since the weekend, so the water flowing wasn't more than a few inches deep. Even with my lack of athletic prowess, due in part to my permanently messed up ankle, I was able to jump across the little water there and scale the embankment on the other side without much problem.

I cut through the baseball diamond's outfield, then a patch of blacktop where a pair of tetherball poles slept. Hopscotch squares appeared here and there. I probably would have given one a try for old time's sake if I hadn't thought I was being watched. A hundred feet later, the blacktop gave way to a mulched playground. A floodlight on the corner of the school building illuminated most of that area, but not all of it. The swings where I saw The Napa Guy sitting hovered just outside the light. That's what we called Arashk at the shop: The Napa Guy.

"What's up, man?" Arashk said, as I approached, the shadows doing his awkward smile zero favors.

"Not much." I took his extended hand and shook it. He seemed to hold on a little longer than normal. I reminded myself he was from another country. Maybe that was their custom. Who knows? I couldn't remember ever shaking his hand before. Regardless, paranoia was going to be the end of me if I wasn't careful. "Just hangin' out."

"Yeah," he said, gesturing at the playground with open arms, "me, too." He laughed a little, then looked around. Despite the late hour, he still wore his uniform, and I wondered if he was one of those guys who wore it everywhere, proud of his position in life.

"You live around here, too?"

"Nah," he said. "Just in the area. Meeting someone in a few."

I made like I was checking the time on my cell. I wasn't, really. I couldn't care less what time it was. I just wanted to move this transaction along.

"Been a long day," I said.

An awkward silence followed, and I spent it watching Arashk. His darting eyes searched the school grounds nonstop. Every few seconds, he wiped the palms of his hands on his dark grey pants. His foot never stopped tapping. He came across like an addict approaching withdrawal.

It had only been a minute, and the guy was already making me nervous. *Give me the damn tickets already.* I started thinking maybe I didn't know Arashk well enough to be meeting up with him on a darkened playground in the middle of the night.

"So, who are ya meeting out here this late?" I asked and started looking around myself.

"Just a girl," he said, and that was all. He wouldn't even make eye contact with me, and that made me the most uncomfortable. In fact, thanks to the vast amount of hours I'd spent watching cop movies, my internal alarm was going nuts. First, he'd mentioned meeting a buddy, and now he said he was meeting a girl? Something was seriously wrong with this picture. This had been a bad idea. Maybe my worst.

Fuck the tickets.

I decided to cut my visit short.

"Hey, man, I forgot," I said, looking back toward my house, "I was supposed to—"

I didn't hear him stand up. There was no rattling of chains, no crunching of the mulch when his boots hit the ground. Before I even knew what was coming, Arashk was on me.

His arm snaked around my neck. Pain surged down my spine as he bent me backward. His breath was hot against the side of my head, making it easy to hear his grunts as he squeezed my throat harder.

I tried to take a breath, but failed. The air wouldn't come. I swung wildly with my elbow, trying to connect with anything soft and sensitive. All it found was empty space. I fought for air. I fought the haze creeping into my vision. I fought to connect the dots. *Why the hell was he doing this?*

Arashk didn't make me wait long to find out.

"Sorry, man," he hissed in my ear. "But Corwin's got something really special planned for you!"

CHAPTER 40

His balls would never be the same. After coming up empty time after time, I'd finally gotten lucky. My wildly swinging elbow met up with something soft and sensitive. He shouldn't have tried getting me down on the ground. All that did was bring critical targets into play. It was an opening Arashk would regret giving me for some time.

Arashk released his grip around my neck and fell to the ground. A sudden rush of air flowed into my lungs. Like a fat kid reaching into a trick-or-treat bowl, I took all I could. I ignored the pain it caused and sucked in as much air as my swollen throat would let pass.

With my hands on my knees, I started to regain my senses. Arashk and Barnes were connected. That fact alone shook me to the core and set the wheels turning. How they were connected, I had no idea. It did, however, explain the sudden attack. I had a feeling it explained a lot more, but I didn't have time to think about it now. One thing instantly clear, though, was the true extent of the danger I was in. Not just as a whole, but right that very second.

I'm waiting on a buddy.

I left Arashk writhing on the bed of mulch. Lying in the moonlight beside him was a long and frighteningly large syringe. The tube was full of something yellow and heart-wrenching.

I ran as fast as my bad ankle allowed. There wasn't any lingering pain in it at this point, but there was no grace in my stride, either. Or speed, for that matter. Hopefully, the shot I'd given Arashk's nutsack would afford me a decent head start.

It wasn't until I'd cleared the baseball diamond's dirt infield that I risked a quick glance behind me.

Arashk was on his feet, heading in my direction. His strides didn't look any better than mine, but I imagined it was hard to run, doubled over and nursing a groin the way he was.

The edge of the creek came quickly, and I almost didn't see it in the dark. I tumbled down the six-foot embankment more than I scaled it. When I hit the bottom, I found myself on my knees in the cold water. I didn't stay there long. I quickly scrambled my way up the other side of the embankment. Only when I had made it to the top did I risk a second look behind me. What I saw made my heart skip at least a beat, if not two.

Arashk was quickly approaching. He was only a few steps from the embankment that lead down into the creek. He was closing the gap fasted than I'd hoped. Without further delay, I turned and headed in the direction of the Richter's shrubs, and beyond that, the beckoning safety of my house.

"You're gonna die, motherfucker!"

The shout reached out to me. And while his threat wasn't exactly original, the desperation in Arashk's voice was hard to ignore. In fact, it ratcheted my fear up a level. I didn't know if the guy had a weapon, other than the syringe he'd dropped. I hadn't seen anything more lethal, like a gun or a knife. But, if Arashk was working with Barnes, I could only imagine what might be up his sleeve. The Spanish Tickler flashed before my eyes. Its prongs, long and sharp. Had he been the one to put it in the truck? Adding that possibility to the fury in his voice just now, and I shuddered at what might happen if I didn't reach the house before he reached me.

I was taught in Geometry that the shortest distance between two points was a straight line. With my lungs on fire, I took that education to heart. I busted my way through the neighbor's shrubs, trampling their purple pansies and stomping down their hostas. I'd apologize later. If I was still around after this was all said and done.

A beacon of light called to me from above my back door. Literally. The porch light encouraged me to focus all my attention on it, to keep running and not look back. While putting one foot in front of the other, I wrung every ounce of motivation from it I could. Only a few seconds more.

Had I left the back door unlocked? I couldn't remember, and couldn't imagine the outcome if I hadn't. I didn't have time to make it to the front of the house now, much less if I were forced to backtrack. Arashk was *that close*. If I reached for the door handle and it didn't turn? Over the last week and a half, I'd accepted the fact that, one way or another, I'd have to face Corwin Barnes. I had to answer for what I'd done to him a year ago. What I'd taken. But I never expected it to go down like this, caught off guard, ambushed by a lackey on a school playground.

My waterlogged shoe slid out from under me with my first step onto the brick patio. I regained my balance with the help of a plastic Adirondack chair. The slip still cost me. One, maybe two seconds. Hearing Arashk's labored grunts behind me, it was a second or two I couldn't spare.

CHAPTER 41

The door was unlocked.

Thank God!

I stumbled through the doorway, spun and slammed the door behind me. Arashk leapt onto the patio. I was amazed at how quickly he'd closed the gap. If he'd had another twenty, thirty yards...

Arashk bulldozed into the wooden door.

My eyes flared. I sucked in a gasp of air. Both the lockset and hinges groaned with protest, and for a brief moment, I thought they'd give me up. Ultimately, they held firm. This time, I thanked God for quality craftsmanship.

I had just thrown the deadbolt when the handle on the door started jiggling. I looked up at the shoebox-sized pane of glass. Would he try to smash it? He'd never reach the lock with the window positioned so high. He couldn't fit through. Strange as it seemed, a thin pane of glass separating us meant everything.

Our eyes met. His blazed with a fury I hadn't seen since that night almost a year ago. These were a different set of eyes, but the rage was the same. Arashk leaned in, trapping his damp hair between his forehead and the pane of glass. He stared at me like a caged animal, its prey just out of reach. Steam formed in a large, oblong circle where his short, hot breaths hit the glass. This wasn't the Arashk I knew. But then, it wasn't like I knew him well. Obviously.

I stood there with my chest about to explode, a throbbing in my temples, uncertain what to do next. I half expected him to break into evil laughter like he knew something I didn't. But he never did. At least I don't think he did.

"What the hell's goin' on?"

The voice came from across the room, groggy and disoriented, yet still familiar. It interrupted the quiet and made me jump. That's when I had a frightening realization. I no longer stood at the door. I sat on the floor with my back against it. My knees were drawn up against my chest with my arms embracing them. I shook my head to regain clarity, a stomach-churning clarity.

It happened again.

I cursed myself with genuine venom.

I scrambled to my feet. My father stood in the hallway in his blue and green plaid boxers, cleaning his glasses with the front of his white undershirt. Rousing him from bed was becoming a habit, but there wasn't time to feel bad.

I turned to the window. Arashk was gone. The only evidence he'd been there at all was the fading circle of steam on the glass. A small part of me felt relief. At least I hadn't been out long this time. Leaning my own forehead against the glass, I looked out into the moonlit night. Arashk's dark form was just turning the corner to the side of the house.

Shit!

"Is the front door locked?" I was still breathing so hard, I barely got the words out.

"Every night. Last thing I check before bed," my father said. "Luke, what's going on?"

My father's voice was calmer now, more concerned. It trailed after me as I hobbled down the hallway, making my way through the front room and into the entryway. I reached for the door handle and finally breathed when I found it locked. I looked around. My father kept a small collection of vintage walking sticks in an umbrella stand beside the front door. I chose a thicker, black one with a silver tip. It wasn't much, but it was the closest thing to a weapon within reach.

The front door was steel and lacked a window, so I watched for Arashk through the long, narrow sidelight beside it. A few porch lights were on across the way. The streets and sidewalks were vacant. The world beyond our front stoop slumbered under a blanket of darkness. I pulled out my cell phone and checked the time.

12:09 pm

"Luke, you wanna tell me what's going on?"

I turned back to the window. There was still no Arashk. My heart leapt. There was no unmarked sedan, either. *Where's Stine?* I turned from side to side, looking as far in each direction as the narrow window allowed. Where the hell was the officer in charge of watching our house? Did he go get something to eat? Did he leave his shift early?

I jumped when my father's hand touched my shoulder.

"Luke—"

"It's happening!" I nearly shouted. "He tried to grab me!"

"Barnes?"

"Yes," I said. "I mean, no. I mean, he had someone do it for him."

"Honey?"

My father and I both turned to see my mother standing at the top of the stairs tying the belt around her yellow robe. I'd gotten it for her for Mother's Day a few years back. The fabric was faded, the seams unraveling. She never got rid of anything.

"It's okay, dear," my father said, leaving my side to meet her on the stairs. I took the opportunity to again survey the scene. Still no sign of Arashk or Officer Stine. I was starting to think maybe the former had given up when a grey paver came crashing through the living room window.

The scream escaped my mother's throat before the rock had even stopped tumbling.

CHAPTER 42

My father sat on the top step beside my mother, one hand rubbing her back, the other holding the telephone to his ear.

"Yes, I'd like to report an attempted break-in."

I'd spent the last five minutes running around every room on the ground floor, making sure all the windows were locked. At each one, I briefly stopped to look out into the night for any sign of Arashk. No shadows lurked behind the Japanese maple between our house and the neighbors. The bushes out front and on the side were likewise free of predatory shapes. As far down the street as I could see, all the driveways were empty, as well as the yards. Since the moment the rock had come through the window, there had been no further sign of Arashk

Like a ghost, he'd simply vanished into the night.

I had just sat down at the dining room table to collect my thoughts when my cell phone buzzed. My heart immediately seized in my chest and my shoulders tensed. Someone didn't want me to take a much-needed break. A voice in my head told me to ignore the phone. I wanted to, but I couldn't. I was pretty certain it was Arashk, and I wanted to hear what the son of a bitch had to say.

I was wrong. The message wasn't from Arashk, and thank God I'd decided to check. It was looking like this was the night Barnes had been planning all along.

"Dad!" I rushed into the entryway where my parents still sat at the top of the stairs.

My father stood abruptly, recognizing the urgency in my voice. "What is it?"

"It's Dallas," I said, swiping my keys off the small, glass table beside the front door. The text message had been short and to the point. I needed to get my ass to Tipsword's Automotive ASAP. "He's in trouble. We have to go to the shop! Now!"

"Whoa, hold on." My father put his hands out like fathers do when they're about to tell you something they know you don't want to hear. "We're not leaving this house. Not until the police get here and make sure that psycho is gone."

"He *is* gone," I said, trying to ignore the landscaping paver sitting among a spray of shattered glass not ten feet away. "I'm sure of it. Let's go."

"Luke!" My father's shout interrupted the thoughts racing through my mind. He didn't continue his own thought until I had turned and was giving him my full attention. "I am not leaving your mother here by herself. When the police—"

"The police haven't done shit!" I immediately recoiled at the indignation in my voice. It wasn't like me to display such anger. "I'm sorry," I said, before taking a deep breath. "I'm sure they're doing all they can, but we can't just sit around and wait. Someone tried to get to Dallas at the shop."

My mother gasped.

"Is he okay?" she asked, clutching her robe.

"I think so. Dallas says he shot the guy. He's assuming it's Barnes, but he's not sure."

My father just stood there, looking at me like a deaf puppy, like I hadn't just given him the biggest news since all this began. He must have been taking time to process this bit of information, because it took him a moment to find his voice.

And it was the last thing I wanted to hear.

"Then he needs to call the police as well."

At least I think that's what he said. By the time I heard the word 'police,' I had already thrown open the front door and was making a beeline for my truck.

As I pulled away from the curb, I passed Officer Stine pulling up in the unmarked sedan. Raising a tall, paper cup, he offered me a head nod and a smile. I left him hanging. I had somewhere to be, and little interest in playing nice.

CHAPTER 43

As usual, Dallas' Jeep was parked next to the tire dumpster. And as usual, I pulled the truck into the spot beside it. Once I shut off the headlights, the world behind the building went dark. The only nearby streetlight had been busted out weeks ago. Despite several irritated calls from Dallas, the city had yet to come fix it. Thankfully, the moon was out, and I could at least see where I was walking.

I made my way to the rear entrance and knocked on the door before entering. The metal rang hollow in my surroundings. I didn't know where Dallas was in the building, and I didn't want to startle him by walking in without warning. He'd already pulled the trigger once tonight, and I didn't know how well his nerves were responding to it. I suspected it had been awhile.

"Dallas?" I asked, poking my head into the storage room. The door was unlocked despite both the break-in and our discussion that afternoon. Old habits die hard, I guess. "Hey, Dallas."

No answer.

I stepped into the room and eased the door shut behind me. The room's other doorway, the one separating the storage room from the office, was always open. In fact, there was usually a thick outdated telephone book propped against the bottom of the door to keep it that way. That night was no different, and because of that, I wasn't going into the office blind. The office lights were on.

"Yo, Dallas!" I shouted this time, standing in the office doorway. The papers and files scattered across the floor earlier in the day were gone. The desk drawer was back where it belonged. Even the mass of outdated magazines with their greasy black fingerprints had been stacked in an orderly fashion on the corner of the counter.

Now I knew what had kept Dallas here so very late. While it certainly wasn't out of the ordinary for him to spend late nights at the shop, they were usually spent under the hood of a car. Quite frankly, since the divorce, I don't think he loved having the house to himself as much as he claimed.

I stepped out of the darkness and into the brightly lit office.

At this point, I had called Dallas' name several times. His lack of response was unnerving to say the least. I was still in shock from being jumped at the school, so my frayed nerves were pulling a double.

I crossed through the office, suddenly uncomfortable with it being so well lit. Unlike the shop, the large front window of the office hadn't been covered with white paper. The glare of the lights on the glass made seeing out into the night nearly impossible. The window acted more like a two-way mirror. Someone could have been standing out front looking in, and I wouldn't have seen them to save my life. All I saw was myself, and I looked very much like a target standing in the middle of the room.

I opened the door to the shop. Compared to the office, the large bay was dimly lit. Only one section of the overhead lights had been turned on. With the sheets of white paper covering the overhead door windows, very little light from the street penetrated. The shop was murkier than I'd ever seen it.

And quieter.

The import sedan still sat in the bay where I left it at the end of my shift. A thought hit me. Arashk had delivered the alternator for it just that afternoon. Something sour hit my stomach. I couldn't believe I'd been so close to him all this time. I saw the guy several times a week. The thought made me sick, and I tried to put it out of my mind.

It was the pool of oil I noticed next, spread out across the concrete floor. The slick had worked its way deep into the room. Black and shiny, my eyes followed the liquid until I discovered its origin: the fifty-five-gallon drum of used oil. It sat against the far wall of the garage, oil flowing over the top. It hadn't been full when I left earlier, but it was full now.

My heart leapt into my throat.

One arm hung limp toward the ground, the other stuffed inside. His head hung to the side at an uncomfortable angle. Only the top of Dallas's shoulders rose above the barrel's rim. The rest of his body was submerged inside the steel barrel. He looked like an illusionist performing an escape act. Thick black oil continued to run slowly down the sides of the barrel and onto the floor.

The urge to run to Dallas was overwhelming, but I held it off. I took a step back instead. I snatched up the nearest weapon I could get my hands on: a ten-inch long adjustable wrench.

The laughter was subtle and amused. It drifted out from somewhere in the shadows. I whipped my head around, and that's when I saw him, sitting on the hood of Dallas' '66

Chevy. He just sat there, nonchalant, like he was shooting the shit with friends while they tuned their engine.

"So, I met your friend here. Heard you met mine."

Corwin Barnes slid off the truck's hood and onto his feet. When his heavy black boots hit the floor, the sound echoed throughout the shop. His smile was the same decaying smile that spent months terrorizing my dreams. The same smile I fought so hard to forget while a team of doctors monitored me, clipboards in hand.

It sent a familiar shiver up my spine.

It wasn't a profound statement, but the words 'fuck you' rolled off my tongue. I took another step back. My eyes left Barnes briefly, long enough to look for something more formidable than a wrench.

My proclamation of hate only seemed to amuse Barnes. His psychotic smile broadened.

"Did you really think I'd forget?" he asked.

Barnes' arms rested at his sides; one hand empty, and one not. The phone made a clicking sound as he repeatedly flipped the lid open and closed with his thumb. There was only one person I knew who still had a flip phone, and it was at that moment I realized who'd really sent me the text message.

"Did you think you could do what you did without paying penance?"

"Is he dead?" I asked, surprised at how calm I was able to ask the question. It certainly didn't match how I felt.

"Who? Mr. Tipsword here?" Barnes tipped his head toward Dallas. To acknowledge him further would have taken his focus off of me. "Not sure. But if he isn't yet, he soon will be. If you're that concerned, maybe you can keep him company."

The motion was brief, barely noticeable in the dim light of the garage: a glance behind me; a subtle nod. It was enough to raise my awareness, and I instinctively took a step to my right.

A rush of air arced through the empty space where I'd been standing. A familiar face grunted from the other end of the tire iron. *Arashk.*

The sudden movement stole my balance. It took a couple of extra steps to right myself. Once I had, my back was to the overhead doors, and I faced the middle of the shop. A good thing since I now had two psychos to keep my eyes on.

My adrenaline spoke before I could stop it.

"How's the sack, asshole?" I pointed the crescent wrench in Arashk's direction, already regretting the words. My indignation over the situation was getting the best of me. I didn't know where this brave charade was coming from, because the odds were definitely not in my favor.

My grip tightened on the piece of forged steel, its narrow edges digging into the meat of my hand.

"You wasn't so funny a half hour ago. Remember? When you was running for your life?" Arashk turned to Barnes. "I don't want to wait until we get back, man. I want to cut his ass up right here and now!"

Apparently, something Arashk said didn't sit well with Barnes. The crude smile faded from his face. His eyes narrowed. Barnes looked at Arashk like he was a stubborn child who'd been told something time and time again, but still wasn't getting it.

Barnes was just opening his mouth to respond when the short chirp of a siren cut him off. The chirp was immediately followed by an abrupt screech of tires. A second screech came next, then a third. Muted red and blue lights flashed across the white paper covering the windows.

The police had finally come through, bringing a sense of relief to wash over me.

But I'd screwed up. I'd taken my eyes off of Arashk and Barnes. Realizing my mistake, I whipped my head back around.

It was too late. Arashk was already gone. One of the two rear overhead doors had been raised about three feet, and Barnes was in the process of rolling under it. Dallas's cell phone slipped and tumbled from his hand. The last I saw of Corwin Barnes was his long sinewy arm reaching back under the door and swiping up the phone.

With more adrenaline coursing through me than I could harness, I rushed over to the barrel of oil that held Dallas's lifeless body. Was he still alive? It sure as hell didn't look like it. I dropped the wrench to the floor with a clatter and gently lifted Dallas's head so I could get a better look.

His eyes were closed, as if they had a choice. His face was busted up pretty bad, already turning various shades of ugly. Blood flowed from a gash across his forehead. It streamed down over his right eye in three distinct tendrils, eventually mixing with the oil in the barrel. His nose was split, swollen, and at an angle that would have made the toughest MMA fighter cringe. The long salt and pepper beard Dallas spent so much time stroking while in thought, was gone. It now lay on the floor beside the barrel.

His open mouth sagged, threatening to take in some of the oil. I slid my hands down into the black liquid and reached under his armpits. I'd never lift him out, but I needed to at least prop him up.

I didn't get far before two police officers burst into the

garage. Like mirror images, both pointed their guns my way and told to me freeze. The exact words were, 'Freeze, motherfucker!'

Assuming I was the motherfucker in this case, I did as I was told.

CHAPTER 44

I woke to the sound of the truck door slamming. He'd done it on purpose. It was his way. As I blinked away sleep, I zeroed in on the energy drink sitting on the dashboard in front of me. I smiled, unable to be mad. It's tough to be upset with someone bearing gifts.

Humidity thickened the air inside the truck. Condensation dripped down the side of the can. Sitting up straight, I worked my neck from side to side to clear out the kinks. Once I could do it without discomfort, I reached out and grabbed the energy drink. I popped the can's tab and was rewarded with the fizzing of tiny bubbles. My dry mouth watered. It had been a long time since I'd had an energy drink. It had been a long time since I'd done a lot of things. Not since...

I drank half the body fuel in one long draw, while an old George Jones song quietly played through the speakers. I rolled my eyes and groaned. New country was at least tolerable. Jason Aldean, Carrie Underwood, and the guy with the first name that's difficult to spell. But old country? I could definitely live without it.

I was happy to make an exception this time, though, because there was only person I knew who liked the old stuff. I opened the passenger side door and stepped out into a light fog.

The rusted trailer was hitched to the truck, and Garrett was busy taking the cover off the boat. I jumped in and started unhooking the bungee cords from my side.

"I see that extra bit of beauty sleep didn't do much for ya," Garrett said. His ever-present smile was, without a doubt, a sight for sore eyes.

"Well, people say I look like my dad, so I'll give him your condolences." We both laughed. It was like the old days. Like we'd never found that church.

Like he'd never died.

With the last bungee cord removed and tossed into the bed of the truck, we each took hold of an opposite corner and started folding the canvas sheet. The next time our eyes met, the usual brightness in Garrett's was gone.

"Do you remember how we met?" he asked, using his hand to iron out a wrinkle in the canvas.

"Second grade," I said, wondering where he was heading.

"Yeah, but do you remember *how*? What brought us together?"

I didn't, and let him know with a slight shake of my head.

"Every day on that damn playground," he said, folding the canvas over once again, "Rocky Blanton would hang around, waiting until Mrs. Ruble wasn't looking. Then he'd walk up and punch me in the arm as hard as he could."

I nodded, as the memory started coming back to me. We folded the canvas over once more while Garrett continued.

"For some stupid reason, I just took it. Didn't tell anyone. Then one day, we were walking back into the school building and you came up to me. You asked how many times I was going to let that son of a bitch hit me before I got mad enough to do something about it. You asked me how many punches it was gonna take."

We had reached the front of the boat, and it was time to fold the cover in the other direction. I took my end and walked it over to Garrett, stepping over the tongue of the trailer. When I handed my corners to him, he looked even deeper into my eyes.

"So? How many is it gonna take, Luke?"

I frowned.

"What do you mean?" I grabbed part of the cover and helped Garrett toss it into the truck bed.

"Barnes," Garrett said, closing the tailgate on the truck. With his foot on the rear bumper, he started counting with his fingers. "First me, then Becca, and now your friend, Dallas. How many times are you gonna let Barnes hit you, Luke? How many times before you get mad enough to do something about it?"

I stood dumbfounded, looking at the best friend I'd ever had, reading the emotion on his face; a face I hadn't seen in so long. Garrett wasn't angry or disappointed. He was concerned, and had every reason to be. He was right. All this time, I'd been a bystander in Barnes's game, sitting back and taking every punch he'd thrown at me. Sure, I was still standing, but still standing isn't always enough. Not by a long shot.

The worst part was I had all the incentive in the world to fight back. A hot core of pain and anger dwelled inside me. It had been there for a while, therapy had helped me see that. But I'd been holding it down all this time, holding it in because the doctors told me to. Move on, they said. It would be better for me in the long run, they said.

They were wrong.

"You gotta let it out," Garrett said, as if reading my

thoughts. "Looks like Dallas may have gotten lucky. Don't wait until it's Claire or your parents. You've got to hit him back, Luke. Hit him fuckin' hard."

Garrett dropped his foot to the ground, and his expression changed. A wry smile broke across his face and his eyes gleamed once again.

"Hit that son of a bitch for me." He winked before turning and making his way to the cab of the truck.

I fought back a sudden urge. I wanted to follow him, not let him out of my sight again. But it had always been my job to sit in the boat as Garrett backed the trailer down the ramp and into the water. Once the boat started to float, I'd crank up the motor and back the boat clear of the trailer. Garrett would then pull the truck up and park it while I idled next to the dock waiting. It was the usual routine, and despite the fact I hated to see him walk away, it felt good to be back at it again. Most of my fondest memories were of us being on the water, and I was eager to get back out there. It had been so long.

As I sat waiting in the boat, the fog thickened. It crept over the landscape, blocking out trees by the second. Water splashed gently against the side of the boat. I looked over the side, but couldn't see anything. The fog had descended on the lake. A chill coursed through me right then. I wished like hell for Garrett to hurry.

When I looked to the parking lot to check his progress, what I saw did nothing to warm the chill gripping my insides. Garrett wasn't parking the truck at all. The blue Chevy continued on toward the entrance to the parking lot, passing parking space after parking space along the way. A moment later, the combination of distance and fog stole the truck from sight altogether.

For the second time, Garrett had left me to navigate the world alone.

A raspy ventilator greeted me as I woke. It swooshed up and down, working oxygen into Dallas' lungs. I sat beside his hospital bed, surrounded by tiny monitors that beeped every few seconds while checking his vitals. The top of his head was wrapped completely with white gauze. It wound all the way down until it covered his right eye.

The beating Dallas had taken was bad, really bad. But I didn't let the doctors sway my thinking. I refused to believe his prognosis was anything but good. They would eventually see things my way. He would be fine.

It was just his recovery would be a long and difficult one.

The longer I sat there looking at my boss, my friend, and one hell of a guardian angel, the more my mood changed. Garrett's words replayed in my mind. With their urging, I acknowledged the anger I'd been suppressing. What the doctors had spent so much time encouraging me to let go of, Garrett had assured me was okay to embrace. Being angry wasn't always a bad thing. Sometimes it was just the fuel you needed.

And I needed all the fuel I could get for what lay ahead.

Barnes and Arashk had gotten away despite the best efforts of the police. Officers had been a few seconds too late in swarming the building. Not surprisingly, Barnes hadn't left a trail for anyone to follow, no leads on his whereabouts or possible residence. For Arashk, on the other hand, I was at least able to provide Detective Morgenstern with a place of employment. He assured me by the time Dallas arrived at the hospital, someone would already be waking the manager of the

NAPA store and gathering information.

Good luck showing up for work tomorrow, dick.

Once I decided I couldn't sit there and look at him in his condition any longer, I rose from the chair, gave Dallas's forearm a squeeze, and exited his ICU room.

In the waiting area, my father stood to the side talking with both a uniformed officer and Detective Morgenstern. All three turned as I walked by. Morgenstern gave me an understanding nod.

"Don't run off," he said. "Got a few more questions for ya."

I acknowledged his instruction with the slightest of head nods. I'd answered enough questions.

My mother sat by herself in a row of uncomfortable-looking chairs reading a magazine. Four seats down, a doctor in a white lab coat had gathered a tearful family. She spoke to the family members in a hushed voice. The women in the group dabbed at red eyes with crumpled tissues, while the men solemnly nodded their understanding of the situation. What that situation was, I had no idea. Though it didn't look good.

I bent and kissed my mother on top of her head. I excused myself for the restroom, but that's not where I headed. I strolled passed the nurse's station, then turned the corner after the vending machines. The hallway took me passed a water fountain and a bank of elevators before ending in what was probably one of the most remote areas of the hospital.

There was nobody around.

It was full of quiet.

It was exactly the privacy I was looking for.

At the end of the hallway, I took a moment to stare out into the night. Through the window, the city of Dayton still slept beneath a blanket of darkness. The sun would rise in a few hours. Alarm clocks would sound throughout the city. Children would head off to learn whatever new curriculum was being taught. Husbands would kiss wives on the forehead while she adjusted his tie. Mothers would exhale deeply as the last door slammed shut. With the house now empty, she could finally get herself ready for work.

I, on the other hand, wouldn't be taking part in the activities of normal people. I had something else to do before the sun came up. Pulling out my cell phone, I thumbed through my contact list, stopping when I got to Dallas's name. With a deep breath and a hard look into the angry eyes of my reflection, I pressed the green call button and put the phone to my ear.

CHAPTER 45

It was 1:37 am.

I rolled the window down on the truck and filled the cab with cool night air. Leaving the radio off, I listened to the gears in my mind sort out its thoughts. The city streets were mine alone. On the outside, everything appeared calm. But trouble was brewing.

The conversation with Barnes had been short and sweet. Like cheesy dialogue from an action movie, I told him this was all going to end badly for him, that I was done running, and I had a message from my buddy, Garrett. He laughed, and I hung up. Like I said, short and sweet. I didn't know what to say to him once I had him on the phone, I just let him know I wasn't scared anymore.

I was pissed.

That didn't mean I had a plan just yet. It was still developing in my mind, and admittedly, in the very early stages. At the moment, the whole of the plan consisted of getting to Dallas's house and finding Prudence. Or, one of her cousins. I didn't know much about guns, but I knew I'd feel better with one in hand.

At the garage, Arashk had come equipped with only a tire iron. I hadn't seen a weapon on Barnes, but I'm sure he had one of some sort. He wasn't planning on just holding me down and tickling me to death. I would, however, have to learn how to shoot on the fly. This was one time I wished Garrett and I had spent a little less time fishing over the years and more time hunting.

Luckily, they'd found Dallas's keys in his pants pocket, which saved me from having to return to the shop. Dallas's clothes had otherwise been a lost cause, oil-soaked and unsalvageable. The few belongings they'd been able to save were given to me until family could be notified. An oil-logged leather wallet, the silver Zippo lighter he carried for some unknown reason, and his set of keys on the Tipsword's Automotive key ring that was also covered with an oily film. I gave his wallet to my mother before leaving the hospital, just in case someone would need his identification. The keys and lighter, however, I'd slipped into my pocket. You never know when things might come in handy.

Turns out, now was that time.

CHAPTER 46

Dallas's house was located in one of those old neighborhoods where cars lined both sides of the street and seeing front yards wrapped with chain link wasn't uncommon. His was a brick single story with brown trim and overgrown shrubs under the windows. A faded terra cotta flowerpot sat beside the steps. Except for the ratty shrubs and a few ambitious weeds, the flowerbeds were as barren as the flowerpot. Dallas always said he wasn't much of a gardener. Said he traded in his green thumb for a black one. The brown shutters around the windows barely stood out against the brick facade, and I remembered Dallas telling me he'd just painted them last fall. Rounding out the old neighborhood look, an ancient porch swing nearly overtook the porch itself.

It was much like the house my grandmother lived in when I was growing up.

I pulled the truck into the short driveway and parked it under the carport awning. I'd only been to the house once and was lucky to have found it again. All the streets in his neighborhood looked the same in the dark. Hell, all the houses pretty much looked the same, too. The day I was here, a car belonging to one of Dallas's elderly neighbors wouldn't start, and I'd ridden along with him to check it out. Afterward, we'd stopped by his house for what he called an 'award-winning' workingman's lunch: thick-cut bologna sandwiches, potato chips, and a Pabst Blue Ribbon. It was the beer that made it 'award winning' Dallas had said, but I'd found that to be debatable.

I stepped out of the truck and gently closed the door behind me so as not to wake the neighbors. After all, their bedroom was only a few feet away. I approached the side door and slid the key into the lock. The knob turned without obstruction, and I gave the door a push. With only a faint protest, it opened into an unlit kitchen. The soft light from the carport entered the doorway ahead of me, revealing a countertop to the left. I immediately started feeling along the wall for a light switch.

A loud grinding sound broke the silence. The blades of the garbage disposal slowed to a halt once I flipped the switch back off. The frenzy echoed throughout the darkened room a bit longer before dying out. My heart raced. I made a mental note to change my underwear when this was all over and flipped the second switch on the panel. The light above the sink came to life.

The kitchen was exactly how I'd remembered, simple and small. On the wall facing the door sat a white gas stove and a yellow refrigerator. I could hear the fridge humming in the quiet. The appliances probably weren't original to the house, but they were older than most you'd find. The only set of cabinets were the ones along the wall with the sink, and I immediately set to work looking for a hidden gun in the various drawers.

Dallas once told me he had guns strategically stashed around the house. Apparently, the neighborhood had seen safer days, and he'd had problems with the local youth more than once; teenagers looking to carry out their own home invasion sales.

After not finding anything in the third drawer, I slid it closed. That's when I heard the floor creak behind me. *Directly* behind me. My blood froze. My entire body stiffened. I was a statue. I couldn't imagine who would be in the house unless...

My mind wouldn't let me finish the thought. It also wouldn't leave it alone. If either of those two lunatics were inside the house, it would be bad. Really bad. I was nowhere near ready. I searched nearby with my eyes for something to use as a weapon. The countertop was bare. The sink was only two steps away. Even if I could have reached it in time, it was empty. No pots, no pans, not even a drinking glass. The only thing within arms reach was an old ratty dishtowel.

Deciding that ripping the Band-Aid off was always the best move, I took a deep breath. With my hands high in the air, I turned around slowly.

I found myself face to face with the business end of what I'd gone there looking for. It wasn't Prudence, but a gun very similar, aimed at the bridge of my nose from an arm's length away. The round, bottomless hole bore down on me. I expected death to come flying out at any moment in a flash of flame and smoke.

Death never came.

I slowly eased my eyes off the end of the gun and trailed them up the arm that held it. To my surprise and relief, I found a familiar face. My shoulders sagged, the tension in them releasing with a deep exhale.

"Luke?"

"Wade." I lowered my arms slightly, but not all the way.

Wade didn't seem to be relaxing as much as I was.

"What are you doing here, sneaking into my uncle's house in the middle of the night?"

"It's a long story," I said. "But I swear everything's on the up and up. Can I sit? To be honest, my legs are shaking a little."

I wasn't lying, and after a hesitant nod from Dallas's nephew, I pulled a chair out from the dining table and plopped in it. Only then did Wade, standing before me in nothing but a pair of boxers and a black USMC t-shirt, lower the gun. With his eyes still focused on me, he took a cautious step backward.

"I'll go wake Dallas."

I put my hands out.

"He's not here," I said, before he could leave the room. "He's in the hospital."

Wade's brow formed three creases before his look of confusion turned to worry.

"You better sit." I used my foot to push out the other chair. "There's a lot you don't know."

CHAPTER 47

As it turned out, there wasn't as much to tell as I'd thought.

In less than fifteen minutes, I'd filled Wade in on the whole disturbing story, sparing no details. He already knew some of the backstory about Barnes and the church and what happened there a year ago. Dallas had shared some of that with him over the past week. Apparently, Wade had been crashing in Dallas's spare bedroom since being let go at the shop. That was pure Dallas: he had no choice but to fire his own nephew, but felt bad enough about doing it he was letting the guy crash at his place until he found another job. Truth be told, since the divorce, Dallas was probably enjoying the company.

"I better call my mother." Wade slid his chair back. "She can help get ahold of everyone that needs to know about Dallas."

Once he left the room, I stood and cleared the table of the two beer bottles we'd emptied during the conversation. I didn't drink very often, but when I did, it seemed to be at Dallas's house. The thought made me chuckle, and I wondered if maybe he wasn't such a good influence after all.

By the time I'd dropped the two bottles in the trashcan under the sink and closed the cabinet door, Wade was back.

"Alright," he said, now sporting a pair of jeans. "I had to

call twice to wake her up, but Mom's gonna head up to the hospital."

"Good," I said. "He could use some family up there."

Wade set a pair of black work boots on the table and sat back down in the chair. Crossing one leg over the other, he started pulling on a pair of white socks.

"Heading up there, too?"

"Maybe later," Wade said, grabbing the first boot. "First, I'm gonna help you get this motherfucker."

At first I questioned why he would want to get involved in a situation with someone as dangerous as Corwin Barnes. Perhaps I hadn't done a good enough job explaining the kind of psycho I was dealing with. Then I realized that not only was Dallas Wade's uncle, but he was a pretty damn good one. Barnes had gone and made it personal for Wade, too.

As I watched him tie his other boot, guilt infiltrated my mixed emotions. I didn't like the idea of exposing yet another person to Barnes, putting them in harm's way. Admittedly, I was also relieved I wouldn't be going it alone. I stopped short of getting excited, though. I still had no clue what I was going to do, or how I was going to go about it.

"That's great," I said. "But I don't even know where to start."

"I do." Wade stood and straightened out the bottom of his jeans. "I know where the fucker lives."

CHAPTER 48

"It's a real shit hole," Wade said from the passenger seat of the truck. "Ran into our Napa driver at a bar one time. Had a couple beers, and I gave him a ride home after. Guy was living in a motel, said he was learning a trade or something, had an apprenticeship worked out. I don't know what for exactly, but I'll tell ya what, the guy's a talkative drunk."

As I steered the truck through Dayton's empty streets, both neon and streetlamps flashed by at a rapid clip. The question of where we were heading had already been answered. Wade was navigating us toward some sleazy motel where we'd hopefully find Arashk. What hadn't yet been answered was what was going to happen when we got there. Wade had given me the handgun Dallas kept stashed behind the refrigerator. With it sitting on the seat between us, I felt slightly more comfortable going in. Especially since we'd be going in blind.

Wade riding shotgun, however, allowed me to sit higher in the seat. After losing Garrett, making new friends hadn't exactly been a priority. Wasn't sure it ever would be. But I had to admit, it was nice having another guy riding in the truck with me again.

It also didn't hurt that Wade was a highly trained soldier.

I brought up the idea of contacting Detective Morgenstern, but Wade quickly shot it down. Even if the cops found Arashk at the motel, it didn't mean he would lead them to Barnes. Especially if he decided 'I want to talk to my lawyer' was his best defense. Barnes could be long gone by the time Arashk eventually gave him up in a plea deal. Then I'd be right back where I started, and that wasn't an option. I was done looking over my shoulder. Wade said he knew faster ways of getting information out of someone, and given his military background, I didn't question him.

Besides, Morgenstern was probably pissed I'd taken off and hadn't stuck around the hospital like he'd instructed. I would have to deal with the fallout from that sooner or later. Remembering the phone conversation in his office, I just hoped it would happen *much* later.

"Don't forget, though," I said, checking my rearview mirror, "Arashk told you he was learning a trade. And he's obviously buddied up with Barnes in some capacity. That could very well mean Arashk has blood on his hands, too. "

"Your point?"

"We need to be careful," I said. "There's no telling what may be going on in that motel room."

"Well, then," Wade said, a poorly hidden smirk on his face, "sounds to me it's not only our civic duty, but we have, in fact, a moral obligation to get into that room by any means necessary."

I looked at him and nodded. "I'd say so." At least we were on the same page.

"Turn right on Singleton," Wade instructed. "Then a couple blocks down, turn left on Bridge. And don't worry. This guy's gonna pay for his sins. I don't care how many he's racked up."

I hadn't been paying much attention to our surroundings

up to that point. My mind had been too consumed with the task ahead. Eventually, it was the names of the streets Wade was calling out that caught my attention. Additionally, I started recognizing some of the buildings we were passing. When the glowing white sign of Tipsword's Automotive flashed by, I knew exactly where we were.

"Are we close?" I asked, trying to calm my growing alarm. I hoped for one answer in particular. Unfortunately, I didn't get it.

"Yep. Almost there."

Shit! No wonder it felt like I was constantly being watched. Barnes' lackey had been close enough to keep an eye on me the whole time. In other words, too close.

I made a left on Bridge like I was told, while Wade checked the rounds in his gun for the fourth time. Were they prone to disappearing or something? Was he nervous, or just really damn thorough? I doubted it mattered either way. Both were good traits. Nerves kept you on your toes.

"So, do you have a plan?" I asked, hoping my anxiety wasn't showing. "Cuz I sure as hell don't."

"Not exactly," he said. "At least not yet. I'll have a better idea once we roll up on the place, and I get another look at it."

I wasn't sure if I felt better with Wade not having a plan, like I wasn't the only one who was clueless, or if it made me more uneasy.

"Pull in there," he said, pointing to a parking lot on the left.

I flipped on my turn signal and waited for a semi trailer to pass before turning into the vacant parking lot of the Lip Service Gentleman's Club.

"Turn around and back into one of those spots on the end."

I whipped the truck around, threw it in reverse, and backed into a parking spot near the corner of the shadowy building. Lip Service appeared to be closed, which wasn't surprising. The city was investigating several of these establishments on the grounds they were employing underage performers. The sting had dominated the news for the past few weeks. Even the large pair of lips above the double doorway that would normally be lit with neon pink were dark.

"Shoot, looks like they're closed." I slapped the steering wheel for emphasis. "No infectious diseases for us tonight."

"There it is," Wade said, ignoring my attempt at humor. His focus appeared to be on something beyond the windshield. He pointed to an L-shaped building across the street situated between a liquor store with bars on its windows and a check cashing place, also with bars on its windows. "That's the shit hole."

"Damn," I said.

"Yep."

CHAPTER 49

There was this time when my father and I drove the two hundred and thirty miles to Detroit for a Journey concert. Even though he'd predicted they wouldn't be as good as when he'd seen them with some guy named Steve, he still wanted to go, and he dragged me along for the ride. It was my first concert. I was thirteen.

On the way home, about twenty miles outside of Toledo, a deer crossed the road in front of us. It made it, but only because my father swerved at the last possible second. Our car didn't fare as well as the deer. Turns out, ditches can play havoc with a car's ball joints.

The ironic part was all week, my mother had tried to get my father to book a room for the night so we wouldn't have to drive back so late. He'd refused, not wanting to spend the money. So, because he insisted on getting home that night, we ended up staying in a motel, anyway. A really bad motel. According to the tow truck driver, it was only a ten-minute walk to the auto repair shop where he was taking our car. I don't remember the name of the place, but we slept in our clothes for protection, and my father made me swear to never tell my mother how bad it was.

I never did, but let me just say, that shit hole on the side of the freeway didn't have anything on the shit hole Arashk was staying in.

The brick building was a single-story with a wavy roof and dimly lit, pothole marred parking lot. There looked to be about ten to twelve units making up the long end of the L, with an office and equally dimly lit vending area creating the short end. None of the vehicles in the parking lot was a white van, and I couldn't decide if I was disappointed or not. I didn't know what it meant. Either Arashk wasn't there, or he hadn't been the driver that night.

One conclusion I came to from the parking lot across the street was the motel had a real problem with their lights. The bulb in the vending area kept flickering like a giant bug zapper. The light behind the letter 'M' in the neon 'motel' sign was completely burnt out. There were twice as many unlit porch lights beside the doors than there were cars in the parking lot. Were those lights burnt out as well? Or, were they turned off for a reason? There was also the theory that maybe the people going in and out of the rooms didn't want to be seen.

It would also explain why the curtains were drawn tight over the windows in every room. Judging by how this place looked, the area it was in, and things I'd seen on television, it was safe to say whatever people were doing inside those rooms, they didn't want the outside world bearing witness.

I could only assume Arashk fit that description.

"Hell of a place to call home, huh?"

"Hell of a place to take a date," I said, shutting off the truck's headlights. I was just about to kill the engine when a dark form passed through my side mirror. Wade must have seen it too, because he had his hand on his door handle before I could say anything. Or stop him.

"Let's talk to this guy," he suggested, throwing open the passenger door.

Finding myself abruptly alone, there was nothing to do except shrug my shoulders and follow his lead.

CHAPTER 50

The old man smelled like piss. Piss and at least two weeks worth of unbathed funk. He wore two layers of identical brown jackets, both filthy, and a salt and pepper beard that was yellowed around his mouth. His face resembled a crumpled piece of paper, and his hair was stringy, long, and in need of an oil change. I didn't know whether we should talk to him or hose him down.

Wade saved me from having to make the decision.

"Excuse me, sir. Can we talk to you for a minute?"

The old man looked Wade up and down, then turned his speculative eye on me.

"What you want?" he asked, putting a hand up to shield his eyes from the floodlight mounted on the corner of the building.

"Just a couple questions," Wade said. "Figure a guy like you probably knows a lot about what goes on around this neighborhood. Specifically, that motel over there."

"And by 'a guy like me' you mean…" The man looked back and forth between us again. After a moment, gave up hope that either of us would take the bait. "Yeah, what about it?"

"We're looking for a guy staying there," Wade said. "A real bad fella."

The old man turned his attention across the street to the motel with a burnt out 'M' in its sign.

"Ain't they all?" he asked, nodding in its direction.

"This guy's worse than most," I said, receiving the eyeball treatment for chiming in.

"Step into my office," the old man said, walking over to a dented, green dumpster sitting conveniently out of the floodlight's range.

Wade followed the guy blindly, while I took the time to look up and down the street twice before stepping into the building's shadow. I hoped it wasn't a bad decision. Same with leaving the gun sitting on the truck's seat.

"So," the old man said, as he lifted the lid on the dumpster and started sorting through an all-you-can-eat buffet of shit, "what this fella do, got you so intent on findin' him?"

"Well, for starters," Wade said, "he put someone dear to me in the ICU earlier tonight."

"For starters?" the old man asked, clearing a large cardboard box out of his way.

"Trust us, there's a lot more," I said. "You have no idea."

The old man was listening, despite the fact he never stopped rifling through the garbage long enough to make eye contact. Until that point. He turned around then and looked both of us up and down all over again.

"You guys don't look like cops," he said. "So, I guess it doesn't hurt to ask, what's in it for me?"

"Maybe a dinner you don't have to hunt for in the garbage," Wade said, pulling out his wallet.

"Hey, now," said the old man. "Be surprised the quality meals I pulled out of this dumpster in particular. A place like this lures guys in with a steak dinner, then distracts 'em pretty quick. 'Fore they know it, steak's the furthest thing from their minds. Can't blame 'em, what with naked women coming up and squeezing your face between their titties."

"Maybe," Wade said, nodding at the building, "but it looks like the place is temporarily closed. That means the pickings have to be pretty slim right now."

The old man hesitated before nodding. "Well, there's that."

"So, how 'bout you help us out," Wade pressed, "and if the information's good, your next dinner will come from down the street at Dina's. On us."

A smile made of teeth that had long forgotten what toothpaste was spread across the old man's mug.

"Always told ol' Reggie, you can't find warm, chicken pot pies in a dumpster, but you can find 'em at Dina's 'round the corner. What do you fellas wanna know?"

CHAPTER 51

The old man, whose name we eventually learned was Jakob with a 'k', knew exactly who we were looking for. All it took was a brief description of Arashk. Turns out, he was an exact match for one of the men he'd seen at the motel on a daily basis. There were several regulars who showed up every few days, but according to Jakob, only three that he'd seen *every* day. Besides Arashk, the old guy speculated that one of the men was either the owner or manager of the place. The third was likely the on-site maintenance man, due to the fact he was seen all hours of the day and night, usually wearing a grey worker's uniform.

What I found most interesting was that the maintenance man's description also resembled Corwin Barnes. The plot thickened at that point. I kept glancing over my shoulder at the derelict motel, each time expecting to see Barnes stomping toward us with his bolo knife in hand. Thankfully, the parking lot remained quiet. Jakob mentioned he thought Arashk might be the guy's lover, since they both appeared to spend time in the same room. While I didn't know if they were lovers, it would have been the best-case scenario for them to be sharing a room. Especially given the fact Arashk had told Wade he was here learning a trade.

Somehow I doubt he was talking about building

maintenance.

"So, how's that plan coming along?" I asked Wade.

We were back in the truck, sitting in the dark, and staring at the last room on the far end of the motel's 'L.' That was the unit Jakob told us Arashk was staying. The longer we sat there, the more sense it made. If Arashk was in fact learning the murder and bone trade from Barnes, it would be only logical they'd not only spend a lot of time together, but maintain a tight-knit unit. When you're doing the sort of things Barnes does, you associate with as few people as possible.

"When you called to talk to Barnes on Dallas's cell earlier, you said it was Arashk who answered, right? Then he handed the phone off to Barnes?"

I confirmed this, which lead to Wade sitting there with his brow creased and his wheels turning. I waited, not wanting to interrupt his train of thought. Within a few seconds, however, he voiced my own conclusion.

"Then we have to assume they're both in there."

I turned away from Wade and focused directly on the room at the end of the building. I'd already entertained the thought. Hearing it said out loud made it more real. Thinking Corwin Barnes might be in the very room I was staring at sent a chill through me. I tried to stay angry, keep my edge for what was coming, but I was finding it more difficult the closer we got. Part of me was eager to get on with things and get it over with. The other part of me feared what Barnes was capable of, and was in no hurry to face it head on. Since I was currently torn between the two, I figured I'd let Wade determine the timetable.

"So, my question is," he said, reloading bullets into his clip for the sixth time, "are you still okay with moving forward before getting the cops involved? Because I sure as hell am. Even if rolling up on one means scaring off the other, I almost don't care anymore. As long as I get my hands on at least one of those fuckers before I have to sit back and watch the court proceedings. I want it for Dallas. He deserves that much."

"Payback sounds pretty damn good," I said, sounding more enthusiastic than I felt. I wasn't sure who I was trying to convince. Maybe both of us. "And there's a hell of a lot they need to pay for. Especially Barnes."

"Alright." Wade slid the gun's clip into place. "I think our best play is to go in all quiet like. No guns blazing. I'd rather hold the cops off as long as possible. Until we're ready for 'em, at least. That'll be determined by what we find."

What we find.

That was the other thing our buddy Jakob had said that caused Wade and me to look at each other warily. He'd seen a handful of young women go into that motel room, but couldn't remember if they'd all come back out. Said it was weird. In my mind, Jakob should be thankful he found it only weird. Because I knew better, and the thought of what we might find started resurrecting old demons.

"You sure you're up for this shit?"

"Hell yeah," I said, thinking about Garrett and Becca. I was using what happened to them for continued incentive. And it was working. My anger was scaling new heights. Adrenaline pumped through me like steam through a locomotive. I was most definitely 'up for this shit.'

Which was good, because the call to action came quick.

Wade had no more than set his handgun back on the dash when something through the windshield caught his attention. He bolted upright.

"Holy fuck," he said, retrieving the gun. "Isn't that…"

I looked up, and just like that, things were set in motion.

Across the street, under the flickering light, Arashk was exiting the motel's vending alcove. He started toward the far end of the building with two orange, 5-gallon buckets at his sides, one in each hand. The way they drew his shoulders down, the buckets appeared heavy.

"Why do they need—" I started.

"So much fuckin' ice?" Wade finished.

We exchanged a look and found the answer on each other's face. And neither of us were thinking margaritas.

I cranked the ignition key and threw the transmission in drive. Blood rushed to my head, flushing my cheeks as I hit the lights and the gas at the same time. The tires spun where we sat. A second later, we shot forward with a chirp of rubber against asphalt. Our acceleration grew at the same pace as my adrenaline, and we crossed the empty lot in the span of a heartbeat.

I barely glanced both ways before jetting into the street. To my left, nothing. To my right, a grin on Wade's face. His anticipation was contagious, and I grinned, too. The truck hit the sudden incline at the entrance to the motel's parking lot and popped the front end into the air.

Arashk turned, caught in the headlights. Either he recognized the truck, or the simple fact a screaming 6,000-pound Chevy 1500 bore down on him was enough to scare the piss out of him. He dropped the two buckets and took off running. Glistening cubes of ice danced across the sidewalk in his wake.

The truck skidded toward an open space, just missing an older model Buick. Either I was overenthusiastic, or I'd underestimated how fast we'd climbed in such a short distance, because I didn't hit the brakes soon enough. The tires went up and over the concrete parking block at the head of the space. The truck jerked violently, then hit the edge of the sidewalk. When we finally came to a stop, the front end of the truck slumped considerably toward the driver's side.

I didn't know the extent of the damage, and I didn't care. Wade was out the door before I could even put the truck in park. As soon as I jammed the lever up, I followed, this time with gun in hand.

CHAPTER 52

Wade pounded his fist on the door to room 112. I don't think he thought it would do any good. We'd just missed Arashk with the truck, and it wasn't like he was suddenly going to open the door for us. Wade just had frustration building from being so close and coming up empty, and he needed to get it out. More like "taking it out" on the door.

"Believe that shit?" he asked, holding his forefinger and thumb about a quarter-inch apart. "That fuckin' close."

I shook my head no because, in fact, I couldn't believe it. What were the odds?

It was the sound of a door creaking open down the corridor that kept me from doing the math. A pudgy naked guy stepped through the doorway holding a pillow over his crotch.

"What the hell?" he asked. The top of his head glimmered with sweat, and the comb over he was trying to pull off looked like a wind-swept bird's nest and wasn't fooling anyone. "Tryin' to concentrate here. Only got the room for another forty minutes."

"Then quit wasting your time with us, jackoff!" Wade pointed in the direction of the guy's room, basically ordering him to get back to whatever he was doing.

The guy shook his head and ducked back inside, slamming the door closed behind him. I was glad, too, because I was here for one purpose and one purpose only. Getting involved with the locals wasn't part of the plan.

"Asshole." Wade turned back to the door to 112 and pounded it one more time. I guess he wanted to let Arashk know we hadn't forgotten about him.

It was when Wade went over to the window and tried to look inside that I realized I was standing out in the open holding a gun. It was such a foreign thing for me to do, yet it felt completely natural. Still, I slid the gun into the waistband of my jeans.

"Nothin' to see here," Wade said.

"So, now what?" I checked the corridor to see if curiosity had brought anyone else out of their rooms. It hadn't.

"Come on," he said, after taking a moment to think. "Most of these types of places have bathroom windows on the back side. We should probably check out that situation. Besides, we've drawn enough unwanted attention out here. Stay out here too long and someone's liable to call the cops on *us.*"

I watched as Wade disappeared around the corner of the building. My confidence in him was still high, but I could tell coming up on Arashk like that had thrown him off his game. Whatever his plan leading up to that point, it had gone right out the window. From that moment on, we were flying by the seat of our pants.

CHAPTER 53

No floodlights reached the side of the building. The structure itself blocked the light in the parking lot. The moonlight helped me keep track of Wade as he felt his way along the wall a couple feet in front of me. I stayed close, trying to maintain a visual on him, all the while thinking if there was a bathroom window around back, I hoped like hell we wouldn't run into Arashk on his way out.

I also hoped like hell we did.

My stomach knotted with contradiction.

A strip of grass long overdue to be mowed, and an eight-foot-tall chain-link fence separated the motel's property from the neighborhood behind it. There was also a narrow slab of concrete that ran the length of the building. A nearby Walgreens parking lot provided enough light to see, but not enough to see well. Wade had been right, though. Each unit had a window in the back, most likely belonging to the bathroom. Unfortunately, they weren't the kind that opened and closed. Four-inch square glass blocks, starting about six feet off the ground, filled the openings.

"Do you have a tire iron in the truck?" Wade asked once he'd had a chance to scope out the situation.

"Behind the seat," I said. "Why?"

"Be right back."

Wade was gone before I could protest. But then, I probably wouldn't have, even if given the opportunity. I didn't know if it was the flourishing seed of newfound anger, or if hanging with the confident Wade for the past hour had helped me grow some balls, but I didn't mind being left alone in a dark and dangerous situation like I had in the past.

It could have also been the fact I had a gun on me this time. It didn't hurt, at least.

"These glass blocks," Wade said, returning with the tire iron, "give people a sense of security. They look thick and strong. Impenetrable. What those people don't know is that, in most cases, they're hollow, not solid."

To prove his point, Wade gripped the tire iron with both hands like you would an axe: one hand on top and one on bottom. Instead of swinging it downward, he reared back and brought it straight forward, ramming the chisel end through the center of one of the blocks. The glass put up about as much resistance as a regular pane of glass, eliciting a sharp clinking sound as it broke. It didn't shatter as much as cave in on itself.

"Good thing that one wasn't solid," I said.

"No shit," Wade laughed. "That would've been painful."

After pulling the piece of iron back out, Wade turned it around and snaked the hooked end of the iron through the hole he had just made.

"When I was in the Army," Wade said, "my unit helped with some of the cleanup in Haiti after the big hurricane. There were buildings that were beyond repair, and since resources were limited, a lot of the demolition had to be done by hand."

Once it was in a few inches, he brought the other end of the iron around and pulled back on it until it hooked onto the glass.

"Saw one of my buddies going around removing sections of glass just like this. You see, the blocks are strong and the mortar holding them together is strong, but the nails holding the entire section to the frame of the building, not so much. Better stand back."

Using the glass block he'd just broken as leverage, Wade pried downward, putting all his weight into it. The entire section of glass came away from the wall with a loud ripping sound. The blocks hit the concrete with a thud. A few split at the seams and scattered.

I pulled the gun, and gripping it firmly, cowered against the brick wall to one side of the window. Still brandishing the tire iron, Wade followed suit.

The crash was sure to have reached Arashk's ears, among others. Whether it would bring him our way was a question waiting to be answered. While we waited, Wade thought of something I'd failed to consider.

"Probably should have had you go around front and watch the door," Wade said. "Make sure he doesn't try to split out the front."

"Shit!" Without delaying further, I returned to the darkness around the corner.

CHAPTER 54

At the front of the building, I stopped and peeked around the corner from the safety of the shadows.

Nothing was brewing in front of the motel, trouble or otherwise. Things were as dead as they'd been earlier. Still, at any second I expected the nearest door to fly open and Arashk to come running out. My nerves were ready. My bouncing foot kept double time. I crouched low with the gun in hand, doing a bad impersonation of a S.W.A.T. officer about to raid. Whether I'd be able to fire the gun, I wasn't yet sure. Any and all thoughts I'd had about using it were reactionary, firing it out of self-defense moreso than hunting one of them down.

Either way, I was ready for Arashk whenever he felt the need to run.

What I wasn't ready for was the guy in the baby blue sweat suit coming around the back of my truck and heading right for me, flashlight in hand. He passed in and out of the intermittent lights, his scowl set firmly in place. The guy definitely had a problem with something. Naturally, I assumed that something was Wade and me.

The man, who looked to be well into his fifties with a receding, slicked-back hairline and potbelly to show for his years, muttered something as he stepped onto the sidewalk a couple doors down. Kicking ice out of his path, he continued up the corridor. His body was ridged. There was a purpose in the way he walked.

I abandoned my crouch. I stood up straight. A confrontation was in my future, and I braced for it. My heart raced. So did my mind. This was a distraction I did not need.

"Hey, assholes!" the guy shouted, as he rounded the corner, "what do you think you're doing parking—"

His words were cut off when he nearly collided with me in the dark. Startled, he took a step back.

"Fuck me!" He quickly brought the flashlight up, training it on my face.

"Calm down," I said, putting my hands up to show I wasn't a threat. It may not have been the best course of action since I still held the gun in one of them.

"Sweet Lord Jesus..." The words crept passed his lips on a whisper. He raised his hands and took another step back. This one returned him to the light.

"It's all good, man," I said, trying to be as reassuring as I could. I needed to deal with this guy while keeping an ear on the door. The situation had the potential to go sideways real quick if I didn't diffuse it in short order. "We're not looking for trouble."

"Says the man with the gun." He swallowed hard. "I've already called the cops, ya know."

The way his cheeks quivered, I figured the guy was most likely lying. There was desperation in his eyes, an unsure tone in his voice. He wasn't acting like someone confident with the knowledge the cavalry was coming.

"Probably a good thing," I said, lowering my hands. "If you hadn't called them, we probably would. Eventually." I was telling the truth, while admittedly hoping he was, too. I wanted revenge. I wanted to get to Barnes before he could get away again. Most of all, I just wanted this all to be over. Thinking about it and doing it weren't exactly the same thing.

That's about the time I heard a door creak. My heart nearly exploded, and my mind told me to move my ass.

"Excuse me," I said, brushing past the guy who I now assumed was either the owner or manager.

Emerging into the light, I brought the gun up and stepped onto the sidewalk. I swung the gun around, aiming it eye level at the open doorway.

"Whoa, don't shoot!" someone shouted. And as the person stepped out into the light, I was glad I hadn't.

CHAPTER 55

"It's empty," Wade said, his forehead creased with uncertainty. "There's no one in there."

I lowered the gun and took a couple seconds to catch my breath, while at the same time, trying to make sense of what he'd just said.

"How's that possible?" I asked. "Where could he have gone?"

Wade apparently thought both questions were rhetorical, because he didn't answer either one. Instead, he had a question of his own.

"Who's this?" he asked, looking behind me.

I turned to find the guy in the sweat suit. He just stood there, trying to look formidable. In the burst of excitement, I'd forgotten all about him.

"I own this place," the guy said, stepping onto the sidewalk with his chest puffed out. He seemed to have recovered from his brush with an armed man in the dark. "Who the fuck are you two, and what the fuck are you doing sneaking around here at night?"

I was formulating some sort of answer when something somewhere crashed. I couldn't tell if it had come from Arashk's room, or one nearby. It was alarming, either way.

Wade must have thought so, too, because he disappeared

back into Arashk's room, gun raised.

"I'm calling the cops," the motel owner said, hustling away.

Knew it. I wish I'd had time to make a smartass comment about the guy saying he'd already called the police, but I had more important things to do than call someone out for being a liar.

The room certainly looked empty when I got my first glimpse of it. The lights on the two bedside nightstands were on, their low-wattage bulbs painting the room a murky yellow. It was enough to see there was nobody but the two of us in the sparse room.

"Bathroom?" I whispered.

"Just came through there." Wade shook his head. "I can check again, though."

Wade stepped slowly around the bed and made his way across the room toward the bathroom. Watching from just inside the doorway, there wasn't much to see: a lumpy, unmade bed, a small countertop with a sink, an area in the corner where a few wire hangers hung from a narrow metal bar. On the floor beneath the hangars sat a black, box television with its cord wrapped around it. There was no dresser, only a large rectangular section by the wall where the dingy brown carpet wasn't quite as dingy as the rest. I didn't waste much effort trying to figure out where the dresser went. Who knows? Maybe you had to pay extra for things like dressers in a place like this. Maybe folks who frequent these motels don't have a use for a dresser because, well, you don't bring a lot of clothes with you when you're only renting the room for an hour or two.

Scattered clothing was about the closest thing resembling

decor the room had. Articles lay everywhere, and from the looks of some of them, they weren't all men's clothing. A black lace bra and matching panties sat wadded atop a small pile of more black clothing on the foot of the bed. The sight of it brought a kick to the stomach as I imagined the probabilities. I didn't know who these clothes belonged to, but I was already sad for her.

The only other object of note was a dark red sitting chair positioned in front of the only window in the room. The shabby cushion looked to be sunken in the center and not comfortable at all, while the fabric covering the arms was worn and faded.

The strange part was the pillow and threadbare comforter that had been haphazardly folded and laid over the chair's back. It was a dead match for the floral-print comforter tangled up on the bed. This seemed odd, having two comforters for one bed. But then something else in the room caught my attention, and the matching comforters were quickly forgotten.

I couldn't believe I hadn't thought of it sooner.

"Still empty," Wade said, returning from the bathroom. "Unless he somehow backtracked and went through the bathroom window after I came through. Seems unlikely, though. Would've seen him. Or heard him. It's a small effing room."

I nodded my agreement, then silently motioned toward the wall beside the sitting chair.

Wade's eyes followed.

The door was painted the same drab white as the rest of the room, blending it nicely, especially in the dim light. The tarnished brass knob was the only thing that really caught your attention, and you would've had to give it more than a glancing look.

"Adjoining rooms," Wade said, coming up beside me. "Could explain a lot."

"Including why there's two comforters," I said, pointing them out to Wade.

"And maybe the missing dresser," he said, motioning toward the empty space where the dresser used to sit.

With a mutual understanding of the implications, we approached the door together. The adjoining room was likely the source of the crash, which meant it was likely where Arashk had disappeared to. I briefly wondered if one of us should go out and make sure he didn't escape through the adjoining room's front door, but I quickly dismissed the thought. I was too intrigued to leave the situation, and I sure as hell didn't want Wade leaving me to check out the adjoining room on my own. Leaving that route unguarded until we could get into the room was a risk we'd just have to take.

Two back-to-back doors stood between us and the other room. The first was unlocked and opened with barely a sound. The second door would be the test. If it was locked, it meant Arashk was trying to keep us out. Which would seem natural. Unlocked would mean he was just fine with us entering the room, and I'd have to wonder why.

With my heart about to breach my chest, I reached for the second door.

The door opened inward.

I stopped pushing once a dark, narrow sliver stood between the door and frame. It was just enough. There were no lights on in the second room. Whatever awaited us beyond the narrow slit hid within a pitch black.

A low hum, like the sound of a fan, came from somewhere

in the dark.

"You ready for this?"

The whisper floated over my shoulder, and though I thought I was ready, their suggestion made me wonder. The need to prove it, to both Wade and myself, spurred me on.

With the toe of my shoe, I eased the door open. A corridor of light burst into the room. As soon as space allowed, Wade and I thrust our guns through the doorway like we'd done this a million times before. More than shadows greeted us.

"Son of a bitch."

It was the smell. It wasn't overly strong, but the familiar stench of iron and gore twisted my stomach into a string of knots. I knew the smell. Unfortunately, I knew it well. It was Barnes' calling card.

Wade wasn't accustomed to the stench and was luckier for it.

I crouched and began searching the void to my right. There should have been a lamp on the nightstand. All I found was empty space. Either the lamp had been moved, or this room wasn't set up the same as the other. My money was on the former. I doubted much creativity was put into setting up shit hole motel rooms.

"No lights," I whispered to Wade.

His silhouette nodded. "Cell phone?"

I checked my pocket, then shook my head. I must have left it in the truck. No surprise considering the rush I was in. I was about to run out and get it when Wade changed my plans.

"We know you're in here, fucker."

Wade was apparently done whispering. His voice cut through the quiet like a bullet through paper. I flinched and cowered.

"And you should know we have guns," he continued. "Maybe you do, too, but I doubt it. By what I've heard, guns aren't your thing."

The sound of continued humming was the only response. That, and our heavy breathing. It felt like a stalemate. Something had to give. We couldn't just stand there in the dark for the next few hours waiting for the sun to come up and shed light on the situation.

That's when I got an idea.

I crossed in front of Wade, making my way over to the room's only window. I was careful where I placed each step. I didn't know what, if anything stood between the window and me, and didn't want to find out the hard way. When I finally reached the wall, my hand searched blindly until I found what I was looking for.

Taking a deep breath, I yanked the drapes hard to the side.

Nothing happened.

The heavy cloth started to move, but quickly caught. I tried again with the same result. I could feel Wade watching from the doorway. At least I hoped it was Wade.

I felt my way to the edge of the drape, and quickly discovered my dilemma: the fabric had been stapled to the wall. All along the edge, thick metal staples imbedded themselves in the drywall. There had to be hundreds of them. Maybe thousands. I set out to find the middle, hoping to pull the drapes apart at the center. That also turned out to be a dead end. The two drapes had been crudely sewn together, making them one large piece of fabric.

Shit!

Sweat broke out on my neck. I started to panic. I'd had my back turned to the room for too long. *Where the hell's Arashk?*

The anxiety of not knowing urged me onto the only other plan I could think of.

After sliding the gun into the back of my waistband, I gripped the fabric with both hands and yanked downward with everything I had.

With a sound like splintering wood, the curtain rod tore away from the wall. The staples still held the cloth to the wall at the edges, but the collapsed curtain rod created a substantial gap at the top of the heavy drapery. Light from the parking lot invaded the room. I crouched below the window and retrieved the gun as I spun around, bracing for whatever the light revealed.

CHAPTER 56

Nothing jumped out at me. No Arashk. No Barnes. No phantom psychos of any kind.

But there was plenty to take in.

As the largest object in the room, my attention was drawn first to the bed. Stripped of a comforter and sheets, the bare mattress sat awkwardly upon a short wooden platform. On the floor beside it, a shattered ceramic lamp lay on its side, the shade crooked and barely holding on. My first thought was of the crash I'd heard earlier. My second was to wonder where the nightstand was, and why the lamp had been on the floor in the first place.

"What in the hell?"

Wade's breathy question caught my attention, and I followed his stare. My stomach dropped. My head started to spin. I had to put my hand on the floor to steady myself until the moment passed.

They were only words, not a physical threat, yet their power had the same impact. They stretched from one end of the far wall to the other. The blood had been fresh, written with what appeared to be a fingertip. The smeared letters had dripped down the wall before drying...

FOR THE HOUR TO REAP HAS COME.
FOR THE HARVEST OF THE EARTH IS FULLY RIPE.

Resembling the writing on the wall at the church, this display was on a much larger scale. Here, the words didn't merely fill a chalkboard, they covered the entire wall; from side to side and from top to bottom. The amount of blood it required filled me with dread. It made my heart hurt. I could only speculate as to how many Barnes had killed this time.

"Do you know what it means?" Wade asked, bringing me back around.

"Yeah." I climbed to my feet. "It means we're about to find some bad shit."

And I was right. The room was full of plenty to see, mostly because half the other room's furniture had been brought in. Anything that could be used as a makeshift workbench. Both dressers stood against the wall, end to end. White towels draped the tops of each.

Approaching the dressers, Wade swallow hard.

Bones were laid out across the towels. Each of the clean, white bones had tiny pieces of paper tucked underneath. Pulling one out, I held it up to the light coming in the window. Not only was the scientific name of that particular bone labeled, but the part of the body the bone had come from was also listed.

Leg.

Arm.

Pelvis.

Everything suddenly made sense. Not only was Barnes back in business and working out of the motel, but he'd replaced his stepdaughter. Arashk was now his protégé. The idea there was someone else in the world just as sick and twisted as Barnes, chilled me to my core. Call me naïve, but I'd hoped he was one of a kind.

"A lamp," Wade said, and from my left, a brilliant light erupted. As soon as its glow illuminated the room, I wished it hadn't. They say the devil is in the details, and none of the room's details were worth seeing.

Stacked against one of the dressers were two-foot by three-foot sections of dark grey heavy foam. A blue caulk gun rested on top. Looking around, it didn't take long to figure out what it had been used for. Other than the blood-painted wall, every other wall in the room was padded from ceiling to floor with sound-proofing foam. I cringed at the need for such precautions.

Before my mind could conjure any maddening screams, I continued my exploration of the room's most closely kept secrets.

Three nightstands formed the shape of an L with the far end leading into the closet beside the sink. On top of each nightstand sat an aquarium, the size you'd find in a child's bedroom. Inside the closest of the glass boxes was another all too familiar sight. It brought back unwanted, yet inevitable memories. A human skull sat nestled on a bed of sand. Thousands of tiny black and brown beetles were busy gnawing away at the few pieces of flesh that still clung to the bone.

Barnes was nothing if not consistent.

The second and third aquariums provided more of the same, only the selection of bones was different. One contained what looked to be either arm or leg bones, and two perfectly intact hands. The finger bones reminded me of the ones I received in that first box.

The third aquarium held the most disturbing display yet. More bugs populated this enclosure than the other two, probably because there was more flesh to devour. The rib cage appeared completely intact. All the half-moon shaped bones were still connected to a section of knobby spine. The feeding was frenzied and plentiful and well underway.

If it had been the first time I'd seen the spectacle, it may have made me sick. But it wasn't, and I was already preparing for the worst. I was certain we hadn't yet seen it.

The smell of death grew stronger.

The door to the bathroom was closed. A thin sliver of light cut along the bottom. Putting my ear to the door, the sound of humming strengthened. Most likely, an exhaust fan. Only it didn't sound like your run-of-the-mill bathroom fan. This one sounded like an exhaust fan on steroids. Judging by what I'd already seen, and what I knew of Barnes's tendencies, I doubted it was airing out someone's bout with bad Mexican food.

I turned and gazed into Wade's eyes. I wasn't surprised to see fear in them. Even in the poor light, his face looked paler than I remembered. This wasn't exactly what he'd signed up for. I doubted he'd seen anything like this during his military training. For me, though, nothing we'd seen so far had come as a surprise, and I found myself shockingly immune to its horror.

"Wanna draw straws?" I nodded my head, indicating the bathroom door. As soon as the question came out, I realized it sounded like I was making light of the situation. The sweat coating my skin, and the tossing and turning in my stomach assured me that I wasn't.

"I can do it," Wade said, seemingly regaining his composure. Looking into his eyes, I couldn't tell if he was telling the truth, or just trying to suck it up and soldier on. Either way, he didn't look ready to face whatever was on the other side of the door.

So, without acknowledging his offer, I turned my back on him and grabbed the handle. It was cold in my hand, and I prepared to duck once I flung the door open.

I raised the gun and took a deep breath.

Over my shoulder, Wade told me to wait.

It was too late.

The door was already swinging inward.

CHAPTER 57

According to plan, I ducked just as the door slammed open. The sound of gagging was instantaneous. Wade had yet to vomit, but I had a feeling it was coming. Considering the scene before us, I couldn't blame him.

The bathroom walls had been white at one time, but now, everything was coated with varying shades of red. And I mean everything. The walls, the tile floor, everywhere I looked, slick with blood. A few splashes of crimson had even reached the ceiling. I stood in awe of the brutally macabre display, but it wasn't an inspiring awe. It was the other kind. The bathtub, specifically, was awash in bubbly, oxygenated blood.

And it was easy to see why.

A woman hung by her wrists over the bathtub. Her naked skin glistened with the same shade of red that filled it. The skin itself looked grey and chalky underneath. Thin cuts lined areas of her body like she'd been marked for quartering. Her feet had been removed and blood still dripped from the stumps.

Overhead, the large fan continued to hum.

"Oh, my God."

This time, the words were mine, and I immediately recalled Dallas's response back at the church:

God had nothing to do with this.

I was also pretty sure God had nothing to do with the message left for me, scrawled in blood on the back wall:

FUTURE SIGHT OF LUKE'S GRAND HARVEST

Taking care not to slip on the blood, I took a few steps into the bathroom. It wasn't until I stood beside the bathtub that I saw what I hadn't been able to from the doorway, what the blood clinging to the body had been hiding. The biggest cross I had ever seen hung around the woman's neck, tucked between her breasts, all covered in red. The sight of it gutted me. I reached up and brushed aside the woman's long black hair.

Even though I knew it was coming, seeing her face stole my breath.

Mackenzie's features were a frozen mask of anguish. Her glassy eyes stared straight ahead. Her mouth hung open in a silent scream. Her bulging throat appeared strained to the point of rupture. I could still hear Claire's laughter coming from the front seat as we drove to the club. I'd only known Mackenzie a short time, but my heart broke right then. Not just for her, but for Claire.

"The hell you doing?" Wade asked from just outside the doorway.

I ignored the question. I didn't have the time to explain. Nor the patience. I had to get her down.

The nylon rope went up and through the ceiling. Plaster tiles had been removed to gain access to the rafters where a steel bar had been bolted in for reinforcement. *Motherfuckers thought of everything!* The rope twisted several times around the steel bar before being tied in a knot. Thankfully, it was a simple knot, like it had been tied in a rush. Problem was, it hovered just beyond my reach.

I once again holstered the gun in the back of my jeans and searched for a somewhat clean place on the edge of the tub. If I couldn't find clean, I'd settle for dry. Finding an area I thought would work, I stepped up onto the edge. I leaned over the tub to grab the end of the rope.

I miscalculated. Dry or not, the blood slickened the fiberglass. My shoe slipped. It was only out of sheer reflex that I shamefully reached out with both hands and caught myself to keep from falling. My arms wrapped around Mackenzie's cold, mucky torso. There was a shallow smacking sound as my face slapped the area just under her armpit. The beer I'd drunk only an hour ago rose up the back of my throat.

And we swung through the air like a pendulum.

Jerking my face away, I stepped down. With my feet on steady ground, I could let go. Mackenzie's body continued to swing back and forth. I dropped my eyes in shame. It took doing so to notice that I couldn't see my right foot. The churning in my stomach turned to physical pain. I was standing on solid ground, alright, but only because I'd straddled the side of the tub. My right foot had splashed down into several inches red blood. I stood ankle deep.

"Shit."

Disgust flowed through me like a rogue wave.

I'd just lifted my foot and started shaking it free of gore when a wail of rage shattered the uncomfortable quiet.

CHAPTER 58

It was like something out of a gladiator movie. The battle cry erupted from somewhere in the room behind me. I realized then that, while investigating all the secrets the room had been keeping, I'd forgotten all about Arashk. Wade's startled shriek told me his focus had also been elsewhere.

I instinctively went for the gun tucked in my pants.

I spun around.

They say that during moments of extreme peril, time slows. Events play out in slow motion. Well, they're not lying, because that's exactly how the next ten seconds went down.

Arashk's face rose up behind Wade in the doorway. His face contorted into something that would make any warrior proud. His eyes were mere slits, his cheeks and nose creased as his open mouth showed every one of his thirty-two teeth. What I didn't see until it was too late, was Arashk's arm swinging down toward Wade just as he was turning around.

A shiny steel claw, the size of a baseball glove, entered the top of Wade's shoulder. All four tines disappeared into him. They didn't stop until half of their length was buried.

The scream that burst from Wade's throat was high-pitched and full of extreme pain. It blistered my eardrums. It echoed off the walls in the cramped bathroom. His head tilted back in agony, providing me with an opportunity.

Without considering the consequences, I raised the gun in Arashk's direction and squeezed the trigger. The blast reverberated through the bathroom, drowning out Wade's scream. The gun's recoil stung my wrist, and through the modest cloud of white smoke, I saw Arashk's head whip backward. His body soon followed, leaving the claw still embedded in Wade's shoulder.

CHAPTER 59

Wade fell face first into the bathroom and immediately began adding his blood to the vile scene. He'd just about added some of mine when I tried to pull the claw from his shoulder. Once he'd calmed enough to speak in structured sentences, he requested that I simply help him get out of "this fuckin' place!"

I didn't blame him. At this point, I was shaken, too. Someone else's blood covered the front of me, and I could still feel her cold, clammy skin against my own. There was also the fact that, for the second time in my life, I'd taken another. I was suddenly in need of a change of scenery and more fresh air than any bathroom fan could ever produce.

With my arm around Wade's waist, and his good arm around my shoulder, we struggled to make our way through the bedroom. He was growing light headed from the loss of blood. Each step a wobbly task in itself.

One look at Arashk's motionless body and it was obvious a coroner would be needed. The bullet had caught him just above his left eye. There was no coming back from the amount of blood that was leaving his head, soaking into the brown carpet. Still, until we were several steps away, I couldn't shake the image of him sitting up and grabbing one of our ankles. I told myself that only happens in the movies, but then, I'd also thought Barnes was dead when I left him beside the snack shop.

As me made our way passed the aquariums and dressers lined with some unfortunate soul's bones, I discovered where Arashk had been hiding. The mattress from the bed was cast aside. The wooden base beneath it was mostly hollow. Why hadn't the guy just taken off? The door to the adjoining room stood wide open. I could only speculate that it had something to do with Barnes; either loyalty to, or fear of.

Wade didn't want to sit on the chair or the bed in the next room. Despite growing weaker by the second, he refused to stop and rest until we were outside and breathing the cool night air. It wasn't until I'd lowered him onto the curb and taken a step back that I saw just how much blood he was losing. A trail of bright red stretched from where he now sat, all the way back to the room. I never would have thought a shoulder would bleed so much. Wade needed a hospital. The sooner, the better.

"Gonna grab my cell." I left him slumped against the metal pole of a handicapped parking sign. It was passed time to hand the situation over to the cops, and I wasn't sure we could depend on the motel's squirrelly owner to do it.

I ran over to where my truck was parked. Its front end slumped to one side, but there would be time to deal with that later. I reached inside the cab and swiped my cell off of the dash.

Thirteen.

That's how many calls I had. Eleven were from Claire. An alarm went off in my head. *Where was Barnes?* Not keeping track of everything and everyone was becoming a habit. Realizing that time was probably very much of the essence, I decided to forgo the numerous voicemails. With my stomach turning itself inside out, I brought up Claire's name and punched the green call button.

She answered on the first ring.

"Luke! Where the hell have you been?" The urgency in her voice was not something I was used to hearing and did nothing to alleviate my growing concern.

"It's a long story." I shot a glance in Wade's direction. He was still slumped in the same position, and I wondered if he was still conscious. "What's going on?"

"I got a call from him tonight, Luke. Barnes."

"What?" Anger ignited heat throughout my body. "How'd he get your number?"

"Heck if I know," she said. "But he got it."

"What did he say?"

There was a short pause before she answered. When she finally did speak again, her voice was softer, cooler by a few degrees.

"He said that if you didn't meet him you know where, he'd be paying me a visit."

I tried to control the rage sizzling inside me, but failed miserably. I slammed my hand on the hood of the truck. Not once, but twice.

"He has my number," I said. "Why didn't he tell me himself?"

"Guess he thought the threat would mean more coming from me."

And he was right.

Neither of us said anything for a moment. I was busy running scenarios in my mind, playing out the ways I would kill that son of a bitch. Every one of them would have been satisfying. Any one of them would do.

How the hell had Barnes gotten Claire's number? As soon as the question crossed my mind, the answer hit me like a shovel to the face. The break-in at Tipsword's. The way the office had been tossed, the officer even said it appeared as if somebody had been looking for something.

Apparently, they'd found it.

My application for employment. I'd put Claire as a reference, and more than likely, her contact information as well. Was her address on the application, too, or just her phone number? I couldn't remember. Please, God, let it have just been her phone number.

"Baby," I said, my voice as convincingly calm as I could manage, "you're safe. He may have gotten your phone number, but he doesn't know where you live. He's trying to scare us."

"Luke," she said, her voice now just above a whisper. "He confirmed my address. He knows where I live."

The silence on my end stemmed from two things. The first being that I couldn't believe how piss poor the night was going, and the second being that it appeared to be far from over.

I started pacing the length of the truck, my eyes darting all around.

"Okay, then, you need to leave," I told her. "Wake your parents, and the three of you get the hell out of there."

"One step ahead of ya," she said, suddenly sounding winded. "Walking out to the car now. They're confused and asking a million questions, but at least they're not resisting."

I felt a sense of relief flutter through me, albeit a small one. Like anything else that had gone right that evening, it didn't last long.

"Luke, I still haven't heard from Mackenzie."

Claire's words cut through my chest like a chainsaw, leaving a hollow space where my heart had been.

"It's not like her," she continued. "We have a very strict agreement. When one of us is out, we keep in touch at all times."

My eyes drifted to the motel room. Given Wade's condition, I'd had no choice but to leave Mackenzie's lifeless body hanging there, suspended in time.

I didn't know what to tell Claire. This wasn't how she should find out about her friend and why she wasn't keeping in touch. I found myself at a loss for anything that would be either appropriate or comforting. Ultimately, I remained silent.

It was Claire who finally spoke.

"Don't do it," she said, picking up the conversation. "Don't go out there, Luke. Call the police and let them go. Maybe they'll catch him this time."

The hope in her voice was encouraging, and for a split second, I considered doing just that: letting the police handle it. Maybe they'd be successful in capturing Barnes this time, and he'd either rot in prison for the rest of his life, or that life would be cut short. And maybe they wouldn't catch him, and I'd spend the rest of my life looking over my shoulder.

I realized there was only one way it would ever truly be over. And only one way everyone I cared about would ever truly be safe.

"I love you," I said, and closing my eyes, ended the call. I didn't have strength enough to listen to Claire's heart break.

With a deep breath and exhale, I put the phone on silent mode and slipped it into my pocket. Only then did I take time to assess the damage done to my truck. It wasn't good. The driver's side wheel sat at a forty-five degree angle. My limited mechanical experience told me either the ball joint or the axel was busted. Either way, the old Chevy wouldn't be making the trip out to the burnt out church. Its fight was over, at least for now. I almost thanked it for its sacrifice, but that seemed a little dramatic.

As I stood staring at the damage, I realized I was letting precious seconds get away from me. Seconds I was fairly sure I might need later.

The faint sound of sirens could be heard off in the distance. Thankfully, I'd just gotten an idea, and it didn't require me sticking around. When I got back to Wade, he was surprisingly still conscious. He even managed a weak smile when he saw me.

"Sounds like the cavalry's coming," I said, kneeling beside him. "But I can't stick around."

"I know," he said, his voice a struggle. "I overheard."

I patted him on his good shoulder and told him to hang in there, that I would come check in on him at the hospital when this was all over.

"Want me to send the police your way?" he asked.

I thought about it for a moment, remembering both the message left for me on the bathroom wall, and the man who'd left it.

"Might not be a bad idea."

CHAPTER 60

The keys were on a hook behind the storage room door, right where Dallas always kept them. Under different circumstances, I would have felt guilty about steeling. But frankly, I didn't have time for guilt right now. Not with so many lives hanging in the balance.

Thanks to the half-mile jog from the motel, my breaths still came in short bursts as I pulled Dallas' prized Chevy C10 onto the road and pointed it in the direction of Corwin Barnes.

CHAPTER 61

I was surprised I didn't get pulled over. Actually, I was lucky. I couldn't have cared less about being slapped with a speeding ticket, but I would have had a difficult time explaining the blood that covered me from head to toe. It all worked out, though, and I got to within a mile of the church in less time than it takes my parents to decide what movie to watch on a typical Saturday night.

I'd spent the majority of the drive trying to erase the motel images from my mind. The rest of the time, I spent worrying about Claire. The direct threat from Barnes rattled me the most. I couldn't bear the thought of something happening to her because of me. That would be some traumatic stress I'd never come back from. The only thing that brought any peace was the fact that, if Barnes was here to meet me, and I had no reason to believe he wasn't, then he was two counties away from Claire.

Sunrise was still an hour away, and the world outside the city was pitch black. But that was fine with me. Like a predator that hunts at night, I liked the idea of tracking without being seen. I killed the headlights as soon as I turned off the road and onto the familiar gravel drive.

I debated over how far I should take the truck. The C10's Flowmaster exhaust system would certainly announce my arrival. Even when idling, Dallas's truck had a decent rumble to it. On the other hand, I didn't like the idea of being out there without it. If I needed some place to escape to, or a quick way out, I'd want the truck nearby.

Eventually, halfway felt like a good compromise. If I could only remember how far halfway was.

My heart wasn't racing just yet, but it was definitely beating faster than normal. But then, I could hardly remember what normal was. It had been a long night. The wave of adrenaline I'd ridden back at the motel had dissipated during the drive, leaving me exhausted and a bundle of nerves. My hands grew sweaty as they gripped the steering wheel. I took turns wiping each of them on my jeans. Some nerves would be beneficial moving forward, I told myself. Too much could be bad.

I steered the truck along the winding drive, creeping past the trees and shadows lining the way. It was with their help that I was able to leave the headlights off and still keep the truck on the narrow strip of gravel. The speedometer barely registered my speed. I rolled the window down and breathed in the late spring air.

It was about the time I started thinking I was nearing the halfway point when the rear of the truck wobbled a little. My immediate thought was that a tire had found a pothole. But a pothole wouldn't explain the rapid shuffling sound coming from within the truck bed.

CHAPTER 62

The truck's rear window exploded, spraying me with a million shards of glass. I glanced up at the rearview mirror while leaning away. Corwin Barnes's snarl greeted me. There was crazy in his eyes. It was the look of determination with a considerable amount of pleasure added in. He thrust his massive arm through the gaping hole.

More out of instinct than plan, my foot stomped the brake pedal. The truck wasn't going more than a couple miles an hour, so it didn't jolt to a stop. The cessation of movement was, however, abrupt enough to cost Barnes his balance.

His body thumped against the back of the cab. He coughed up a grunt while his eager hand searched blindly. I crouched further against the door, watching in horror as the gun that had been sitting on the seat beside me slid forward. It dropped onto the floorboard a second before I could grab it.

With no time to mourn my loss, I jumped on the gas pedal. The truck responded. Its engine roared to life. The chassis buckled, then rocketed us forward. The change in direction threw me back against the seat and sent Barnes tumbling ass over elbows.

Trees rushed by on both sides. I fought blindly to keep the rambling truck in the space between. With the steering wheel gripped in one hand, I reached down with my other and fumbled for the switch that would bring the headlights back on. No use hiding now. The element of surprise was no longer an option.

The lights came alive just in time. I jerked the truck back onto gravel a second before the front end clipped the trunk of a large tree. The C10's bumper was spared by only inches. A low-lying branch slapped the windshield. With the tires back on gravel and the driveway revealed before me, I glanced once again in the rearview mirror.

Shit!

Despite hurling through the night down a winding drive, Barnes hadn't lost much ground. He was working his way back up the bed on his hands and knees. His strength and determination scared the hell out of me. The rate he was going, I had only seconds before he was at the window again.

I needed a plan.

I steered the truck around a hard curve. The gravel couldn't hold the tires and the truck slid off the edge of the drive. Rocks pinged against the undercarriage. Dirt and leaves went airborne. I cranked the wheel, let off the gas. Once I'd gotten the truck back under control, I hit the gas and gauged Barnes's progress. His demented smile filled the rearview mirror. I'd seen this view before, so I already had a plan. Hit the brake, throw Barnes forward. Hit the gas, throw him back. Repeat until I could think of something better.

The church's parking lot couldn't be much further. I'd have more options then. If I could just hold him off.

Trees flashed by.

The road to salvation lay ahead.

I suddenly couldn't breathe. Barnes's arm clamped around my throat, squeezing, cutting my airflow. The urge to panic was overwhelming. I fought it best I could.

"What now, hero?" Barnes's ground up words came through the window, loud enough to be heard over the roar of the C10's engine and the wind rushing through the cab. "Wherever I go, you go!"

Up ahead, the trees opened up. The parking lot spread out.

And still, I couldn't breathe.

Slamming on the brakes wouldn't work this time. Barnes's grip was too tight, the truck's speed too high for the gravel to bring it to a stop with any real force. My problems were mounting, and at the top of the list, I was failing miserably at not panicking.

If I didn't think of something fast, it would all be over.

We burst from the canopied driveway. The parking lot welcomed us and we kicked up its gravel. When the headlights caught sight of something on the other side, a plan formed. It wasn't a good plan, but it was a plan, nonetheless. I braced myself. The seat belt was the old kind that only went across my lap, but it was better than nothing.

Sorry, Dallas.

I gunned the engine.

CHAPTER 63

The concrete steps were all that remained of the burnt-out house of worship. It was either desperation or a lack of oxygen to my brain that kept me from thinking clearly, because it really was a bad idea. It went against every one of my instincts. Still, I fought the urge to slow down, and instead, pressed the gas pedal all the way to the floor.

Barnes's arm tightened around my throat as we bore down on the steps. While gagging, I adjusted the steering wheel to the left, keeping the concrete slab directly in our path. Disastrous results lay fifty feet ahead, but what else could I do?

Thirty feet.

The impact would pull Barnes through the back window and into the cab of the truck, if not all the way through the windshield. At least that's what I hoped.

Fifteen feet.

The point of no return came and went. It took all my strength and more foolish courage than I thought I had to not let off the gas.

Barnes cried out in fear, realizing too late what was about to happen. He released his grip. I gulped the first full lungful of air in a long time. As the corner of the steps disappeared below the truck's front end, I braced for inevitable impact.

And I closed my eyes.

Both tires ruptured on contact. This was immediately followed by a concussive jolt of metal sheering and crumpling in on itself. What glass remained of the rear window shattered as Corwin Barnes came crashing through.

The abrupt stop rattled every bone in my body. The lap belt held, but threatened to cut me in half. My knees rammed the steering column, cracking the plastic. My teeth knocked, chipping several. The horn burped as my chest took the full brunt of the steering wheel, leaving me once again gasping for air.

In the midst of the sonic chaos, I sensed something else happening; something completely wrong and out of my control.

And it was happening fast.

The bed of the truck lifted off the ground. Everything around me took on a look of confused surrealism. The view out my window changed to something I'd only seen while on a roller coaster.

What had been below was now above.

I'd underestimated the ramifications. I hadn't taken all possible consequences of the collision into account. The truck somersaulted through the air. The seat belt continued to hold as I rotated upside down. The gaping black hole that used to be the church glanced up at me briefly, then disappeared. A second impact approached at break neck speed, and I braced for it best I could.

CHAPTER 64

They say that when you dream, there is no color, only black, white and shades of grey. I didn't know if I was dreaming, but my world was entirely black. I found myself wishing for some white, or a hint of grey. Even when I was pretty sure I'd pried my eyes open, I couldn't see a thing.

My body hurt in places I didn't know it could. But, I was alive. At least, I thought I was. Even as the cobwebs began to clear, a trace amount of doubt still lingered. It took the smell of charred wood and the metallic taste of blood in my mouth to assure me that I'd indeed survived the crash.

The sensation of blood rushing to my head told me I was upside down. The truck had catapulted, landing on its roof in the church's basement. Things hadn't gone as planned, and the jury was still out whether I'd achieved my objective.

I shifted slightly. A million shards of broken glass rained from my chest and disappeared into the abyss below. The roof had caved in. The lap belt cinched even tighter. My right arm was pinned against something, but my left arm was free. I reached across and started feeling for the latch that would release the restraint.

What I found was a boot. Its rugged heel dug into my hip. Amid the chaos and pain, I'd momentarily forgotten that I wasn't alone. The collision had done a number on me, and I'd had the benefit of a seat belt. I had to imagine that Barnes had fared much worse. The way the last twenty-four hours had gone, I didn't bother hoping he was dead. It would have been nice, but I knew better.

Carefully nudging the boot aside, I pressed the release button and felt gravity take over.

In my haste to get free, I failed to think things through. I wasn't prepared for the subsequent free fall. It was only a few inches to the collapsed roof, but it sent a bolt of lightning through my neck when the top of my head hit metal. I tried to roll onto my shoulder, but it took more effort than I would have thought. The cab of the C10 hadn't been all that roomy to begin with, and now it was downright confining.

A sound came from somewhere in the darkness. It was a short, muffled groan, and I froze. I held my breath. Nearly a minute later, the sound hadn't repeated. Had I really heard it? If Barnes was even breathing, I couldn't tell. Silence surrounded me. Silence and darkness.

And gasoline. The faint odor was growing stronger. Overtaking the charred wood scent, it was now all I could smell.

Great, something else to worry about.

I remained calm, despite the mounting threats. I'd heard somewhere that cars didn't usually blow up in real life. Not like they did in the movies. I only knew that, at the shop, Dallas had a very specific method for storing flammable chemicals. He'd explained that there were three things required for combustion. The fact that I could only recall two of them at the moment—fuel and oxygen—bothered me. I needed to escape the truck and find my way out of that hole in the ground the sooner the better.

With both hands now free, I quickly found the driver side window. Like everything else in the truck's cab, the opening was smaller than before. If I was lucky, I would still fit through. I wasn't sure about the larger Barnes, and I didn't care.

Shards of glass scraped the palms of my hands as I felt for a section of the door to pull up on. I ignored the new pain simply by adding it to the old ones. There would be plenty of time to deal with them all once the risk of blowing to pieces had passed. I still hoped that the movies had it wrong, but I wasn't hanging around to find out.

Gripping the doorframe, I began pulling myself toward the window. Glass pieces scraped my back along the way, and I had to try to lift my body up and over. I leveraged my heels against the seat and pulled myself along with my arms.

My head had just cleared the opening when a hand seized my knee. My breath caught in my throat. My heart stopped. The hand started working its way up my thigh. I suddenly couldn't breathe and had to force myself to inhale deeply. The strain stung my sore throat, bringing me to tears.

Panicked, I kicked the black space around my feet. I couldn't see Barnes, but knew he was down there somewhere. I kicked wildly with both feet, like a toddler in mid-tantrum. Most of the time, they found nothing but truck. Twice I heard Barnes grunt on contact, but he never gave up my pant leg.

It was about the time he started pulling me back into the cab that I realized I needed to do something more than just kick my feet. I frantically grabbed for something, anything that might offer more leverage. I found the short metal post of the truck's side mirror. Clutching its base, I pulled hard enough to gain some ground and start inching my way back out the window.

I pulled with everything I had, fatigue and physical agony working against me. My body begged to give in, to let it all be over, but my heart wouldn't consider it. There was fight left in me, and I planned on riding it as long as I could.

Just as my shoulders breached the opening, a searing pain shot through my side. I screamed, torturing my throat, and for a brief second, loosened my grip on both the doorframe and the mirror. A tugging sensation pulled at the burning area, quickly followed by another wave of hot torment.

The anguish in my throat paled in comparison.

Upon releasing the doorframe, my hand immediately went to my side. My shirt was warm and damp. My fingers flirted with something cold and hard and sticking out of me. Four somethings, in fact, all brutally curved in the shape of a claw.

How many of these fucking things did they have?

Tears flooded my eyes, and I let them come.

Once again, I felt the sensation of being tugged on as the claw's steel tines tore deep into my side. I cried out for the second time. When I thought the agony couldn't get any worse, the claw proved me wrong. I felt it pull from my side, taking a decent amount of flesh with it. The sound it made as the steel opened me up was like the tearing of paper.

My stomach revolted, giving up its contents right then and there. What the scene in the motel bathroom had failed to do, excruciating pain had accomplished. The overwhelming stench of stale beer, stomach acid, and gasoline filled the cab.

Despite my injuries, I had the mental wherewithal to realize I was momentarily free. I grabbed the side mirror and pulled as hard as I could. This time I made substantial headway, working my whole upper body through the opening.

Behind me, I heard the clang of sharpened steel striking the truck's roof.

Missed, fucker!

I don't know if it was the pain, or the overpowering fumes of the gasoline, but my head wasn't right. I could feel the Earth tilting on its axis. Light-headedness came and went, and I prayed my worst fear wasn't happening. *Not now.* There couldn't be a worse time for a blackout.

Hang in there, Luke.

The words rang hollow in my head.

Hang in there, dammit.

CHAPTER 65

The third time wasn't a charm for me. The claw caught me below the thigh. This time, the steel tines struck bone. I screamed, suddenly very alert. Shock contracted every one of my muscles. My body went rigid, stiff as a board. The mirror didn't stand a chance. Its screws made a crunching sound as I ripped it free of the door.

Shards of glass scraped my side as Barnes drew me back into the truck. At that point, the claw was putting up more of a fight than I could. With my free hand, I reached for the claw in the hopes of relieving some of the pressure on my leg. What I grabbed onto instead was Barnes's large mitt-like hand.

His skin was cold to the touch, clammy, and my natural instinct was to let go. Every voice in my head screamed at me to do so. The things I'd known him to do, the detestable crimes those hands had committed. Touching them repulsed me beyond words.

And scared me to death.

But I didn't let go. I held on and used the leverage to pull myself closer. This relieved some of the pressure from the claw. More importantly, it brought me within striking distance. Night surrounded us, but Barnes's eyes glowed a dull white as they glared up at me. I didn't have to see his twisted smile to know it was there.

Removing that smile became priority one. I brought the mirror down, smashing Barnes in the face. The tempered glass shattered against something hard. Possibly a cheekbone. Maybe his jaw.

Barnes grunted. A curse shot passed his lips, and his head jerked sideways. The pressure in my leg continued. If anything, it intensified.

Laughter taunted me from the black void of the truck's cab. I found it more irritating than the smile, so I brought the mirror's steel plate down on Barnes' face again. This time, instead of hearing the sweet sound of shattering glass, a dull clank rang out, followed by an honest to goodness howl of pain. More satisfying than shattering glass, it encouraged me to bring the mirror again. And again.

And then again, until the metal plate broke away from the stem and disappeared in the darkness. The jagged metal shank was all I was left with.

Barnes wasn't laughing anymore. He was grunting and pulling himself up using the claw in my leg as leverage. The torture it brought resulted in another scream, this one from the deepest pit of my soul.

I felt the muscle rip free of bone. What escaped me then was less of a scream and more of an anguished wail. I almost would have welcomed a blackout at that point. I just wanted it to be over.

Then Barnes was on me.

I could feel his hot breath. Warm spittle dripped from his mouth to my lip, adding insult to injury.

"Finally."

His voice was low and gravelly. If I hadn't known better, I'd think he was talking only to himself. The threat behind the word, however, was definitely meant for me.

You better do something, I told myself. *And do it now!*

I turned the mirror's arm around, wielding it like a stake. With the little energy I had left, I cocked my arm and brought it hard, driving the jagged piece of steel through the soft fleshy part of Barnes's cheek.

His shriek was deafening in the confined space.

As he jerked his head away, I let go of the handle and let him have it. He fell away from me and started to slump back toward the depths of the cab. I sent him the rest of the way with a kick to what I believed was his shoulder. I heard his body slam against the passenger door.

I seized the opportunity by grabbing the doorframe and hoisting myself back through the window for the third and final time. I didn't leave the cab empty handed. The steel claw tagged along, still embedded deep in my thigh. I scrambled away from the truck and immediately started searching for a way out of the burned-out basement.

CHAPTER 66

A handful of charred wooden planks lay scattered amid the moonlit ruins. I envisioned makeshift ramps leading up and out. It was the only way. As handy as they would have been, the stairs were gone, contributing to one of the numerous piles of grey ash that filled the basement.

I grabbed the nearest plank—which happened to be one of the longest, as well—and propped it against the edge of the church's concrete foundation. It was destined to be a steep climb. After checking the board for stability, I started crawling my way up on my hands and knees.

The wood bowed. It creaked and threatened to split under my weight. Two-thirds the way up, and the sound of splitting wood rang out.

It was a harrowing sound.

But, not as frightening as the sound that filled the night air.

"For the hour to reap has come!"

The shout was hoarse and came from below. It was immediately followed by a report from a firecracker. Beside me, a chunk of concrete foundation disintegrated into a puff of dust. Pebbles peppered my face.

As I reached for the top of the cinder block wall, I used my feet as much as possible to hoist myself up. Even using both my arms and legs, I struggled to pull myself over the edge. The crash and struggle with Barnes had left me weak. My growing list of injuries wasn't helping.

I was bleeding strength.

When another firecracker ignited from below, something punched the back of my shoulder. The force of it threw me forward, onto the burnt grass lining the edge of the foundation. As I dealt with the sudden shock of cold, wet dew against my face, I realized two things: one, Barnes wasn't dead. And two, he'd found the gun.

Like a man on fire, I immediately started to roll, staying as low to the ground as I could. In my rush, I didn't think about the instrument of torture that still hung from me like a vestigial appendage. As soon as I rolled onto my side, a searing pain lit me up like no other. The pressure pushed the tines sideways, and I felt them tear through muscle. My hand instinctively went to my thigh. I couldn't relieve the pressure or make the pain stop, but through it all, I was able to make sense of something that was maybe more important. Something inside my pocket.

I still had Dallas's silver Zippo.

In that brief moment of clarity, I remembered the third element needed for combustion to happen: *ignition source.*

A third shot rang out. This one grazed my shoulder as I struggled to my knees. I faltered, fell backward and had to catch myself. I shoved my blood-covered hand into my pocket. It came out holding the lighter, its finish dull with oil. The side was dented, and the lid was cockeyed from being struck by the claw, but it was a beautiful sight for my sore eyes.

I flipped the lid back my thumb and found the flint wheel. With a deep breath, I spun it.

Nothing happened.

The slightest whisper of smoke rose up, but that was it. Two more tries earned the same result, and the hope that had energized me a moment ago began to vanish.

"Come on!" I shouted, as if all the lighter needed was a little encouragement.

I held the lighter up to the moonlight. Both the flint wheel and the piece beneath it were damp, streaked with glistening black oil. I brought the lighter to my chest and feverishly rubbed it back and forth on my shirt. When I started getting woozy again, I put my hand to the ground to maintain balance.

Breathe, I told myself.

Slow it down.

Concentrate.

An all-too-familiar laughter rose up, literally, from the ashes. My attention was immediately drawn to the gaping hole in the ground where Barnes was making his way up onto the overturned truck. He moved slowly, like an old man, like some of the fight had been knocked out of him. He crawled across the undercarriage and used the C10's frame to push himself to a standing position. The moonlight glinted off the gun clutched in his hand.

I ignored the voices in my head screaming for me to run. Instead, I tried again to spark a flame. Nothing.

Barnes was at eye level now, and as he raised the gun, I realized why he'd felt the urge to laugh.

I had nowhere to go, and nowhere to hide.

"Light, damn you!" I spun the wheel again. "Light! Light! Li—"

Persistence paid off. A one-inch flame erupted from the lighter to dance in the night air, devouring oxygen like a starving beast.

Another shot rang out. The bullet clipped my hand. I dropped the lighter in the grass beside me. Apparently, the best thing about Zippo lighters is that you don't have to hold anything down for it to stay lit.

I dropped to my stomach and rolled onto my side, picking up the lighter as I did. The brass case was getting warm, and I didn't know how much longer the flame would stay lit. With my heart racing, and expectations of another bullet being sent my way, I turned just enough to see the truck.

You got one shot, I told myself. *Make it a good one.*

The moon caught the lighter in its glow. It arced through the air, tumbling end over end. The flame flickered. I held my breath. There came a succession of clinks and clanks as the lighter hit the edge of the driver's side door and tumbled through the open window.

It was a good shot.

A heavy whoosh sucked the air out of the night. A beat later, a massive explosion shook the ground.

It was a *very* good shot.

A brilliant fireball shot toward the sky, taking metal, wood, and even some concrete with it. The framework of Dallas's truck rose about a foot above the basement's rim before dropping back into the fiery abyss. I rolled backward, shielding my eyes from not only the bright light, but the intense heat. What followed was an apocalyptic rumble that swallowed Barnes in the process, returning him to Hell where he belonged.

As the initial concussion faded, I struggled first onto my knees, then my wobbly feet. Then I smiled. I couldn't help myself. I actually smiled. Finally, something had gone my way. Something big. A moment later, the dam broke, and I literally burst out laughing. Overwhelming relief had to be the sweetest feeling in the world.

And as I stood above the seared crater with the flaming truck as its centerpiece, I closed my eyes and basked in the woeful shrieks of a man being burned to death.

CHAPTER 67

The screams lasted less than a minute before falling silent. "That's for Garrett, asshole."

I watched the truck burn in the fiery pit, the heat on my face a reward for a job well done. And while the job might've been done, my ordeal was far from over.

A dark haze threatened my vision. My energy level was running frightening low on reserves. My entire body ached, and I'd lost track of how many holes I had in me. I could actually feel the blood exiting my wounds, streaming down my skin and seeping into my clothes.

I took one last look at the flaming wreckage that used to be Dallas's prized possession, then spit a wad of phlegm in the hole and turned away.

I'd seen videos where people place their foreheads on one end of a baseball bat, stand the other end on the ground, run around it until they're dizzy, then try to walk. It's hilarious to watch. Especially when alcohol is involved. I didn't have a bat, and I sure as hell didn't have any alcohol left in me, but I felt the way those people looked. And there was nothing funny about it.

The world spun sideways as I limped toward the mouth of the driveway. I faced a long walk to the main road, and even then, who knew how soon a car would happen by. Especially at this time of night. *No*, I told myself, and brushed aside the creeping negativity. I had to remain positive. I was heading in the right direction, and that's all that mattered.

I'd only stumbled a few yards into the canopy of trees when I thought my mind had finally cracked. I didn't trust my eyes, but a pair of headlights appeared to cut through the trees up ahead. It looked like a car. It could have been a UFO for all I knew.

My head went from spinning to drowning in a sea of dense fog. I found myself unable to think straight, and my steps were just as meandering. I'd hit a knee a couple of times, and wasn't even out of earshot of the crackling fire. All the while, the headlights kept coming.

I was bent over, hands on my knees in the middle of the winding drive, when the car came around the last curve and caught me in its high beams. Like a baby deer, I just stood there watching as it approached at a high rate of speed.

The car suddenly braked. The sound of tires sliding through gravel interrupted the quiet of the woods. When it eventually came to a stop, and not a moment too soon, I found myself face to bumper with a silver Prius.

Whether it was overwhelming relief, or I'd simply lost too much blood to remain upright, I dropped to my knees in the harsh pool of light. When my knees proved just as unstable, I ended up sprawled on a rough bed of gravel.

I heard a car door open, then another. A familiar voice screamed my name. When two strong arms slid underneath mine and lifted me off the ground seconds later, I wondered if I was dreaming.

"Get the door." The second voice was rushed, different, but not entirely unfamiliar. "We'll put him in the back seat."

Claire's father had one of those deep, yet comforting voices, and even though it seemed filled with tension at the moment, it still did the trick. I felt my body relax. Not a little, but completely. Like there was nothing left to fear, and no reason to worry. So, like a newborn with a full belly, I gave in to the unconsciousness that was all too eager to claim me.

The next time I opened my eyes, I could see the sky rushing passed the rear window. It was lighter than it had been, but not quite daylight. Upside down tree tops came and went until they were eventually replaced with buildings and billboard signs. Street lamps reflected off the glass in succession, creating an ethereal strobe effect. Unlike the trees, the scenery in the city changed constantly, never showing the same scene twice. I turned to the front seat where Claire sat on the passenger side.

"I'm sorry," I said. My mouth and throat were dry. The words barely made their way out. Claire turned in her seat and offered a small grin through tear-stained cheeks. I saw her reach back, felt her stroke the hair off my forehead. What I didn't do was hear what she had to say. Just as her lips parted, everything faded to black once again.

EPILOGUE

The sun coming through the window was so bright that Dallas asked me to close the blind. It was a good problem to have. Not only had the Ohio skies been crappy and full of rain the last couple weeks, but this was Dallas's first day in his new room. There were no windows in ICU.

"Thanks, kid," he said. "Now I can see everyone's smiling faces. At least those of you on this side of the room."

A black patch covered Dallas's right eye. The jury was still out on whether the loss of eyesight was temporary or permanent, but as far as Dallas was concerned, the patch at least was temporary. Even if his sight didn't return, he vowed to get a glass eye. 'I'd rather make people uncomfortable with my googly eye than see a pirate every time I look in the mirror,' he'd said.

Dallas didn't remember much from that night. Much like his eyesight, the doctors said the chances his memory would return were 50/50. Dallas hoped it did. I secretly hoped otherwise. The ordeal was over, and quite frankly, nothing good could come from reliving it over and over in his mind. There are just some things that are better left forgotten.

"So, how's the food around here?" Claire asked, straightening a stack of car magazines beside his lunch tray.

"Food? Is that what they call it?"

"Hey," I said, "if I had to eat it, so do you."

On the other side of the bed, Wade laughed.

"You're just used to bologna sandwiches and frozen pizza," he said. "This is a good opportunity for you to try a vegetable or two."

Wade's shoulder was healing pretty well. The sling was supposed to come off in another week. He'd actually been the lucky one. A full day and a half in the hospital and he'd been given his walking papers. I'd had to spend three days, and Dallas was going on two weeks and counting.

Which meant that someone had to run Tipsword's in his absence. Ironically, that someone was Wade. It was actually nice watching him take charge around the garage, dealing with customers and running the business while Dallas was laid up. He certainly didn't know cars the way Dallas did, but he was doing a good job. Alcohol didn't appear to be an issue anymore, and he was always the first one in and the last one to leave. He even mentioned maybe going back to school and taking some business management courses to help Dallas with that side of things. It sounded more and more like his temporary stay was going to be more permanent, which I didn't mind. Wade was a good guy. I just hoped there would be enough work for me, too. Dallas assured me there would be.

"So enough about me," he said, his expression darkening just a bit. "How are you doing?"

I told him I was good, which I was. The nerve damage in my thigh was irreparable, but with continued physical therapy, the chronic pain would be manageable. A lifetime of pain was an acceptable tradeoff for putting both Arashk Dimir and Corwin Barnes where they belonged. However uncoordinated it made me look, at least I could still walk. Which was more than I could say for the two of them.

Dimir.

I hadn't even known Arashk's last name until the cops told me a couple days later. Ironically, even though he'd been in the country illegally, he'd been easier to identify than most of their runaway and homeless victims. I told Detective Morgenstern that I thought it spoke volumes about the way things were done in our society. He didn't agree with me, but he hadn't argued, either.

The only victim they'd identified so far was Mackenzie. I saw her distraught mother on the news one night, tearfully thanking the community for their support during this trying time. Through her tears, I could see the resemblance. It was a face I would always remember, and not for what Mackenzie would have wanted.

Six.

The police estimated there were six victims in all. The motel had been temporarily shut down, and they were taking their time processing the scene for evidence. Morgenstern said they probably wouldn't know for sure for quite some time. Besides Mackenzie, the initial estimate was that there were bones from at least three different victims remaining in the room. A stash of boxes, bubble wrap and shipping labels were found in the motel's maintenance closet. He may not have been working out of the old church, but Barnes was back to selling worldwide again.

If he'd ever stopped.

Luckily, we'd gotten to Arashk before he could return to Romania and spread the disease. A fake passport and an airline ticket were found in the room, along with a photo of his mother and a decomposed finger wrapped in a silk tie. The airline ticket was for an early morning flight scheduled two days after the night Arashk jumped me. After investing all that time stalking me, he must have figured it was either now or never, regardless what Barnes's plans for me were.

This time, the police found Barnes's body right where I told them they would, or at least what was left of it. They'd had to use dental records to identify the charred remains. Remembering the sorry state of Barnes's teeth, I felt sorry for whoever had that job.

"Well, I'm glad it's all over," Dallas said. "I like my life nice and boring." I knew it was a lie. He'd hoped to get his hands on Barnes, and truth be told, he was probably more than a little disappointed he'd missed out on all the action. Especially since he was in need of payback himself.

"Me, too," I said, meeting Claire's gaze and giving her a wink. "I'm ready for things to settle down. Speaking of which—"

"We're getting an apartment!" Claire blurted out. The smile on her face matched her level of excitement. "It'll be really nice, at least until I have to go back to school in the fall."

"Well, there you go," Dallas said, motioning toward Wade. "Maybe Luke could use a roommate in a couple months."

Wade smiled and threw up his hands.

"Hey, right now, let's just worry about getting you back home."

With smiles all around, we nodded in agreement.

"So what are you most excited to get back to?" Claire asked.

"Probably just getting back to work," Dallas said, after

taking little time to consider it. "Getting back under the hood of some cars and getting my hands dirty. Especially the C10. I can't wait to get that thing painted and finally out on the road."

Wade and I exchanged a look. He had been the one to fill Dallas in on everything that happened. Apparently, he'd left out one critical detail.

"Well, old man," Wade said, throwing Claire and me a quick smile, "I'm out. But Luke here's got something to tell you."

Grabbing Dallas's toes through the thin, white sheet, Wade gave them a wiggle before excusing himself from the room.

And it was at that moment that I changed my mind. Maybe Wade wasn't such a great guy after all.

About the Author

Tim McWhorter was born under a waning crescent moon, and while he has no idea what the significance is, he thinks it sounds like a very horror writer thing to say. A graduate of Otterbein College, he is the author of the horror-thrillers, *Shadows Remain, Bone White*, its sequel, *Blackened,* and a collection of short stories, *Let There Be Dark.* He lives just outside of Columbus, OH, with his wife, a dwindling number of children and a few obligatory 'family' pets that have somehow become solely his responsibility. He is currently hard at work on one of several ongoing projects and relies on interaction with readers for those much-needed breaks.

www.timmcwhorter.com

Email: tm5to1@live.com

Twitter: @Tim_McWhorter

www.facebook.com/pages/Tim-Mcwhorter-author

Also by Tim McWhorter

Shadows Remain
Bone White
Blackened
Let There Be Dark
The Winding Down Hours
The Opening

Continue reading for a sneak peek at
The Opening.

A new novel from Manta Press…

PROLOGUE

A crowd had gathered.

Some were tourists, in town for only a week, soaking up as much sand and surf as they could before returning to the city for another year. Residents of Angler Beach made up the rest. He knew most of the pained faces staring up at him. Many for as long as he could remember. Some seemed eager to do something, to stop what could never be undone. Maybe it was the acrid fumes or the fear of getting caught in the fray that kept their feet rooted in place. He only hoped they would stay away long enough…

"Don't do it, Floyd!" one of them shouted.

"It's not worth it!" cried another.

He heard the pleas, but ignored them just the same.

Raising the red gas can above his head, he drained every last drop before tossing it aside. The empty container tumbled end over end down the concrete steps. It came to a stop on the sidewalk, landing at the feet of those brave enough to stand witness to what was certain to be a horrific display.

One everyone would remember.

The fuel streamed down his face, stinging his eyes. He coughed as the fumes constricted his throat. He choked on the lack of clean air. His lungs threatened to collapse. To simply breathe became a struggle as he reached into his pocket for the second half of the equation.

He pulled out the lighter.

"Somebody get help!"

"Somebody call Helen!"

He held the lighter—a gold zippo he'd had since Korea—down and away from his body. He didn't want to see it. The mere sight of it might cause him to second-guess.

Meanwhile, the pleas kept coming.

"Somebody, please! Do something!"

He turned his back to the crowd and looked upon the doors of The Chamberlain Theater. *His* theater. A rusted chain snaked through the long, gothic-styled handles. The two ends converged at a padlock that hung in the middle. Taped to the glass, a simple, white sheet of paper, bank letterhead across the top, barred him from entering as much as the chains. He'd owned the theater for over forty years. A damn lifetime. Memories were one thing the bank couldn't have. No, he'd take those with him.

Gasoline dripped off his nose, his chin, and pooled at his feet. He remembered the day they installed the heavy, custom-built wood doors that opened to the auditorium. Remembered the morning the marquee sign arrived, polished and majestic, strapped to the back of a flatbed truck. It had been a proud day, one the entire village of Angler Beach had come out to share. From that day forward, The Chamberlain Theater was no longer an afterthought, sought only when rain had washed out the summer sun and surf. It had become the anchor of the town center.

His beautiful wife aside, the theater was his life; the patrons his lifeblood. He'd needed nothing else. The Chamberlain filled his hollow, childless void.

He wiped his face with his shoulder, coughed into it.

Now, those days were gone. Thanks to an economy in the toilet and bills that never stopped coming, even after the customers had. Countless afternoons he'd spent alone in his office, brainstorming ways to bring in more business. He'd failed at every turn. And when the bank had foreclosed, repossessed and sold the theater out from under him, they had done no less than fill the gas can and hand it to him.

An hour ago, he kissed his wife's cheek while she slept beneath the roof he could no longer provide. He was too proud, too ashamed to see his failure reflected in her emerald green eyes. He'd fed the cat, scratched behind her ears the way she liked, then quietly closed the door behind him.

On the sidewalk in front of the theater, the crowd continued to grow.

It was time.

He raised the lighter to his chin.

Sensing the end was near, the crowd's chorus of pleas swelled. Cries of his name filled the crisp morning air. And as a lone brave soul, unable to stand idle any longer, charged up the steps, the Floyd took one last stagnant breath.

He closed his eyes.

He spun the flint.

The story of Floyd Cropper setting himself on fire on the steps of his beloved theater made the nightly news all along the Eastern seaboard. Self-immolation wasn't something that happened in everyday America. The fact that this tragedy occurred in such an idyllic coastal town made it all the more sensational. The press ate it up. Arriving by the vanload, they stuck cameras and microphones in the faces of anyone who had something to say about ol' Floyd. And it seemed everyone had something to say. Even those who didn't know the man, knew someone who had. It was the most attention the town of Angler Beach had received since the late Eighties when the young Perry brothers' skiff capsized and their bodies were lost.

But, seventy-two hours later, when word broke of sexual assault allegations against a powerful media mogul, everyone outside of the quaint, coastal town forgot all about Floyd Cropper, and the restoration of The Chamberlain Theater by its new owner quietly began.